1982

THREE WEEK BOOK

DATE DUE

AP 29 '82		
JE 17 '82		
SE 29 '82 1983		
FEB 5		

A LIVING DOG

By Peter Somerville-Large

Fiction

A LIVING DOG
EAGLES NEAR THE CARCASE
COUCH OF EARTH

Non-Fiction

DUBLIN—A SOCIAL HISTORY
IRISH ECCENTRICS
FROM BANTRY BAY TO LEITRIM
THE COAST OF WEST CORK
CAVIAR COAST
TRIBES AND TRIBULATIONS

A LIVING DOG

PETER SOMERVILLE-LARGE

PUBLISHED FOR THE CRIME CLUB BY
DOUBLEDAY & COMPANY, INC.
GARDEN CITY, NEW YORK
1982

Library of Congress Cataloging in Publication Data

Somerville-Large, Peter.
A living dog.

([Crime club])
I. Title.
PR6069.043L5   1982   823'.914
AACR2
ISBN: 0-385-17861-1
Library of Congress Catalog Card Number 81-43283

A living dog is better than a dead lion.
Ecclesiastes 9:4

A LIVING DOG

CHAPTER 1

Drury looked out of the carriage window at the curve of Killiney Bay which Victorian travellers used to compare to the Bay of Naples. They would not have if they had seen it that afternoon. Grey waves splintered and fell on the deserted gravelly beach. Further out, on a sea polluted with suburban garbage, a small oil tanker came south behind Dalkey Island, and headed towards the Kish lighthouse on its way to Arklow. The double curve of mountains punctuated by the two Sugarloaves, each as dramatic as Vesuvius, was covered in drizzle.

When the diesel spluttered out of the station, the fifteen boys in his charge raised a feeble cheer. They all wore dirty blazers whose pockets were adorned with a ridiculous crest, a lozenge held up by two allerions, eagles displayed without beaks and feet. The motto said Virtute et Labore. He who can, does, sang the train wheels, he who cannot, teaches.

Drury was thirty-three. He had done a degree in General Studies at Trinity College, Dublin, followed by a Diploma in Higher Education. Then for a long time he had been unemployed apart from a couple of spells in non-respectable (and in retrospect amazingly well-paid) jobs like barman and factory hand. At the end of that period he had considered himself extremely lucky when he was picked out from the crowd of unemployed teacher graduates to work in a small private school.

Prospect Preparatory School had been established nearly a century before, and had soldiered on ever since, sternly Unionist, ignoring the fact that Ireland had severed its links with England for more than half a century. Conservative virtues were emphasised in its curriculum and boys were coached for Common Entrance to English public schools. There are tribes of Indians in Brazil who struggle to maintain their beleaguered societies while all around them forests are cut down. Prospect survived in modern Ireland by paying its masters starvation wages. Drury taught Latin and English and supervised cricket and rugby.

Today the gaping hole of the afternoon had to be filled, and once again he had been shouldered with the task of bringing a selection of the Upper School on an outing. For a moment the boys sat docile, look-

ing out at the sea. He did not join their solemn stare, but turned the
other way to gaze towards Killiney Hill scattered with big houses set in
steep luxuriant gardens. This was one of the most affluent suburbs of
Dublin. Various members of his family had lived there, and the fact
that several of his relatives had enjoyed the era of croquet, tennis and
cheap deferential maids serving tea in the garden emphasized his current poverty. Indeed his great-aunt still had her house high on Killiney
Hill, and if he shifted his head he could make out the turrets protrud-
ing from eucalyptus trees. But the lifestyle that she enjoyed was not
shared by her neighbours. The old order had given way to the world of
rich accountants and builders who had taken over the pseudocastles
and red-and-white Betjemanesque villas, and filled them with Jack
Yeats pictures, foreign au pairs and microwave ovens.

He glimpsed the daring elegance of Sorrento Terrace, a row of spacious nineteenth-century houses built at the beginning of the railway
era and perched on a rock above the sea. The train entered Dalkey tunnel to a chorus of whistles and soprano screams. Two scuffles broke out.
Beamish thought he could get some satisfaction by putting his hand
down Switzer's trousers, and O'Keefe imagined he could light up and
smoke a cigarette all in six seconds. When the train emerged out of the
darkness, there was a rush to the windows to view the place where the
Dalkey train crash had taken place. He took no notice of any of them.
He began to read a paperback thriller he had confiscated at prep.

He read for twenty minutes, ignoring the boys running up and down
the carriage, until the train pulled into Pearse Station—Westland Row,
Headmaster persisted in calling it, although the change of name had
taken place in 1966. This afternoon he had recommended a tour of the
National Gallery. "Concentrate on the Dutch School . . . landscapes,
interiors . . . an essay afterwards . . ." The Dutch School was wholesome, and the boys were to be encouraged to admire the cheerful Frans
Hals and the portrait by the Master of the Tired Eyes of the woman
who so resembled Matron, in preference to other schools of painting
with pictures like the half-naked wanton by Goya. That had been
bought at unnecessary expense with funds from the George Bernard
Shaw bequest. Shaw would turn in his grave. A little levity could be tol-
erated, and they were allowed to smirk at the coarse Dutch joke of the
pissing horse, which was the most popular painting in the gallery.
Drury listened, but he had no intention of taking the boys to the National Gallery. It had a restaurant, and he did not intend to provide tea
for fifteen, since he knew from experience that he would never be
refunded. The National Museum, on the other hand, was quite safe,
because no refreshments were available there at all. Headmaster would
never query the change, would not even read the essays the boys wrote.

After they were marshalled in a ragged line they walked up Westland Row, past grey St Andrews, past the plaque that commemorated the birthplace of Oscar Wilde.

"Who's he, sir?" Poor Oscar. Headmaster maintained a prejudice against him. Drury, who had read many of the scores of books about him published year after year, had rather come round to sharing it. Anyone so consistently over-publicized in life and in death deserved two years' hard labour. He amused himself for a few moments by devising a list of those dead and alive whom he would send to Reading Gaol for the offence of attracting endless devoted maudlin publicity—Adolf Hitler, Mohammed Ali, Jackie Kennedy, Pope John Paul II. His preoccupation was a mistake, for the boys seized the opportunity of racing across the road and diving into a newsagent's. There was a nightmare ten minutes pause as they bought sweets and cigarettes, ignoring his threats of beatings. Notes crackled; in his own school days he had had to make a pound last a whole term. Then out again past the Dental Hospital where students practised half-learnt skills on impoverished Dubliners. He once had a filling there himself. They had to pause and wait for fat Kingsmill, puffing and blowing, to catch up. The boys called him Speedy. Their nicknames were cruel; Headmaster's wife with her prominent teeth was known as Jaws, while Drury himself had been christened Fireball.

Longing for a rhinoceros-hide whip, he escorted them under the windows of the poor old Kildare Street Club. His father had belonged. He himself thought the place hideous, but dutifully pointed out the carvings, including the famous monkeys playing billiards. A few steps further on they reached Leinster House and noted the line of concrete flower basins placed on a site that had attracted ugliness ever since the Duke of Leinster had departed, taking his lawns and fountains with him. Drury was too young to have seen the toadlike statue of Queen Victoria which had been nicknamed Ireland's Revenge. Headmaster remembered it with nostalgia.

"Remember not to rush around and get lost," he shouted as he marched them through the colonnades of the National Museum. This was essential. He remembered the near disaster at the zoo outing three weeks before. That afternoon had promised well. Zoo outings were always popular, even if they had lost the panache they once had in the time of Mr Hemmings. Mr Hemmings died decades ago, but stories, assuming the aspect of legend, had lingered about the days when he was in charge of zoo parties. He had been a member of the Zoological Society with some sort of entrée backstage. The chicken pushed into the crocodile's pen; was it true that boys had watched it strut and peck its way down the scaly back oblivious to danger, until there was a lunge and a shriek? And did they crowd around as Mr Hemmings fondled his favourite python, draping its coils around his arms and shoulders, and feeding it a live rabbit in the privacy of the keeper's room? Watching sea lions dive for dead fish could never be so interesting, and Drury did not notice when Erskine wandered off. He half hoped a lion had eaten him when he found him two hours later, devouring doughnuts in the restaurant which he had made a point of avoiding.

Today he kept counting the blazered figures running around the glass-roofed main hall of the Museum.* (Where was Erskine now?) They peered without animation at gold torques, chalices, croziers and other glories of Celtic art. He took them into the exhibition of Viking remains and failed to rouse interest in a mound of small black shoes made for medieval Dubliners. They paid a brief visit to the big room full of relics of the heroes of 1916; the school curriculum paid little attention to that glorious episode in Ireland's history. Back in the hall they were more enthusiastic about the big skeleton nursing a rusty sword who, according to the label, had been a Viking warrior.

"He's not as nice as the people in St Michan's, is he, sir?" The outing to shake the leathery hand of the grinning mummified Crusader in the vaults of St Michan's had been a great success.

Looking at his cheap Timex he found that less than half an hour had passed. They would have to go upstairs. This was one of the drawbacks of coming to the Museum. Most exhibits upstairs, the Waterford glass and the silver medals celebrating faded victories of shorthorns and heavy hunters at the Royal Dublin Society showgrounds, were displayed on an open balcony protected by a wrought iron railing running round the main hall. He had not heard of any child climbing over it and crashing down on the Ardagh Chalice or the Cross of Cong, but it would be just his luck if a boy from Prospect became the first. He could not remember if there was a room of Egyptian antiquities upstairs as well. A mummy would provide a welcome distraction.

Switzer whined, "Sir, I want to see the shrunken head."

"What shrunken head?"

"There's a shrunken head down here, sir. So big." For a moment he concealed his bitten nails by clenching his fist.

"No there isn't."

"Yes sir, there is. Daddy told me. There's Indian stuff, bows and arrows. And a super necklace of shark's teeth. And someone else's head with tattoos on it."

He tried to stop the jabber of excited voices. "Quiet. Shut up. Or we'll leave."

---

* The Museum has changed a lot since Drury's visit.

Malcomson, a know-all, joined in. "I think he's right, sir. Some chap who sailed with Captain Cook brought back things. They showed them in Trinity a while back. Masks and headdresses."

"Nonsense."

Some of the boys were surrounding an attendant. "Where's the shrunken head? Where's the shrunken head?"

"That oul' fella? He's not on display. The room he's in has been closed to the public these ten years and more."

Drury recalled how the museum was always short of money. Since it could not afford to pay enough attendants, various exhibits remained unseen in locked rooms while collections of incredible interest and value were stored unopened in the basement, or dumped in various decaying storehouses elsewhere in the city. All available funds were spent in polishing up Celtic artefacts and displaying brown photographs of old IRA brigades. Your Irish heritage . . . we can't afford to show you anything else.

"We're particularly interested," he lied. "It's a school project." Anything would be better than touring the silver teapots and glass pigeens upstairs.

The attendant was young and new. He hesitated.

"You can have a word behind if you like . . ."

They gathered outside an office. After a long time a bald-headed man poked his head out. "Sorry, not a chance."

"We're doing a special study of Melanesia." That was not quite untrue, since Headmaster was always setting essays on Captain Cook.

"No."

It would have to be the upstairs balconies after all. He began rounding up the boys when someone else appeared.

"Hi there, Jim." A familiar face, and evidently they were on first name terms. Who the hell was he? Drury always had trouble remembering people's names.

"Hello . . ." He could vaguely recall meeting him at one of Michael's parties. Presumably he was employed here in some capacity. An archaeologist? He smiled ingratiatingly. "I'm afraid we're intruding . . . just a sudden nostalgic desire to see the old Jivarro head . . ."

"A pity it's not on view," the man said. Brian? Denis? "It doesn't seem all that long ago since it was the most popular exhibit in the Museum."

"I told them the gallery was closed, Mr Broderick," the attendant said.

Ah. Memory creaked. "There's not a chance, Maurice, that an exception could be made?"

The boys were blocking the corridor. Another attendant wished to pass carrying a tray with a tin teapot and some digestive biscuits. Maurice was actually smiling.

"Oh, I don't think we should always be so harsh. Just this once . . ." Perhaps he made the exception because of their mutual friendship with Michael.

Grumbling, the attendant they had first approached led them to a big room lined with showcases crammed with junk. This was the ethnographical collection. Among the feathered cloaks, decorated war clubs and New Guinea masks was a big deal table covered with files, open notebooks and cardboard boxes filled with potsherds and broken pieces of comb. Evidently the limited facilities of the Museum had obliged someone interested in Viking Dublin to work in here. Thankfully he was absent for the time being.

The attendant shouted as the boys ran round making all the cases rattle.

"Keep them brats away from the table in the middle. You don't want any knocking over them bits of pots. Isn't there enough mess without making more?"

Lonergan found a preserved Maori. A century and a half ago he had been murdered for the sake of his tattoos, his head cut off and preserved. "Pretty good, isn't he, sir?" The swirling patterns on the papery skin covered cheeks and forehead. "Looks like O'Keefe, doesn't he, sir?" O'Keefe had bad acne.

For a century the poor dead New Zealander had been second best to the Jivarro in the opinion of every small boy who visited the Museum. "Here he is!" A whoop from Beamish brought them all running. The shrunken head was preserved under a bell jar like a stuffed bird. It was black, the size of a grapefruit, its eyes closed, its thick lips sewn together. The boys struggled, fighting to get a glimpse of the diminutive showpiece. They shouted questions; Drury was not sure of the answers.

"When you killed your enemy and shrunk him like this you acquired his virtues. Some people ate their enemies for the same reason. Yes, cannibals. Yes, there still are cannibals. But shrinking his head is an even more obvious demonstration that you've got the better of the poor fellow. No, they don't shrink heads any more. Yes, I'm quite certain. How did they do it? They used hot sand. They'd put it through there, into the cavity at the neck. Then they'd swing him round and round by his long hair . . ."

"Sir, sir . . ." Kingsmill, who was too fat and too feeble to push his way through the scrum to gaze at the horrible thing, was shouting from another case of exhibits.

"Sir, is this anything to do with you?"

He went over to where Kingsmill was standing by a case full of African masks, voodoo objects and the like. It was dominated by two magnificent Benin bronzes, noble contrasts to the objects that were attracting the attention of the twittering boys. Kingsmill pointed to a yellowed label whose inscription was written in ink that had faded to brown. "Oba or chief. The hole in the top of the head is for the insertion of an ivory tusk. Late Middle Period. Mid 17th Century. Donated by Major James Drury, MC."

"Look at that, sir."

He was aghast. How did Grandfather come to be in possession of things of such quality? Of course!

"That's my grandfather."

"Oh sir! Where did he get them from, sir?"

"He didn't get them himself. His father did. My great-grandfather."

Other boys drifted over from the Jivarro head and caught the bronze stare of the imperious Africans.

"My great-grandfather was a soldier." Up until this generation many male members of his family had been in the British army, behaving with a persistent inconspicuous gallantry that had got them nowhere.

"Did he loot them, sir?"

"They were souvenirs. He was in the Ashanti wars."

"Where were they, sir?"

"In West Africa. Nigeria. About a hundred years ago. The chap who ruled the place at the time was pretty savage . . . like Idi Amin. Human sacrifices, bodies all over the place . . ." He'd have to look up details. "The English had to send in an army to clean up, and my great-grandfather was on that campaign."

"And the clever old fucker grabbed these, sir?" Schoolboy slang had deteriorated. Whatever happened to golly and crumbs?

"They were spoils of war."

"How did they end up here?"

That was the question. "I suppose someone in the family thought that they were things that everyone ought to see."

"But sir, how can everyone see them?" They weren't even on display. Only in Ireland, preoccupied with its own miserable little heritage, would a national museum hide away treasures like these.

He rounded up the group, which was becoming tired, and led it back to the station. In the crowded rush-hour train the boys did not feel like giving up seats they had fought to obtain. As he stood swaying to train rhythms, he thought about his grandfather. He remembered how the old fool had sold off his mansion and farm to the Land Commission for less money than would now buy a large car. Hardly a man of business. Here were old wounds bursting open afresh. He imagined the scene when the African objects were disposed of. The Major, retired, self-righteous, eking out a pension on his run-down estate. Every penny accounted for. He had never been wrong about anything. Cellars or attics being cleared out; the bronze heads lying in the dust.

"Ugly brutes . . . I wonder if the Rector would have them for the Bring and Buy?"

And then some other ass, most likely his grandmother, would have thought of the Museum. In those days it had still been the dumping ground for colonial cast-offs, associated with military men and district officers in topees. If only someone in the family had had some sense and held onto these things, they would have been his by now. They were worth fifty thousand pounds at least.

Rain began as he cleared them off the train at Killiney Station and led them back to the school. Past the lodge where Mandeville, the maths master, had been allowed to reside and endure the damp for the past decade, a "sleeping policeman" had been built across the pitted tarmac drive. Beside it was a DEAD SLOW sign. Someone had painted out the SLOW so that it read DEAD. Prospect, a Victorian mansion, was cold even in summer, but endurable in July. During the winter the sufferings of all who had to move through its lofty rooms were not alleviated by Headmaster's jubilation that the oil crisis was a justification of his Spartan policies.

"You might have caught an earlier train," wailed Jaws. The maids would threaten to leave if they could not get off by five-thirty. She had to do most of the cooking, since domestic staff was difficult to recruit. Prospect paid maids and cooks the same wages as the teaching staff, but only the subnormal were prepared to accept menial work in a boys' preparatory school, when they could get just as much money by working in any supermarket. (Why didn't he obtain a job in a supermarket?) Drury glanced into the dining room, surveying the memorial notice board in the shape of tablets from Mount Sinai, and the pitchpine walls spotted with the customary photographs of sadistic or homosexual masters sitting among sportive small boys. He sniffed the grease hiding in the cracks of the scrubbed wooden tables. Tonight there would be toad-in-the-hole. It wasn't a duty evening for him and he didn't have to stay.

He bicycled home in drizzle to the little three-bedroomed house that had been grudgingly picked out for him by his family trust. Even though his family had kept up the grandiose concept of a trust, it had not been able to afford the ten thousand outright that should have been his inheritance, and he was paying off a mortgage. Nearly all his father's estate had been used up to pay the cost of the nursing home where his mother had spent her last years.

The house was semi-detached. He could often hear his neighbour's television through the dividing wall and the shared laughter of a comedian's jokes. It had been built by a contractor who had put forty-two living units in a space for which he had only been given permission for forty. He had squeezed in the extra two some months after the others were completed, and no one in authority had come along to check.

The entrance to the estate was marked by a boulder like a dolmen on which its name, Goleen Park, was chiselled in deep lettering. Drury's abode, along with a dozen others, was in Moorish style with Spanish arches and some rudimentary iron work. Another group had been given a neo-Georgian gloss with Doric columns on each side of the panelled front door (Doric being easier to mass-produce than Ionic or Corinthian), and multifaceted windows like spider's eyes which caught the sun's rays and were fire hazards. The more expensive featured a small bay window and a bottle-glass pane. In America such accessories come under the heading of camp architecture, but here in Goleen Park they were regarded with great seriousness. Georgian or old Spanish extras were hallmarks of respectability. All the houses had roofs made of tiles that resembled burnt toast. The contractor had skimped on building materials and labour, and there were problems with drainage, plumbing and electrical fittings. It was no use trying to sue him, because he had retired with a fortune to the south of Spain.

There were other reasons why in an era when house prices had risen spectacularly the houses in Goleen Park had not kept pace with market values. Just opposite, the local Corporation had built a massive council estate. The Corporation houses were much prettier and better built, with carefully laid-out courtyards and squares. Old trees had been preserved, now defaced with literature cut into their bark. The inhabitants of this estate included a good many children and unemployed youths, who spent their time either proclaiming their sympathy for the IRA in aerosol spray or stealing. They broke into respectable people's homes, peed on the floor and took away the television. In lighter-hearted mood they stole cars and spare parts. The battery from Drury's Morris Minor had disappeared a couple of days since.

He went into the kitchen and threw down his brief case containing uncorrected exercises under a poster of Middle Earth. Agnes sat at one end of the deal table making jewellery. She was surrounded by pieces of shaved copper, dried bubbles of superglues, plaited bootlaces, horseshoe nails, springs, hammered discs, pieces of leather and what looked like scapulas. Some finished examples of her work were thrown into a shoebox. She was no Fabergé.

She was a lumpish girl with thick coarse hair that she plaited every day in the little plaits and then undid. She had big breasts and dark eyes that managed to look languid and inquiring at the same time, an expression that he had once mistaken for intelligence. Six years ago when his mother had condemned their intention of getting married, she had been right for the wrong reasons.

Theirs was a mixed marriage. He was a Protestant, she a Catholic. They had met in circumstances that had been far from ecumenical. He had attended a tennis club dance given by the Church of Ireland in a parish down in the country. The dance had been just as terrible as any other he had ever been to. He often mused on the legend that such functions were enjoyable. There had been the usual plain sweaty girls, the band too loud for the confined space, the conga, the raffle and the balloons spilled out of a net and exploded by drunkards. But the evening had been made enjoyable by the presence of one pretty, bright-eyed, sarcastic gate-crasher. The local Rector, terrified of the threat of mixed courtships, had firmly forbidden any Catholics to attend. Agnes had been smuggled in by her partner, who pretended that she was a Protestant cousin instead of a Catholic girlfriend. The partner drifted away during the course of the evening, leaving Drury to fall in love.

Both his family and hers were horrified when they expressed a desire to get married. The Doyles were losing a daughter to a jobless Protestant arts graduate, while Drury was agreeing that his unborn children should be brought up as Catholics. His mother called upon a clergyman, a distant cousin, to dissuade him. (Many of her relatives had gone into the Church of Ireland, thus contributing to the family's impecuniousness.) Mr Tweedy lectured him at length, mumbling into his sherry a number of times, "I hate to see an old family go this way." His remarks were typical of the behaviour of the Protestant clergy in general, who spent their time making endless feeble protests about mixed marriages and never coming up with their own version of *ne temere* in order to embark on the politics of confrontation.

The wedding in a cathedral-sized triumphal neo-Gothic church had been a dismal occasion. Afterwards both sets of relatives endeavoured to console themselves with champagne. His family was represented by Aunt Hatta (his only close relative, and the only member of his family to have hung onto her money) and his mother. The Doyles became merry, as indeed did Aunt Hatta, for whom champagne was a favourite tipple. But in his mother's case, it proved to be a depressant and she wept, spoiling the fun. Two years later, when she emerged from her nursing home to see her grandson baptised with oil and water along with a dozen other infants, she wept again. Shortly afterwards she died.

It was only a few months after her death that Agnes ceased going to Mass. She took down the Infant of Prague on the return of the stairs and the framed certificate in their bedroom proclaiming that the third Pope ago granted a dispensation for their marriage. She gave up rhythm, Billings and prayer, and took the Pill. She became interested in alternative cultures.

He had ceased to keep track of the fringe religions, cults, philosophies and various solutions to life's problems in which Agnes had been involved. At very brief intervals she had investigated different forms of meditation and had absorbed the teachings of successive oriental seekers of enlightenment. It seemed to him that she and her friends failed to take any of these enthusiasms seriously, since they skipped from one to another so easily. Involvements in cults could be expensive. He remembered the visit to the commune that had concluded that the world's energy impulses were concentrated in the Scottish Highlands. It had taken more than the profits from making leather jewellery to pay for that trip. Was that the lot that believed in reincarnation? Agnes was already interested in primal memory and prepared to tackle the concept of rebirth.

Her change in lifestyle made her earnestly promiscuous. She had a succession of lovers whose values she respected and who were interested in the same things she was. Most of them were on the dole or drawing assistance, which amounted to about the same money that Drury earned. They specialized in accomplishments like ornamental lettering or hacking out jewellery. He made little attempt to tell them apart, but thought of them by number, like items on a Chinese menu.

He had gone some way towards accepting the lovers. They came and went. Almost worse was the food. In the early days of their marriage there had been an emphasis on trying to get her weight down and she had involved him in some cruel alimentary regimes which he had thought of as the Leningrad diet and the Bangladesh diet. Recently, she preferred to eat things that brought understanding of the living environment through which man may acquire health and happiness by achieving harmony with the world around him.

"What's for supper?"

"Cassoulet."

He glanced at Kevin his son, who was hugging his Action Man and spooning in Mr Heinz's variety of beans. Kevin was having his revenge and would eat nothing else. When he was a baby his diet had been faddy, a whole year on mashed potato eaten at breakfast, lunch and tea, another on natural yoghurt and honey. Now he scorned Adjuki beans, mung beans, black-eye beans, red beans, broad beans and kidney beans. Such delights were for Drury.

Sometimes he protested about her menus. He did now. He said, "I could do with a steak." She pouted. "I said I would like some meat once in a way."

"I wish you wouldn't keep harping on it. You want steak, you buy it yourself. Right? And cook it. Right?" She prepared to dish up. "I ran into Yvonne Nolan today in my lunch hour. She gets her holidays in a couple of weeks. Why don't you?"

"Holidays in National Schools start at the beginning of July. Prospect follows the schedule of English private schools and does not break up until three weeks later."

"Yvonne's bought herself a new car, a neat little Golf. Do you know she earns over six thousand a year. Double what that skinflint gives you. Right?"

"I've told you over and over again. Yvonne Nolan works in a National School. National Schools pay their staff properly. They get government grants at junior level. Private schools do not get the same grants if they teach children under thirteen."

"I thought you got a grant for teaching Irish?"

Stupid cow. How many more times did he have to tell her. "That's right. Without it my salary would be even less." He was shouting; Kevin crept away. "Parents can allow their children to opt out of learning Irish by paying the equivalent of the grant in addition to school fees. A good many do. They prefer their boys to learn another dead language. Latin. I work at a reduced rate for the privilege of being in a corner of a foreign field that is for ever England." He reflected that the premises of Prospect offered a new dimension to the phrase "a richer dust concealed."

"Then isn't it time your headmaster hauled down the Union Jack?"

"You know perfectly well we no longer fly it on Founder's Day . . ." he bellowed before realizing that she, too, was speaking metaphorically.

The plate before him was filled. In addition to the beans there was the usual rabbit food dressed with sesame oil and cider vinegar and something with the texture of string.

"What's this muck?"

"Carrageen. It contains iodine and most of the B-complex vitamins."

He poked at it with a fork. "It looks like entrails. The auguries are not good."

"I told you about it yesterday. You agreed to try it, right? It's nothing faddy or trendy, Jim. It's just part of a practical approach to things which includes the awareness of the effects that various foods have on the body processes . . ."

"I don't want it."

Her face became blotched with anger. "Cook your own dinner!" She picked up her plate and made for the door, followed by Kevin. Soon he heard her heavy footsteps tramping upstairs and the sounds of the transistor she carried about with her. He sat for a few moments surveying the glass jars of beans, lentils and dried herbs, the black molasses and dark brown sugar. Her herb garden stood in the window. When the time came to bury her murdered lover's head in a pot of basil, she would need a larger container. Behind it were other straggling pieces of greenery, not potted plants, but pot plants, ho ho. The mind-expanding qualities of cannabis had never been apparent in her case. Would he sweep up the whole lot, together with the packets of seaweed and put them all into a garbage sack? That would make her really angry.

No, he'd give himself a treat.

He went outside and down the road past the Corporation houses and the vandalized playground. The supermarket stayed open until eight. A butcher wearing a white throwaway forage cap sold him a big steak. He bought frozen chips, a bottle of wine, mushrooms and remembered a jar of French mustard. He spent all the money he had with him and came back to the house whistling. Kevin and Action Man leaned out of the window aiming a machine gun at him. It gave him pleasure to supplement Action Man's lethal wardrobe. Being a peace lover, Agnes disapproved of toy guns and soldiers.

In the empty kitchen he fried up the meat and threw in chips. Oh, the pleasure the smell gave! He was taking the frying pan over to the table when he caught sight of some things on the dresser. They were pieces of broken china. Trembling he put down the pan and examined the designs on the shattered fragments—a little bit of a peacock, some sprigs of plum blossom.

"Agnes!" No answer. "Agnes!" He could hear the hysteria in his voice. "How did this plate get broken?"

She called down, "Kevin did it."

"Do you happen to know how much it's worth?"

"You shouldn't have left it lying on the settee."

How he loathed the word settee. He remembered now he had rung Michael to get his opinion about the plate. And then he had replaced a broken light bulb and watched the news. He must have forgotten about it.

"Why the hell didn't you put it in a safe place when you were tidying?"

"I wasn't tidying." She was fanatical about sharing household duties. "Anyway it's stolen property. And Michael wouldn't give you more than twenty quid for it."

She came down stairs carrying a poncho.

"Where are you going?"

"Out." She slammed the front door shut. Because of Kevin he couldn't even leave the house now for a drink. Not that the local pub was much fun nowadays, being crammed full of youths tanking up before departing on their nightly routine of pillage.

He ate his steak which had grown cold and put Kevin to bed. Then he went into the sitting room which was dominated by a big fireplace surrounded with simulated marble. Over it hung the Paul Henry reproduction and the string picture that had been wedding presents from her relatives. The curtains had a violent pattern featuring Greek keys which Agnes considered "striking". The adjective "striking" applied to decoration invariably meant hideous. He had never bothered to impose his own taste, which he considered to be very good. Taste was like pitch in music; you had it or you didn't. He allowed Agnes's preferences to dominate, the Indian wall hanging studded with pieces of mirror, the Art Nouveau Celtic poster by Jim Fitzgerald.

He switched on television. All his neighbours had colour, and their pictures emerged crystal-clear because they chose transmission through a piped system he could not afford, which carried programmes from Britain as well as those broadcast locally. Lack of colour was only an occasional handicap, say during a programme about tropical fish or about Turner. Lack of the pipe was more serious, particularly in summer when reception tended to become blurred, like this programme beamed from Cardiff showing a group of voluble old men talking Welsh. He changed to the only local station he could obtain and looked for a moment at some bearded musicians in Aran sweaters. He disliked Irish traditional music. He could not understand why the work of Sean O'Riada was regarded locally with the same reverence as that of Beethoven. He hated Gaelic singers with their wailing that sounded Arabic, the beat of the bodhran and the lilt of bagpipes pounded from sweaty armpits.

He switched off, poured out some wine and relaxed a little. Agnes was technically correct when she said that the Famille Rose plate was stolen property. Even though it would be his anyway in due course. But beggars could not be choosers, and he had no alternative way of augmenting his salary. He could not live on what he earned as a schoolmaster, a sum that kept well behind inflation. Agnes pocketed the pathetic profits she made from selling her handwork in seedy stalls in markets crowded with the type of dropouts that made up her friends.

He refilled his glass, going over in his mind all the ways he had tried to augment his income. Invariably they had involved antiques. Since his childhood he had had a passion for old things. He always lacked capital and had never been able to get an opening in a shop, apart from those weeks during the school holidays when Michael had allowed him to mind his place for a small wage. He was unsuccessful on his own.

Perhaps he was incapable of absorbing the necessary knowledge to make quick correct decisions.

He recalled some of the purchases he had made at auctions. How Agnes had laughed at the case of stuffed foxes still upstairs in the spare room. The trouble was that he had so little money, and the price of antiques increased year by year. He could only afford to buy items like pieces of damaged Staffordshire, stone porter bottles or old hand-irons. One year he had given all his rejected stock to Lover Number Four for his stall in the Dandelion Market. It had not sold, no man, no way.

Then there were the things whose value had escaped him, like the curious little mechanical dolls made out of bone that moved jerkily when the wheels beneath the platform on which they stood were revolved. After he had resold them to Michael for a five pound profit, they turned out to have been made by French prisoners during the Napoleonic wars, and the sum they were sold for at Christies was staggering. It was true that Michael gave him a commission, but as he kept saying you had to be tough in the antique game.

Another time at an auction in Ennis he had passed over a stained silhouette which was later identified as a portrait of William Smith O'Brien. The National Gallery paid several hundred for it. He had acquired the Harris and Mooney parchments in the same auction. They were also upstairs in their black tin box, legal documents from a defunct solicitor's office. Conveyances, wills, land deeds, indentures, part of Ireland's history.

He had bought them with the idea of making a bit of money in an unusual way. He sent two hundred letters to lawyers in America, getting the addresses out of an International Legal Directory. He typed them himself on a hired typewriter, a task that took weeks. He had been proud of the letter which was brisk and friendly. He could still remember how some of it went.

"Dear Snooks, I have recently managed to acquire for fun and a little profit some authentic Irish parchment (handbeaten sheepskin) deeds going back a couple of hundred years. They make excellent office decor, and I enclose a photograph of a newish one dated 1853." (The photograph and the Xeroxing had to be paid for.) "The indentures—the word is derived from the indentation on the top of the deed—were all handwritten by scriveners (Charles Dickens was one in his youth). The seals at the bottom were usually red and the scalloped top was to prevent fraud. . . . My prices are forty dollars for nineteenth-century deeds, sixty dollars for eighteenth-century deeds. The air postage is not that cheap, so that I suggest a minimum order of sixty dollars . . ."

You'd think hick American lawyers would jump at the chance of having an old Irish legal document on their office walls. Perhaps they would have been more interested in evidence of ancient property transactions in County Clare if the postal strike had not intervened. Only seven replied, and he did not cover his costs.

It was no wonder that he had come to rely increasingly on Greataunt Hatta for incidental expenses.

The rooms in Aunt Hatta's large house were filled with good pictures, furniture, glass, china, clocks and silver. She had never been burgled. The house looked shabby from outside, and she kept eight dogs. Antique dealers knew about her possessions, but she did not receive them when they called on her. One or two had been bitten. In the trade legends had risen about her house, legends which he could have substantiated if anyone had asked him. The Urbino Istoriato dish used as a dog's drinking bowl. The Meissen dessert plates hanging by their lattice work on rusty nails in the bathroom. The stains caused by the dogs on the Konya Ladik prayer rug.

Although few strangers visited her without her express invitation, she liked to receive her great-nephew. He would spend the occasional afternoon with her, and just before he departed she would offer him some gift with the graciousness of a Turkish sultana bestowing a diamond—a brown paper-bag full of cooking apples or a pot of jam. During the course of the afternoon he usually managed to supplement her generosity. Arthritis prevented her going upstairs very often, if at all, and her bedroom was now installed on the spacious ground floor. He would make a trip to the upstairs lavatory which he would combine with a quick forage in one of the spare rooms. Usually it brought some result, a Rockingham sheep perhaps, or the little dish that had contained pins and haircombings which he smuggled out under his shirt. She never suspected him, and he thought it was because he was not greedy. The most ambitious thing he had brought away had been the eighteenth-century miniature that had paid for his car.

His thefts were modest, but the risks he ran were enormous. Aunt Hatta was old, and with luck and justice she would eventually leave her possessions to him. She had even told him so. But he never felt secure since, even though he was her nearest surviving relative, other more distant connections existed. Suppose she found out? She might very easily alter her will in favour of someone else, someone who was rich already, like Cousin Jeremy over in England who was a Lloyds broker. Or she could leave her fortune to charity.

That was why he always took the objects he purloined to Michael. He did not tell him where they came from. He did not like to go elsewhere because although it was unlikely that other dealers would seek out the origins of the antiques he brought them, the fewer people who knew about his activities the better. They all knew about the existence of his aunt's treasures. Did Michael guess that the little objects Drury brought him came from her? Since he was his friend, and had been his friend for years, he preferred to trust him rather than take risks. But he wished that he did not give him such stingy prices.

Meanwhile he enjoyed knowing him. His own life was so dull. Michael was fun, he brought him into the world of antiques and was generous. At Christmas he gave lavish presents, a bottle of Black Bush or Courvoisier or a side of smoked salmon. (Aunt Hatta had given him a book token for the last twenty years.) He was always throwing parties. He was having a party tomorrow night to which Drury and Agnes were invited. However highminded Agnes's enthusiasms, they did not prevent her from enjoying extravagant entertainment.

She could buy the new car battery. She could pay for it. She was the one who insisted on driving it during the summer while he went around on a bicycle. This insistence dated back to the time when she had a proper well-paid job. Incredibly, she had been a qualified social worker, but had given that up for the time being for motherhood.

The wine was finished, and he might as well go upstairs. He checked Kevin sleeping in his room full of broken toys. It was only ten o'clock. His last thoughts before he dozed off were of his grandfather and the Benin bronzes and of the exercises he had forgotten to correct.

CHAPTER 2

A train roared in the distance and milk bottles clinked. The dog next door resumed its howling that had only ceased at daybreak. All over the estate and across the road among the Corporation houses other large dogs began barking. They were always worse in summer when prowlers were at their most active.

Downstairs he heard a voice. "The *Independent*'s leading article reflects the caution over economic policies in the Taoiseach's speech . . ." My God, it must be *It Says in the Papers* . . . after five past eight. School started at nine. Bitch, she hadn't woken him. She usually got up early to do exercises or meditate or greet your man, the sun. Somehow such mystical pursuits were reconciled with the drone of the radio.

He dressed and shaved hurriedly with a blunt throwaway razor in the bathroom, whose state of filth verged on disgusting. He brushed his teeth, taking care as he searched among hair combings, tampon applicators and Valium tablets that he used toothpaste and not cream for removing her moustache, as had once happened. He ran down to the kitchen where he filled a bowl with muesli, settling beside Kevin to crunch it. Although her muesli was really quite good, it had to be well chewed, and eating it rapidly was like swallowing jacks. Her bread was coarse, very coarse. She left her herb tea and made him a cup of Nescafé. They did not always quarrel. He kissed her as he got up to leave.

By cycling furiously he was just in time as the bell rang for Assembly and files of boys pushed into the main hall. Prayers rang out, Headmaster's voice striking the usual note of blended unctuousness and severity. Morning had broken, to be greeted by Latin with Remove and English poetry with IIA. The momentum of the summer syllabus, culminating with cricket practice and a spell of prep in a hot classroom buzzing with flies, took him through the day.

When he cycled back to Goleen Park at six o'clock, Agnes was already dressing up. She wore a garment that had been designed for a poor Asian woman, long-sleeved with a quilted bodice, navy blue and decorated with sprigs of flowers. Around her neck she had fastened a beige painted Bagru scarf. There were silver rings on all her fingers, silver earrings in her pierced ears and a gold zodiac sign hanging round her neck. To her regret she had been born Libra, the least decorative of zodiac symbols. Librans were sunny-tempered talented people. She cleansed herself with milk of lilies and splashed her face with gillyflower water which did not contain the glands of a poor civet cat.

"Got a babysitter?"

"He's spending the night with the Bradys." The problem of babysitters was a bourgeois one, and there had been times when she did not bother about it at all. When he was a baby she'd go down to a pub leaving Kevin by himself. Social worker, family therapist, heal thyself. The Bradys were a fairly recent discovery. Years ago in her professional capacity she had contact with Mrs Brady who was a battered wife. In the last year she and her family of delinquent sons had moved into the nearby Corporation estate and the acquaintance had been resumed. Drury did not mind; friendship with the sons was a defensive ploy that might well prevent their house from being burgled. Kevin enjoyed himself at Maison Brady, sitting up until midnight, watching television, drinking strong tea and the occasional sip of stout.

Michael's party was scheduled for eight-thirty. Around nine they got to work on the Morris, whose new battery did not seem to work much better than the one that had been stolen. Maintenance on the car was neglected; it would never pass one of those MOT tests they insisted upon in England. It was very old, old enough to have two illuminated arrows as indicators. Tyres were bald, rust was thick and brown, and the windscreen wipers did not work so that the driver had to stop when rain fell.

They started with difficulty and went across to the Bradys, where they left Kevin, together with Action Man and his comfort blanket. Then they chugged over to the steep slopes of affluent Killiney and ascended to the misty heights where Michael lived in his castle. This was an imposing building that had been erected by a prosperous nineteenth-century draper. It had cut granite facing, mullioned windows, and a dried moat which had once hidden unsightly servants going about their business from the view of their masters. A flagpole and television aerial competed for prominence above the east tower.

The tarmacadamed drive was lined with old-fashioned street lamps whose glow was muted because of the floodlighting. On both sides, flowerbeds that appeared to have been stamped out of the lawns with pastry cutters were piled with fertilizer smelling of dirty feet, and nurtured nursery-grown annuals and marmalade-coloured roses. Scattered here and there were ferro-concrete reproductions of Roman sarcophagi, and urns shaped like the Portland Vase filled with geraniums. Arrows directed cars towards a steep field whose value as a site was nearly as much as that of the whole housing estate where the Drurys lived. The floodlighting bathed the lines of cars. The Morris Minor is a cult car, he thought sadly, as he manoeuvred between a Porsche and a BMW.

Mooney fawned on him as he stepped out.

"Hello, Mooney, how's life?"

"It's not like old times, Mr Drury, sir." Drury had to agree. Michael had acquired Mooney with the castle. His old employer, Mrs Willoughby, had left a quarter of a million pounds to charity, and at the time of her death had still been paying the old malcontent fifteen pounds a week. Michael paid him five times as much, yet he snivelled for the past.

They climbed the castle's big steps and entered the hall where Michael, wearing a dark blue velvet dinner jacket and frilled shirt like a crooner, stood greeting guests, the Gatsby of Killiney. Drury had known him for about ten years. The hair and sideburns had become tinged with white, the paunch under the shirt was filling out. They met some time after Michael had left the bank, for improbable as it now seemed, he had begun his career as a humble bank employee. (Not that bank employees were humble nowadays.) He had not been a cashier, but one of the people at the back who went around carrying statements and cheque books here and there. No, that was not correct either, because he must have had access to the computer and understood its working.

Once when he was drunk he had confided to Drury the details of his working career. He entered banking when he was very young, at exactly the same time the new computer was installed. Those were the days before bank managers became cringing slaves to computers and their dictates, and still had power to bully their customers and their employees. It was because his boss was such a so-and-so, Michael said, that he first challenged the system. The method he used was not original; in the United States it is one of the commonest types of computer crime. But Michael thought it up all by himself. Primitive man probably discovered how to make fire in many different places at many different times.

Michael's way of embezzling involved what is known in America as the salami or thin-slice-at-a-time technique. It relied on stealing tiny sums of money from other people's accounts which he programmed the computer to pay into a dummy account of his own. They were minute amounts: seven pence from Customer A, three pence from Customer B, sometimes as little as a farthing (this was in pre-decimal days) from Customer C. When he first began he had been cautious enough merely to round down sums ending in fractions to the nearest whole number.

All he had to do was to wait for these small increments to accumulate in the bogus account. It was surprising how quickly and satisfactorily they added up. He was careful never to divert sums from any particular account more often than once a year. As far as he knew no customer ever queried the small discrepancies in his statements. In by far the largest majority of cases they never noticed them. If they did find a sum did not add up, either they thought their maths was at fault, or they could not be bothered to contact the bank and argue about it.

Later, Michael became bolder and the salami slices became thicker. Over some years his account grew fat, until he was able to invest it in a couple of lucky real estate ventures that made him rich. He described his final interview with his manager.

"The old fart knew that something was going on."

"Oh?" said Drury, disappointed, since he had hoped to use the story against him some time.

"It wasn't worth his while to investigate. The cost and effort of prosecuting would end up more than the amount I'd nicked."

"You didn't get all that much, then?"

"Enough for the old property deals. And after that, home and dry. It's the first hundred thousand, Jim, that's the hard bit. When that's been earned the money comes easy. It earns itself."

It certainly did. Now he greeted Drury casually, slapping his shoulder. He kissed Agnes, embracing her and pinching her bottom with the hand that did not hold his cigar and whiskey glass. Beside him Orla, his new mistress, watched coldly. Three years ago he had left his wife for a succession of beautiful girls. It had been an ungrateful action, because he owed a lot to Maire. She had been his childhood sweetheart, even more adept at social climbing than he was. She had smartened up the farmer's son, taught him to dress, smoothed some of the rough edges from his voice, traced his descent from a High King and told him to call himself Michael instead of Mick. Now he paid her a huge allowance and she lived alone and unhappy.

More guests were coming up the steps, the skins of the women's mink coats rippling in the floodlighting. (Michael himself had a mink coat to ward off winter chill, or rather, a coat lined with mink. He said it had cost four thousand pounds.) As Drury went through into the barrel-vaulted hall, he reflected how his host's taste had influenced his secondary career. Most of his money had been made in property deals. Nearly everyone in Ireland speculated in property, the way people in America speculated in stocks and shares before the Crash. But his real love was the antique business. Even in his banking days he had bought and sold antiques. He became adept at prising good brass grates from the bedsitters of improverished old women and replacing them with gas

fires. Everyone was happy, the old women with their new easy source
of heat, Michael with his profit. Aladdin's uncle had pioneered that
racket, new lamps for old.

For more than a century antiques had been one of Ireland's principal
exports. Michael was among the first to recognize when the traffic
began to flow the other way, and when it would pay him to import furniture from the continent. Men of Ireland, enriched by an economy
that was momentarily buoyant, clamoured to fill their newly-acquired
mansions with old things that provided a hedge against inflation. Michael toured England, France and Germany to bring back the furniture
that he sold to the new rich. He knew exactly what they wanted. His
house, a showcase of the things his customers liked, was filled with ornate tables, bureaux and cabinets in rosewood, satinwood, bronze and
gilt. In the hall, which contained a number of these pieces, a bureau
had disappeared since Drury was last here, for Michael could not resist
a profitable sale. It had been replaced with something just as gilded and
ornate, on top of which was displayed the Vincennes clock acquired at
the Mentmore sale.

Raising his eyes, Drury examined the row of stag antlers that, together with a large painting depicting the slaughter of hunted animals,
hinted at baronial opulence. This was blended with an ecclesiastical atmosphere imparted by some artefacts which appeared to have been
acquired from a church that went modern after Vatican II. A font was
being used as an ashtray. There were also touches of modern taste in
the big bronze bust of Michael done by a local artist, the inevitable
Jack Yeats painted in colours resembling Neapolitan ice cream, the
wrought iron screen which divided hall from drawing room, and the
soft red carpet underfoot which was ornamented with the Kenny crest
repeated over and over again.

In the dining room a fine old Waterford chandelier hung from the
hammerbeam roof. Under still lives of a strangled pheasant and a
disembowelled hare, the whole length of the back wall had been laid
out as a bar where six barmen were dispensing limitless drinks. Most
of the male guests joking with them and addressing them all by their
Christian names would be drunk before the evening finished. Their
wives would drive them home, defying the menace of the breathalyser.
There used to be a theory that it did not matter how drunk women got,
since the garda seldom stopped them at night time. A ban-gard or po-
licewoman had to be present when a lady was required to urinate for
forensic purposes. And all the ban-garda went home at eight o'clock. Or
so people believed until the story went around of the trapped tippling
woman driver who only escaped punishment by substituting Chanel
Number Five for her urine sample.

Drury pushed to the bar and ordered a Paddy. Agnes had slipped away and joined a group of girls who stood around a television celebrity who had exchanged some sort of feeble show-biz career in England for local stardom. Although he was mobbed everywhere he went in Ireland, he could obtain easy oblivion by slipping over to London or going off on a continental holiday when he would be unrecognized. Presumably there were celebrities like him in Albania. Drury speculated on the conceited fellow's personality problems as he watched adoring women around him sipping Blue Nun. Was the popularity of Blue Nun connected with its religious emblem, which hallowed suburban drinking problems?

Moving among the guests he observed how Dublin had produced another new aristocracy. He recalled the peevish reflections of Jonah Barrington and other nineteenth-century observers when they complained about the lawyers, doctors and attorneys who replaced the milords and viscounts fled to London after the Act of Union. The current group of parvenus who formed the crust of a provincial society had achieved wealth and prominence even more rapidly. Many had climbed from levels of bare subsistence through the recognized gradations of display and power within ten or fifteen years. He saw several politicians whose faces, bland or boozy, appeared frequently on the front pages of newspapers. No doubt their appearance here indicated into which party coffer Michael was pouring funds that would benefit him sooner or later. There were plump building contractors who had made their fortunes in England and regularly spent part of them gambling during Cheltenham race week; farmers whose land had become as valuable as if their acres supported city centres; accountants who earned fat percentages sorting out the finances of shady clients; property developers hungry to flatten yet more Georgian buildings and replace them with office blocks; architects whose success was gained by bonhomie in city bars rather than by the flair and accuracy of their designs; a spotty pop star or two. He reminded himself that they were all fun-loving generous people enjoying their wealth. There was no meanness about them; they had made their money and now they were spending it joyfully. These were the men with one foot still in the bog, whose difficulties in adjusting to wealth so fascinated sociologists. For example, that property man talking to Michael had knocked down numerous quiet residential streets, but still liked to accept luck money at business deals. Drury would have been delighted to wrestle with the traumas induced by newly acquired wealth, known, he believed, as the Mercedes-with-the-bald-tyres syndrome.

He took another whiskey to soothe the envy that burned in him. He noticed other guests who had yet to make their first hundred thousand.

Michael cultivated a number of writers and artists to appease his cultural snobbery, not only imported writers getting ever richer on tax concessions, but Irish men of letters. A few of these had written extraordinarily successful historical novels dealing with the gloomier periods of Irish history. Any work of fiction that brought in Cromwell or the Famine sold like hot cakes. But the majority of native writers, well represented here, considered themselves fortunate if they made five hundred pounds out of a book that took several years to complete. Michael had also invited along some people from the National Gallery and the Museum whom he liked to have around so that he could pump them about his purchases of paintings and antiques. Like Duveen he had some Berensons on tap. Drury ran into Maurice, whom he had met in the Museum the day before.

"Thanks a lot, Maurice, for letting the boys in to see the ethnographical collection."

"Hello, Jim. I'm glad they enjoyed it. Seems a pity a lot more of those things aren't on display."

"Why aren't they?"

Maurice looked wary. "There have always been problems of space at the Museum. And of course, we're desperately short of funds."

"A funny thing. You know those Benin bronzes? They were donated to the Museum by my grandfather."

"Is that so?"

"I had a good look at them yesterday. Long time since I've seen the dear old faces."

"They're nice pieces all right . . ." the other said cautiously. Obviously he had never given them a second glance. A Celtic chauvinist uninterested in any work of art created outside Ireland after around 1100 AD. The Sistine Chapel and the Mona Lisa would never inspire in him half of the enthusiasm he felt for the Tara Brooch or the Ardagh Chalice.

"I suppose that those bronzes *were* donated? They weren't by any chance merely lent? What I mean is, if they are only on loan, my family would not be too pleased to learn that they were hidden from view the way they are."

Maurice shook his head. "No, they were given all right. The Drury bequest was recatalogued a year or two back. It contained quite a lot of interesting material from West Africa."

"Do you mean to say there was more Benin stuff?"

"Oh, quantities. Not as fine as those heads, of course. Most of it has been returned to Lagos."

"I beg your pardon?"

"Surely you know the Museum has a policy of handing back certain parts of its foreign collection to their countries of origin?"

"What on earth for?"

"There's a widespread feeling that such things shouldn't be here. They are largely the spoils of colonial exploitation."

Drury was furious. "I thought that was a view only held by Marxists? or by impoverished museums eager to clear a bit of space in order to exhibit a few more kernstones or trial pieces or other local artefacts? You're hardly handing back the Elgin marbles."

Maurice was unruffled. "It's a debatable point. As you say, not everyone thinks it's a good idea to dispose of museum material."

"I should think not."

"But it makes for good foreign relations. Recently we shipped some items from the Pacific collection back to Hawaii."

"Hardly a matter of returning something to an ex-colonial society since Hawaii is now a part of America."

"It's a debatable point."

"What about Grandfather's bronzes?"

"Oh, they're under discussion. I should imagine they will be off to Nigeria one of these days."

Drury said angrily, "Would it not be better to sell them and use the money to pay the salaries of extra attendants to exhibit some of the things that lie in the Museum's offices and cellars?"

"You should write to the *Irish Times* about it." Maurice drifted off to talk to a French film producer eager to make yet another film that demonstrated Ireland was a beautiful place filled with simple garrulous peasants. Drury attempted without very much success to talk French to his wife. Then a heavy hand shook his arm. "How's the little school?"

"Not too bad, thank you." What was his name? Ah, he remembered from the son who was at Prospect. Kestervan. Not an attractive boy. Father a career diplomat attached to the American embassy.

"Sandy's settled down at last. He thinks the school is great. So different from High School back home."

"At least he's stopped running away."

Mr Kestervan laughed loudly. "You know people often ask me why I like sending Sandy to that weird little place. But I'm an Anglophile, Mr Drury. I was over in London as a young GI more than thirty years back and I saw the courage of those British. I share your headmaster's admiration for Winston Churchill. Helen, I said to Mrs Kestervan when I saw Prospect, here is a place which may appear to be quaint, but where Sandy will learn the proper old-fashioned values."

Drury was wondering if he should mention the problem of Sandy's pot-smoking, when Mr Kestervan was suddenly swept into conversation by the wife of an EEC official eager to talk about high prices in Brussels. He wandered to the far end of the room where doors opened onto a terrace above the swimming pool that Michael kept heated all summer long. Little lamps slung on eucalyptus trees illuminated the surface. Already, though midnight had not struck, a blonde in a long pink chiffon dress was being thrown in.

"Stop . . . please don't . . . please don't . . ."

He wondered if she would be saying that if her escort got her upstairs. At the last party much use had been made of Michael's Imperial bed, trimmed with eagles and sphinxes. Next day a girl had been found lying in his marble bath clad in a black bra. ("Isn't a convent education a great thing? A hangover from the boarding school days when she had to wear a shift when she wanted to bathe.")

Michael had style. Out on the lawn a band played from a marquee. Listening to the shrill notes of disco music, Drury decided he would look for a girl and go dancing. But first of all he would eat. And what was more, he would eat well. He obtained another refill of whiskey before going to the small back dining room, where among modern Waterford bowls piled with pyramids of rosebuds and stephanotis, a lavish buffet was spread on Irish linen table cloths. He knew that it must have been prepared by Orla. When she was not exercising her hunter in suburban fields, lying out before her masseuse or impulse-shopping at Dublin couturiers whose prices, if not their fashions, kept pace with those of London and Paris, Orla spent time doing Cordon Bleu cookery. She stood directing three old women dressed like maids in a French farce, who dispensed thick cuts of cold roast beef, elaborate salads and dishes of lasagne and quiche. He piled his plate and found a chair.

There were few people about. The heart of the party would remain close to the long bar, and much of Orla's lovely food would remain uneaten. Many of the guests who drifted in here came in for confidential reasons. Some politicians were talking slander, while a supermarket owner and an importer of shirts from Taiwan, having ceased to discuss ways of avoiding bankruptcy, were comparing strings of polo ponies.

"Hello, James."

Here was Mrs Hackett, wearing a long foxy brown dress and discreet jewellery, a string of pearls hung beside a regimental badge that showed a grenade picked out in diamonds. Behind her Colonel Hackett was throwing back whiskey sharply, like a Russian drinking vodka.

"I forgot you were acquainted with Michael Kenny. Can't say I approve very much of what's been done to the Castle."

They were neighbours of Michael's and, like Mooney, they regretted the old days. Sometimes the Colonel looked out of the chilly little drawing room of Darjeeling and spied on Castle Xanadu through a telescope.

"Poor old Maud must be turning in her grave. I'm no snob, but good God, look around you . . ." His voice was loud. "An even more dishonest lot than usual." He glared at a bleary-eyed member of the government.

"Now Denis, not while you're eating another man's salt." They had been coming to Michael's functions for years. He liked to invite the odd Protestant as ornament like black men at liberal parties in America.

"Jolly good salt too . . ." Like Drury they had heaped their plates with food. "Mr Kenny has always been kind to us old fogies," Mrs Hackett said. They were silent for a time while they tried to cut the beef with the side of their forks. Then they talked about weather, gardening, the Colonel's work for the British Legion and the current Test Match. Between mouthfuls of red meat, Mrs Hackett enquired in tones of icy patronage after Agnes. She had never ceased to have the suspicion that Agnes was not only a Roman Catholic, but had once been a nurse. For her nurses remained unacceptable, sisters of Sarah Gamp. A neutral ground for conversation seemed to be social work, although she had not approved of Agnes's sort of social work, which had been for a proper wage. (Ah, happy days!) She herself still worked harder than Agnes ever did and for nothing, keeping alive the tradition of Lady Bountiful.

Drury drifted over to the supper table to get puddings, laden plates of chocolate and meringue. Michael appeared with a train of revellers like Dionysus. His arms were around two girls, one of whom was Agnes. "Hello there!" Orla, Drury, the Colonel and Mrs Hackett glared at him. "Isn't it a great party?" he shouted. "Isn't it a great life?" He was gone in a minute. Mrs Hackett remarked, "This may well be the last party here that we'll be attending."

"Oh?"

"We've been giving some thought to the idea of moving. We can't manage much longer. And the burglary has made us rather aware of how vulnerable we are. You heard how Denis lost all his shooting cups?" She went on to describe the flat they were thinking of buying which would be protected from intruders by a porter as well as being centrally heated. The oil stoves and single storage heater at Darjeeling did not help her arthritis. The snag was the awful price of flats in the Dublin area . . . She began bleating about inflation and Drury thought he would never get away. Luckily the television celebrity came into the room. Aware that the eyes of Killiney and Foxrock were upon him, he was sober. As he helped himself to a modest meal, mindful of his figure, Mrs Hackett prepared to offer him discreet homage. Drury escaped to the bar.

He downed another whiskey and tried to enter into the spirit of things. He made a pass at a girl whom he knew slightly, whose name escaped him. He fancied that his ill success was connected with his dull plimsolled image. He had a dance with the French film producer's wife in the marquee that vibrated with sound, reminding him of the old tennis club dances. He talked to a pretty woman who turned out to be Australian. In his life his score with Australians was zero—he had never met one he liked. After ten minutes of listening to her nibbling her vowels, he decided that he had not broken his duck. Back at the bar the hired barmen looked more sober than ever as they dispensed drinks at an unabated rate. The Hacketts, who had arrived promptly at eight-thirty, went home long before people began to really disgrace themselves. Two girls slipped off their clothes. The splashes in the swimming pool got more frequent. Mooney stood by with a pole to prevent anyone from drowning.

Agnes reappeared dishevelled on the arm of a bearded man whom Drury recognized as Number Four. He was on Michael's visiting list because he was an artist who painted huge ugly pictures of the sort that banks and insurance companies loved to buy. This was the one who, she once confided, was entirely passive in bed. He had a wife and children, and passivity went some way to soothe the guilt he felt as a result of his Catholic upbringing. "Step aside," Drury murmured, and threw him into the pool. With the glow of satisfaction he felt, the best thing to do was to go home.

"I'm off. Do you want to come?"

She was still laughing at the plight of the man in the water, waving at him as she trotted away. The spotlit clock on the castle turret said half-past three, and beyond the floodlighting the dawn was coming up on Killiney Bay. A peacock, already awake and striding round the ferro-concrete urns, gave loud cries, waking many of Michael's neighbours. Colonel Hackett's plans to shoot it had not been finalized. Other guests were striding or swaying down the tarmac, the light making their shadows tall. From the field where the cars were parked came the purr of rich pampered engines.

The Morris refused to start.

"Where did you get the battery?"

"Mm . . ." she murmured, giving him a big wet kiss. "Sean Brady sold me one . . . very cheap . . . ten quid . . ."

"You bloody fool, don't you see it's more than likely he's sold our own one back to us?"

"Get another!"

She waved to a Porsche snapping into gear.

"Why don't we get another car? Fucking Protestant meanness!"

He tried again.

"I'm walking back." She climbed out and went down the drive, her vodka-regulated pace an alternative stomp and stagger.

It was plain that he needed a push. He stopped several guests who good-naturedly agreed to lend a hand.

"Put her into gear."

"Try a bit more choke . . ."

There was a tremendous backfire and a chorus of cheers as they reached the turreted gateway and the engine broke into life. He picked up Agnes halfway down the hill, who climbed in without protest, rested her head against his shoulder and fell asleep. A little further on he heard the blare of a horn and a Mercedes with lemon-coloured headlights pushed by him. A woman rolled down the window and gesticulated. He had to brake sharply and stop. She was the French film producer's wife.

"Mr Drury, Mr Drury, your fleek is out!" He realized she was talking about his indicator. When the Mercedes roared onward he found that once again he could not start. He freewheeled downhill and got going at last with a lurch. The garda waiting at Church Road to catch drunken drivers did not stop the little vehicle weaving past them. They may have had pity on it.

Next day was Saturday. Drury had to take classes on alternate Saturdays, but luck was with him and it was Trimble's day. Although his throat ached from smoking, he found that sticking to good Irish the whole evening had been fairly successful and he had hardly any hangover. An envy pang formulated the fact that Michael could help himself to the best ten-year-old slurped into a crystal glass any time of day or night. In the kitchen he found a tin of fruit juice and brought a glass to Agnes.

"I didn't think you wanted anything to eat."

No reply.

"The herb tea seems finished."

"What time is it?"

"Half-past nine."

"Fucking Protestant."

"Should anything be done about Kevin?"

"Go away. Go to hell." She could retrieve him later. He ate a hearty breakfast downstairs. Just as he was finishing the phone rang.

"Hello, Jim, how ya feeling?" The tenor voice, made more so by the filter of the phone, sounded like John McCormack.

"Michael, you're amazing . . ."

"I just came in from a swim."

"No-one lying at the bottom of the pool?"

"Ha, ha, you're gas, Jimmy. There's a couple of fellas laid out in the sitting room though, never made it back to their cars. And I'll leave you to guess what I found upstairs . . ."

"It was a great party, Michael." Drury's voice was prim.

"Listen, Jim, would you ever do me a favour?"

His heart sank. "Anything you say, Michael."

"I was wondering . . . you a friend of the Hacketts?"

"My family's known them for a good many years."

"I noticed you were talking to the Colonel. And the gracious lady." There was a longish pause. "Did they mention anything about selling up their place?"

"Well . . . Mrs Hackett did a bit of her usual complaining . . . You know, the size of the garden, the cold and so forth."

"Listen, that's a sweet little property."

"Oh. Yes, I suppose it is."

"Right slap bang beside Castle Xanadu. I'd love to lay my hands on it."

"Well I suppose if they're selling they'll put it in the hands of Jones and Beamish. Old Bob Beamish's daughter is married to Alan Hackett who's a nephew of the Colonel." He kept up fairly well with what was going on within his tribe's black tents.

"I'd like to get in there early, Jim. I'd like to be in on the ground floor before the place comes up for auction. There's a good chance it might go high, and maybe I could tempt them beforehand."

"You plan to make them an offer they can't refuse?"

"You're gas, Jim. It's just that people like that like to see ready money. I don't mean anything dishonest, mind."

"Just a little sharp practice?"

"You took the words out of my mouth. Would you come along with me and see them?"

"You know them as well as I do."

"Just as neighbours. I've made a point of seeing them now and then. I'd like to go along and have a chat with the Colonel Sahib. On his home territory. And if you were there it might smooth things."

"I really don't honestly think I'd be any help."

"I'd make it worth your while, Jim, if any deal comes off."

"Oh. What exactly do you want me to do?"

"Get us invited over."

"You want me to set it up?"

"That's it."

"Oh. Okay, Michael. I'll give the Colonel a ring some time next week."

"I'd prefer if you did it this weekend."

"What's the hurry?"

"Oh, I just like to get things settled."

Drury didn't enquire further, but speculated that during the countless conversations the night before some information had been gained. Quite likely a rumour about planning permission. Most of the land on Killiney Hill was marked out by the Corporation on its plans as SRX, the symbol for "solely residential". That was apart from the park, which was POS or "public open space". Michael might have heard about a proposed change from SRX to a slightly different category which could give permission for the erection of a discreet block of flats on the Hacketts' land. That might be fouling his own nest, but it would make him a good deal of money. He could always move on; he was ripe for buying a Georgian mansion down in the country. The garden of Castle Xanadu together with the Hacketts' place would make a fine site. He might even have engineered some sort of arrangement. Like everyone else Drury heard rumours of dealings in high places, of sums of money paid to the right people. The fiddle rather than the harp should be the symbol on Irish pound notes.

If that were so, his haste was explained. He would offer the Hacketts a generous price, well above market value for their small bungalow, and try to rush a contract through before old Beamish had a chance of sniffing things out. A verbal agreement to sell was enough in a court of law nowadays, and Drury himself would be there as witness to it. Probably old Beamish would never cotton on. He was always conservative about house property prices in any case. Drury's own house had been purchased through Jones and Beamish, not only because his family liked to deal with Protestants, but on the assumption that its price would be cheaper than the current market level. Always buy through Jones and Beamish, people said, but never sell through a real estate office that skimped on advertising and consulted last year's prices when they made their estimate.

The Hacketts might lose out, but if there was something in it for him, Drury didn't mind.

"I'll ring them right away if that's what you want."

"Have us asked over tomorrow if you can. You wouldn't get a meal out of them?"

"Not possibly."

"Then the lunchtime sherry will have to do. You arrange things and I won't be ungrateful."

The Colonel was quite pleased, though puzzled. Michael? That fel-

low? That damned party. Never in my life seen such a waste of money.
Can't be acquired honestly. Agnes coming? Sorry about that. Expect
you some time after twelve, after church.

Michael called for Drury in his Rolls, a potent symbol of power.
During the worst of the petrol shortages when Drury had to queue for
hours to fill up the modest tank of the Morris, Michael had boasted
how fawning attendants kept the Rolls satiated when he slipped down
to any garage in the area after hours. Now, although it was raining,
neighbours came out and examined the car and its owner, noting his
striped Yacht Club tie and the cigar stuck out of his podgy mouth like
a lighthouse. He blew the melodious horn and they glided away, small
boys who had been waiting for an opportunity to scratch the paintwork
waving after them. They drove past families returning from Mass carrying Sunday newspapers, and came to the curve of the coast where the
sun shone on Dalkey Island. Darjeeling, located just above Castle Xanadu, resembled a dak bungalow. Dripping fuchsia and shrubs and
creepers jostled for room. Michael parked beside a clump of bamboos.
The rain emphasized the atmosphere of tropical jungle.

When Mrs Hackett opened the door an inviting smell of roast beef
accompanied her. Drury, who could expect couscous and bean salad for
his lunch, sniffed appreciatively.

"Go straight along into the drawing room. I'll be with you in a moment. I've just got to heat up the joint." When the Colonel was in the
United States as some sort of attaché after the war, prim grey-haired
Mrs Hackett had puzzled Americans by that statement which they had
interpreted otherwise than her simple intention of warming the roast.

The drawing room was brightened by an elaborate flower arrangement in which puce and scarlet flowers rose out of vases filled with
chicken wire and sponge. Mrs Hackett's form of artistic expression received public recognition when she did the flowers in church. She was
always given difficult times of year, those Sundays in November and
January when the garden did not have much to offer in altar fodder. It
was a question of honour never to resort to florists.

Some family miniatures and a carriage clock suggested old decency.
On top of a bookcase filled with Wodehouse rested the ukelele on
which the Colonel liked to entertain guests after curry dinners, strum-
ming "Goodbye Dolly Gray" and suchlike. There was evidence of foreign travel, a line of ivory elephants diminishing in size, an ebony cabinet containing brass toys and Kashmiri trays, pottery Chinese fishermen
balancing buckets on poles. Automatically Michael examined everything, while Drury seized the opportunity of reading the front page of
the *Sunday Times* which he could not afford to buy.

"A lifetime abroad and look what they bring home," Michael said loudly. "That's nice, though." He went over to a chest of drawers that was very much to his taste. "They never got that in Darjeeling." He put on half-rimmed spectacles and squatted down to examine the squiggly bits. "Nice marquetry. Lovely, lovely. Looks like the real thing. Louis XV I'd say . . . I wonder who the cabinet maker was?"

Mrs Hackett came in again. "How splendid your party was, Mr Kenny."

He got up, his knees creaking. "Call me Michael." He had been trying to persuade her to do so for years.

"The Colonel is still out in the garden. James, perhaps you'd like to take Mr Kenny out to retrieve him."

Drury led the way down the side passage lined with engravings of pictures by Lady Butler into the kitchen. On the deal table stood a line of thermos flasks. Since the Colonel hated waste of heat and energy, when he boiled a kettle he put any surplus water into a flask to be used on another occasion. Plastic buckets and bottles of clear yellow liquid pierced with glass tubes indicated that he still made wine. Drury shuddered as they passed the big white trough of a sink with the buckets underneath for selected types of refuse. The Hacketts stuck to the habit of making guests wash up. A guest was put in front of the sink where he set to work without any sort of detergent. The Colonel would tell him how the rivers and lakes of Ireland were polluted with Fairy Liquid, which had ruined the rise of the mayfly. Detergent was unnecessary for getting china clean. All you needed was hot water, he would shout, pouring out dribbles from the flasks. Drury had once broken a saucer and carried away the pieces in his trouser pocket rather than confess.

They went out of the back door into the walled garden where every inch was cultivated. Gooseberries, raspberries, strawberries, peas, runner beans, even courgettes were grown. At long last the Colonel had been converted from the idea that courgettes were nothing more than pansy marrows. Apple, pear and peach trees splayed, tied, spliced, pruned and nailed against scarred brick had yielded under torture and were prepared to give up generous harvests.

"A JCB would clear all this away smartly enough." Michael would see the Hanging Gardens of Babylon in relation to a bulldozer.

An old Labrador barked at them. When he was a puppy, Labradors had been proper working dogs, not yet symbols of middle-class affluence. He looked sad, perhaps because his master woke him every morning by throwing a tennis ball at him as he lay in his basket. The Colonel prodded a compost heap. He was protected from the rain by a coat that reached down to his ankles. He always maintained that this was the logical length for rainwear. His baldness was concealed by a khaki bush hat such as Australians, Chindits and Patrick Pearse once wore, its folds decorated with fishing flies.

"Hello, James, how's life in the coolie lines?" He nodded at Michael. "I'm coming in now. Sorry not to have been there to greet you. Awful lot to be done round the place. Have a man in one morning a week. Lazy beggar. Do you know he asks for five pounds? Five pounds just for a morning's work! And the fellow actually drives up here in a car. A car!"

He led them back through the downpour into the house to rejoin Mrs Hackett, who had poured out small glasses of sherry. Both Drury and Michael had noticed the whiskey and gin at the back of the drink cupboard, but Drury was relieved, fearing parsnip wine. The Colonel ranted about apples, proper apples, not foul French Golden Delicious. He expounded on the disadvantages of joining the Common Market. He said that the transition from pounds to kilos was a swindle, just as the transition from shillings to new pence had been. He insulted a number of Michael's political friends who had been at the party. He had been scathing about Irish politics for more than fifty years. His long life abroad had led him to the opinion that Ireland should be closed down. Drury remembered the time when he had brought up the subject of fairy rings in his presence. "Fairy rings! You never see any nowadays because there are no fairies. There haven't been any in this country since 1933. They all left when de Valera came into power."

Michael felt he had to interrupt.

"I believe you're thinking of moving," he said abruptly. Smoking that cigar was a mistake.

"Moving? What on earth gave you that idea?"

"Jim here passed me the word."

Drury received a furious glare.

"It's like this, Colonel Hackett, Mrs Hackett. You can see that your Darjeeling is right behind my own place. You can understand how handy it would be for me to expand out this way."

"Quite so. We'll let you know when we intend to put it on the market."

"I'm prepared to make you a substantial offer now. A good deal more than the current market value, plus an agreed further figure—whatever you and your legal people consider reasonable—for disturbance. You could get it valued by an estate agent. Save you all the auctioneer's fees. I'm telling you, you'd find it plain sailing if you dealt with me beforehand."

"Ah," the Colonel said. "I'm having a talk with Henry Beamish one of these days."

"Eighty thousand?"

The Colonel glanced at his wife. Mrs Hackett lied gently. "We haven't really made up our minds about anything yet. I know that James heard us murmuring about a little flat, but that's just an idea we like to toss up and down from time to time. There are so many snags . . . the garden, I couldn't bear the thought of being without my garden. Perhaps when we come back from our holiday in Scotland we might begin to think about the future. There's poor Roly as well . . . I really think we'll have to wait until Roly is gathered to his fathers before we consider leaving here."

Michael looked at the dog's white muzzle and lower eyelids dragged down to reveal areas of red.

"Ninety?"

Drury knew it was hopeless. Michael couldn't understand that the Hacketts felt the idea of his purchasing their beloved Darjeeling was something like sacrilege. They were new to the idea of selling property. It would take the exposure of an auction combined with the natural growth of greed for them to be converted to the idea that money speaks louder than finer feelings. Meanwhile they were behaving as if Michael were offering for the Petit Trianon. It took many more refined lies before he got the message. He contemplated putting out his wet-tened cigar end in a bowl of potpourri before pressing it into a silver ashtray won by the Colonel at Dehra Dun in 1938.

"We'll be off, then. If you change your mind, will you give me a buzz?" On his way out he paused beside the chest of drawers. "That's nice. You wouldn't think of parting with that, now, would you, Mrs H? Before you get down to the rough and tumble of moving?"

"Oh, no, no . . . really Mr Kenny . . . a family piece . . ."

He pulled out a wad of money, a roll tied with a rubber band.

"When I really want something, I'm prepared to be generous. Let's say seven hundred pounds? Seven hundred and fifty? It would go well at the back of my lounge." He smiled.

"No."

The money was slipped back into his trouser pocket. "Any time you change your mind you know where to find me."

In the Rolls Drury asked, "How much was that bureau worth?"

"It's tempting to make an open-and-shut offer when you see a good piece like that in the middle of a lot of junk. If they had any more decent furniture they would bring in the experts. There was one very like that went recently in Sothebys for eleven thousand."

Agnes thought the episode a great joke. Drury told her, "You realize that Michael would have given me a thousand or fifteen hundred pounds if the Hacketts had agreed?" That quietened her laughter.

CHAPTER 3

On Monday afternoon he had to take the scouts on a tracking expedition near the leadmines. Headmaster had pressed him into scouting. The failure of Prospect Troop A some years ago had not put him off permanently. Now that the fuss had died down and most of the boys involved had gone on to other schools, he felt it was time another generation learned about knots and hunter's stew. The new troop was amalgamated with others which were church sponsored and had become ecumenical. Drury owed some sort of debt to the Boy Scout movement, since he had got his job at Prospect after Mr Bailey was dismissed.

Mr Bailey's peccadillos had not harmed his career permanently, for he obtained a post in England as housemaster at a minor public school. Drury envied him; if only he, too, had the courage to get away from here. He would really like to leave teaching altogether. The worst mistake of his life, apart from his marriage, had been to take that diploma. He was stuck with it. He must try again to escape. The best thing he could do was the same old round of answering advertisements for teaching posts in English schools. Was it still the case that each job attracted a hundred applications? He might write to the British Council again. A year's teaching in, say, Malawi, could offer some measure of freedom.

Michael was irrepressible. Here he was on the phone again on Monday evening.

"Did you see Saturday's *Times*? Did you read about the auction at Harmony Hall?"

Drury had, although he had not followed the sale of the house itself. He seldom bought the *Irish Times* on weekdays. However, he sometimes treated himself to Saturday's issue, which had a literary page and a regular article about antiques and furniture auctions. From this he had indeed read about Harmony Hall and its owners, the Sherlocks.

"Any connection to you, the people selling?"

He nearly said, of course. What Anglo-Irish family was not connected to another?

"They're distant cousins. Not close enough to be of any direct benefit."

"Didn't your grandfather own a house near there?"

He could not remember having told him that, but supposed he must have talked at some time or other about the proximity of the inheritor of the Benin bronzes.

"About twenty miles away. In the same county." Mention of his grandfather made him remember how the old man had sold up at the very worst time before property values began to rise. His land had gone for fifteen pounds an acre. The Sherlocks had held on to their Georgian mansion until now. The house and farm had gone for a quarter of a million pounds, and according to the article in the *Times*, the furniture should fetch as much again.

"Did you see the catalogue?"

"No." Not at the price the auctioneers charged for it.

"Grand things in it. The English dealers will be there and they won't miss a trick. And the boys from the continent. Care to come down with me, Jim?"

Yes, Drury would. Curiosity was one motive. It was years since he had been inside Harmony Hall, and there were few enough of these old country houses left to go under the hammer in this way. The Sherlocks' place was virgin. Since the day that Cassel or Nash or Ducart or Adam or maybe an amateur ancestor sketching on the end-paper of the *Gentleman's Magazine* had designed and built it, not a stick of furniture had been sold out of it. When a period or a style went out of fashion, the condemned chairs, tables or chests of drawers went upstairs to the governess's room or the housekeeper's parlour and eventually to the maids' rooms. It was reported that several presentable pieces of Regency furniture had been found in the attics.

He had a faint hope that he might make some money. His salary had been paid recently and he had about fifty pounds. If he were sharp, he might seize the opportunity of buying some little bits and selling them for a quick profit. With luck, he would buy and sell on the same day. He could earn a bit by bidding for someone or keeping an eye on other bidders. Or by being Michael's dogsbody, just as he had been at the Malahide Castle auction and all the others. He supposed he would have to do him the favour of introducing him to the Sherlocks just as he had made him known to other owners of run down Anglo-Irish houses.

There were difficulties. The auction was spread over two days, Thursday and Friday. If he stayed at a hotel, that would be a minimum of six or seven pounds a night.

"Be my guest."

"That's very kind of you . . ." But Michael sometimes forgot his promises, and then Drury could end up with an unwelcome bill. He'd rather be independent. When Michael put down the receiver, he rang the Sherlocks, getting through after an hour's delay. Easier to ring Botswana than the Irish midlands.

"Who? James who? Oh, James! Stay for a couple of nights? We're rather busy, you know."

"Anywhere would do, Cousin Isabel." He knew they had thirty-two bedrooms. "You see, I've tried the hotels in Ballyhack, and they're booked up, all of them. And I'm bringing down this very well-known dealer."

"Does he want a bed as well?"

"Oh no. But he's rather counting on me."

He obtained reluctant consent. "Bring a sleeping bag." The next problem was school. He would have to be ill. In January he had taken a few days off by pretending to have flu, and then a couple of weeks later had caught the real thing. A relapse—Headmaster had not liked it. Now he arranged for Agnes to ring up on Thursday and describe an unspecified range of symptoms.

Wednesday was half day and he departed after lunch. Travelling with Michael was eventful, for old habits died hard. Before he specialized in eighteenth-century furniture, his taste in antiques had been more catholic, and he still liked a simple bargain. Ten miles out of Dublin he suddenly braked and pulled the Rolls into the side of the dual carriageway. Then he walked back three hundred yards, pushing aside hairy-hoofed piebald horses and freckled red-headed children to where some tinkers kept their stall. Drury could see nothing but rubbish—a glass fisherman's ball, a chipped china candlestick, and oil lamps, mixed with pieces of electric flex, a battered refrigerator, scrap metal and three baths. But as the Rolls sped by Michael had spotted a copper jelly mould. He beat down the shrill woman with the red boots and the brown buck teeth from twenty pounds to sixteen in a raucous argument where they competed as equals. The roll of money appeared from his pocket.

"I make a point of keeping friendly with these people . . ."

Later he pulled up again, a few yards beyond the entrance gates of a house in a grove of trees. To Drury's surprise he went round to the boot and pulled out a plastic bucket.

"Do us a favour, Jim, and go up and ask for some water. Say the engine is overheated."

"Overheated? This?"

"You never know, do you? And if the old lady lets you in, have a good look round. You'd be surprised how many of these small places contain one or two good pieces."

How did he know about the old lady? Drury trudged past the field with the retired donkeys and the neat flowerbeds and heard the benevolent cawing of rooks in the grove of beeches. He was invited to have a cup of coffee. He declined and while she retired with the bucket to the kitchen, glanced around her hall and peered into the drawing room. There was nothing memorable in the drawing room, but in the hall a grandfather clock showed a caricature of the full moon. He looked up the staircase and noted a walnut chest.

"Anything interesting?" Michael put on his dark glasses and they drove on. Drury told him about the clock and the chest. "On the way back, maybe." He switched on the quadraphonic cassette which filled the interior with strains from *The Merry Widow* as they bowled through the midlands.

In due course Drury was able to point out the ruin in the middle of a field that had belonged to his grandfather. The outline of rooms and fireplaces showed on a ragged wall like a ludo board. They came to a thirty-pub town which displayed large red auction signs and big arrows pointing down a winding country road. They followed it for some miles until they reached an elaborate gateway. The capitals on the pillars were carved with swags and topped with balls sitting firmly on the capstones. Sweeping curtain walls leading to outer pillars were disfigured with more red notices containing information about the auction.

Rhododendron bushes darkened the potholed avenue until they opened out on boggy fields filled with cattle and stumps where the Sherlocks had chopped down their park trees. Beside the high walls of the garden a patch of field had been roped off and marked out as a parking lot. Drury ran his eyes over the cars. A lot were local; one of his useless accomplishments was the ability to recognize regional licence numbers. They probably belonged to sightseers taking a day off to come and see the death of an old house and look inside it for the first time in their lives. Mingled with them were a number of Dublin cars belonging to antique dealers. Some continental buyers had brought pantechnicons.

Michael parked beside a canary yellow Mercedes from Dublin in which a man wearing a pork-pie hat was studying a catalogue.

"How's things, Gus?"

"Not so bad, Mick, how's yourself?"

"Struggling. You been round yet?"

"There's one or two bits worth following up." He showed his catalogue full of coded biro marks beside the lots. Michael pulled out his own and they made comparisons. Their tastes were similar.

"Have a look at these. Ormolu wall brackets of Louis XIV design, the demi-baluster back plates with putti playing trumpets centred by lion masks."

"Here's a lovely thing . . . walnut and marquetry commode mounted with cased ormolu escutcheons and toes in the rococo taste."

"I have my eye on this French Empire ebonized dwarf cabinet with red boulle spandrels mounted with gilt-metal foliate borders."

The house was big and grey, buried in trees and the twilight of history, with outstretched wings that tapered into bushes. A garda sergeant stood beside the marquee where the auction would take place the following day, while two security guards in blue uniforms with bright yellow peaked caps complemented the stone lions beside the hallway.

The pillared main hall was full of English voices, loud and insistent, belonging to people from Boothroyds, the London auctioneer. The Dublin real estate firm that had already sold the house had been allowed to come in on the auction in a subservient role, supplying porters and such-like, auctioning some of the bedroom ware and seeing that the bar was run properly. But quality such as that offered by the contents of Harmony Hall called for English expertise. Drury looked enviously at the young men and women whose elegance proclaimed their public schools, their years at the Courtauld, their apprenticeship at the V and A or Spinks. The women, he knew, were not paid very well, no more than twice his own salary. There were too many prestige jobs in fine arts and other fun professions like publishing and journalism, and too many women graduates from Oxbridge and other seats of learning competing for them. But the men were more privileged and looked sleek and successful. A languid aesthete in casual summer clothes sat behind a table piled with catalogues, three pounds or five pounds with illustrations. Greatly reluctant, Drury paid out five pounds from his little reserve. Illustrated catalogues held some of their value. He asked for the Sherlocks. The Englishman looked dubiously at his frayed tweed jacket which could hardly be more shabby than that worn by Cousin Gerald.

"Are you a friend?"

"I'm staying the night."

"I saw Lady Sherlock not so long ago. Sir Gerald's been wandering here and there. I'm afraid you'll just have to keep an eye open."

He located Cousin Isabel in the morning room by her voice, which was audible over immense distances. In her entourage he could recognize Billy Skibbereen who had been at prep school with him. He had gone on to Eton, while Drury attended a Dublin day school for sons of Protestant tradesmen. Irish representatives of the London fine art world tended to be titled. The Skibbereens were Union peers. He decided that now was not the time to make himself known, especially as he could see Michael nearby turning over a chair and examining its bottom for identifying marks. (Only very inferior dealers looked for worm.) He couldn't bring himself to make introductions at this moment. He sidled away and wandered round the big rooms that had so quickly been made uninhabitable by the rearrangement of furniture garnished with numbered labels. The crowd made it difficult to examine any lot in peace. Pickings. He looked at the uniform of a knight of the defunct order of St Patrick, a chandelier whose dusty garlands had been cleaned with spirit for the first time in years, prints of horses clearing fences by opening their front legs very wide, and a marble copy of the first Lady Sherlock's foot. They would all be far too expensive for him to buy. He wandered from room to room looking for bargains.

In the north-facing library the books had been unread for centuries. Book dealers, in general rather more decrepit than the furniture specialists, turned over big leather-bound volumes in mint condition that contained coloured engravings of birds and tropical animals. The remarks that Drury overheard them make were derogatory.

"A bit tatty round the edges."

"Only a second edition."

"Pity the spine is rubbed."

Elsewhere picture dealers were taking paintings down and turning them over, a Nativity, a still life featuring slivers of lemon peel and a disembowelled hare, family portraits by provincial artists and a number of canvases which Boothroyds claimed were old masters. Amidst the priceless furniture were ranged bottled gas stoves that ran about on wheels and provided the only heating in the house. Outside the dining room a two-ringed burner allowed Cousin Isabel to do her meagre cooking. The kitchen below with its anthracite burning Aga had been abandoned for two decades. Drury wandered downstairs and through the big room with its great pine table that had once seated a staff of twenty. On top, plastered with black numbers, were various archaic kitchen gadgets and a *batterie de cuisine* consisting of numerous copper saucepans engraved with the Sherlock crest.

In the scullery he found Cousin Gerald with his butler Mick Finnegan, a tiny old man who addressed his employer as "Boss". After a minute Cousin Gerald recognized him. "Hello, James. Come and give a hand, there's a good chap." Drury had not seen him for years, but this did not prevent him from having to spend the rest of the afternoon following in his wake doing useful things. He climbed a rickety ladder, a pair of pliers in his hand, arranging electric flex over hooks like Christmas garlands. Up the same ladder screwing cheap lightbulbs into en-

amel sockets. Giving an authoritative opinion about some frayed and
rubbishy pieces of flex that Cousin Gerald wished to incorporate into
the electric system.

"Tell you what, James. There are some spare fuses in the cupboard
in the housekeeper's room."

The housekeeper's room was far away, very far, the other side of the
kitchen. The great cupboard to which he had been directed was built
in and therefore could not be sold. He opened a sagging door and
found the interior clogged with jam jars and Gentleman's Relish jars.
In the old days the servants' condiments were always served in Gentleman's Relish jars. There must have been a hundred. Where were the
fuses? He pushed his hand in behind. Rusty cocoa tins with nails. Piles
of dusty straw punnets fitting into one another. A mousetrap containing a mummified corpse. What was that, thinking of corpses? A body?
He got a bad fright. It seemed to be something very like a corpse or a
mummy. Something huge lying along the back of the shelf like a
seasick passenger in an old sailing ship.

He pushed his hand in, breaking jam jars in the process. It was a
garden statue just under life size, covered over with silver paint. It was
very heavy. Trying to heave it out and underestimating its weight, he
could not budge it. He picked at the silver paint and decided that it
must be marble. Half a leg was broken off. On the remaining leg the
silver had run in bulges and blobs, like a skin disease. He had seen a
statue very like this somewhere else. Where? He remembered—in his
Aunt Hatta's garden in Killiney overlooking the goldfish pond. That
one, too, was also painted silver. He supposed he could get the paint
off, and if so, in spite of the fact it was broken, he would have quite a
nice garden ornament. People paid good money for this sort of thing.
He arranged the jars carefully in front of it, in the process finding a
punnet filled with cobwebby fuses.

On the way back to Cousin Gerald he retrieved his catalogue from
the saucepan where he had hidden it and looked through the last
pages. The statue appeared to be unlisted. There was no relevant lot
apart from "Contents of Housekeeper's Room". Hidden away behind
all that rubbish it had evidently not been seen. Worth keeping an eye
on.

"You've been a long time!" By now Cousin Gerald had abandoned
interest in lighting and was off on quite a different tack. He had found
a blocked lavatory. There were only three lavatories in the whole house
so this was serious. The nearest plumber was forty miles away. Drury
knelt down and pushed a series of implements, wire coat hangers, bam-
boo sticks and umbrella spokes, in the direction of the S-bend, releasing

antique excrement. Mick Finnegan swept away flood water over the mossy flagstones.

"What you want, Boss, is an eel. Put an eel down and it would clear in a minute."

In the end they had to abandon the sorry old jakes and leave it weeping. Cousin Gerald took him to his study where he produced a paintbrush and a box of stencilled letters that delighted him like a child. Drury was set to work to write negative notices, PRIVATE, NO PARKING, NO ENTRY, DO NOT TOUCH, OUT OF ORDER. He toiled, disturbed by streams of people coming in and wandering round to examine the Spy cartoons on the walls and the old copies of the *Illustrated London News* from which dust flew up in clouds. The fact that the rolltop table at which he worked was also for sale did not make his task easier. It was evening before he got his reward—a gin and tonic served in an old Waterford tumbler that was damaged. He cut his lip on a chip on the engraved rim. All the intact glasses were ranged in numbered ranks on the dining room table. The gin was in honour of the Boothroyds people, dominated by Billy Skibbereen, who exuded charm as only a man who expected a commission of fifteen thousand pounds knows how. All the dealers and the curious had left the house, which was now guarded for the first time in its existence by the security men hired by Boothroyds. Round about now Michael and his friends were crammed into the Commercial Hotel at Ballyhack.

For dinner the Sherlocks offered boiled chicken served by Mick Finnegan on card tables in the study. Billy Skibbereen listened patiently to Cousin Gerald grumbling about the lavatory, and to Cousin Isabel who was worried about the vulgarity of the purchasers. On the way back from gardening she had examined the cars in the parking field and noticed all the imitation tiger-skin seat covers.

"Cars!" said Cousin Gerald. "Do you know there are people who change their cars every year?" The Sherlocks had only possessed three cars in their lifetime, excluding the 1903 Daimler that had lain in the shed for seventy years, which Boothroyds had unearthed and sent to a special vintage car sale in London where it was expected to fetch forty thousand pounds. Cousin Gerald's grandfather had brought it to Ireland, the first car in the county. Soon after it arrived it had been lent to a royal personage over on a state visit so that he could tour more easily among his still loyal subjects. Drury's parents had firmly believed that the Sherlocks were given their baronetcy as a reward for this favour.

"Do you remember the Alvis before the war? We'd fill her up with fourteen gallons and still get change from two pounds. Keep it, I used to say to the man at the pump."

"Those bloody London chaps wanted me to prepare a field for planes and helicopters."

"You should have taken our advice," said Skibbereen. "You might well have attracted more foreign buyers."

"I won't have my cattle mucked about any more than need be." He owned pedigree Charlerois. It amazed the neighbourhood that although he was so thrifty about his own comforts, he was prepared to pay several thousand pounds each for the animals in his herd. Drury wondered about their fate after the house was sold.

"We're moving in with poor Muriel to look after her," said Cousin Isabel. "She's very seedy, I'm afraid."

He knew that Cousin Muriel was dying of a hideous disease. "What about your herd?" Surely not in Cousin Muriel's suburban garden.

"Oh, we're auctioning that too." Right up until the last moment the animals' welfare was paramount, just like the state of the walled garden, where Cousin Isabel had just spent a couple of hours weeding.

Before retiring, Drury, Mick Finnegan and a security guard accompanied Cousin Gerald in procession as the house was locked up. In the drawing room the furniture looked as if it were rearranged for a dance. Pretty well everything was being sold, apart from some silhouettes, miniatures and smaller family portraits. Cousin Gerald, who had been writing a history of the Sherlocks for thirty years, indulged in the usual Anglo-Irish mania for ancestor worship. The great mahogany doors of the drawing room closed smoothly; the powder closet, the library, the boudoir with its plaster ceiling were shuttered one by one for the first and last time before tomorrow's final dispersal.

Drury went off to bed carrying his sleeping bag, the little case with his overnight things and a saucer of Whiskas. The room he was allotted had a four-poster bed (Lot 731) on which were laid some numbered scarlet uniforms (Lot 750—Uniform of the Lord Lieutenant of the County and Lot 751—Uniform of the local Militia) which he was instructed to move to the chaise longue (Lot 747) close by. The washhand basin was draped with a grey blanket on which lay a cat nursing a litter of kittens. On the walls were two prints with more black numbers pasted at their corners, Wellington and Blücher after Waterloo (Lot 755), a royal visit to Punchestown with a numbered key (Lot 756), and a small, dark, damaged, unedifying oil painting of Lot and his Daughters (Lot 758). Starlings sounded in the chimney like rattling tin. He slept badly; midsummer it might be, but his sleeping bag could not disguise the fact that the bed was damp. He got up as the clock on the landing (Lot 240—AN IRISH MAHOGANY LONGCASE CLOCK with painted dial, the hood with scrolled cornice supported on fluted columns . . .) wheezed six o'clock. From his window he could see the marquee and further off the precious Charlerois. A cloud of cawing rooks greeted the weak June sun.

Breakfast was served on the same card table. Eggs were boiled in the electric kettle and picked out from where they lay beside the element. The tea was full of rags and bulbs of egg white that had squeezed from cracked shells. Afterwards, Drury helped Cousin Gerald stack plates and mugs in the small dishwasher which until a very short time ago had perched on a fine carved mahogany table in the back hall. (White rings from wet glasses had not improved its value.) The washer was the old-fashioned sort with a window. They switched it on and stared at the swirling water for some time.

"Damn marvellous machines!"

In the main hall bentwood and folding chairs were packed close together. There was not room for all the bidders, and those who could not find a place here would have to broadcast their bids from adjoining rooms. A pudgy young man in a pinstripe suit tested a loudspeaker while another tinkered with the closed-circuit TV that would aid bidders banished to drawing room and study.

Michael arrived early, already smoking a cigar. He looked aggressive, hair sleeked back above his velvet collar. He waved his mauled catalogue. "I couldn't stand that hotel a minute longer. They had the nerve to put a couple of extra beds in my room."

His friends were drinking in the bar in the marquee where they had assembled to arrange procedures for the auction they would carry out when the main auction was over. Some of the marks in their catalogues meant "Bid" or "Do not bid", since one or other of the syndicate would be assigned different lots, and the others had to refrain from boosting the prices. Drury was given the task of making several bids on Michael's behalf, since the sight of his flashy friend waving his catalogue or a pudgy finger often had a mercurial effect on prices. He noticed that the limits he was given were far higher than the Boothroyd estimates.

"They're English auctioneers and they're new to Ireland. Firms like that always estimate low out of caution. Boothroyds lacks Irish experience. If Christies or Sothebys were handling this sale, they'd know by now what happens when the adrenalin starts flowing in Irish veins."

"It won't affect their commission."

Then Michael and his friends began to criticize and disparage the things they were about to bid for, just as the book dealers had shown their contempt of the books they were about to buy the day before. It was as if by sympathetic magic they would keep the prices pegged. Perhaps they wanted other bidders to overhear their loud comments.

"That hunting table in the library . . . did you see the join in the legs? Crude job. Estate carpenter most likely."

"The Judith and Holofernes is no more a Caravaggio than last week's pin-up in the *Sunday World.*"

"Nineteenth-century copy . . . they know that themselves."

"Then why did they give him his initials?"

"Trying it on the continentals."

"The little landscape in the boudoir must have been repainted by the maiden aunt or the governess. I picked off a bit of varnish and it was fresh as a daisy."

"The table with claws and devil's mask. Millar and Beatty 1911."

By eleven all the rooms on the ground floor were crowded and the sofas in the drawing room and boudoir were comfortably filled with plump women. In the hall where the main action was taking place, Michael and his group found prominent standing positions in the back facing the rostrum. They were a small seasoned pack. There was an expectant buzz of conversation like a theatre on a first night. Among those gathered under the octagonal glass lantern were some peers interested in the conservation of Georgian buildings, many of the guests at Michael's recent party and a visiting American film actress. Foreign dealers had brought along ravishingly pretty wives and mistresses.

The loudspeakers spluttered and the auctioneer, another smooth-tongued Englishman, looked down on the crowded room explaining the terms of sale and mumbling about buyer's premium. Counterfoils in the catalogue must be completed, a deposit was necessary, all goods were to be dismantled and collected by Saturday, pounds mentioned in bidding referred to the Irish punt and not sterling. A man in an apron held up a battered chair. In moments the bidding reached hundreds before it was sold to an equally battered old woman sitting near the front. There were complaints that the loudspeaker wasn't working properly in the drawing room, and a pause while the circuit was checked. To Drury, used to auctions in Dublin where every object was fulsomely described and bids were sobbingly pleaded for, the style of the English auctioneer was unusual. He did not need purple passages. Everything was noncommittal, understated. It was like selling cattle. Prices were high; they made records. But Drury was familiar enough with the antique world to know that this year's records were next year's buttons.

After an hour he made one of Michael's bids and was alarmed to find himself the owner of a George III mahogany bureau with sloping front forming a secretaire, that cost over nine hundred pounds. Some time later he made his first bid on his own behalf for a silver gilt meerschaum pipe. Boothroyds' estimate was fifteen pounds; he knew a man in Dalkey who collected meerschaum and would willingly pay twenty-five or thirty. He opened at ten pounds and raised; within seconds the auctioneer's plummy voice was saying, "Against you, Sir." A squeak from the powder room pushed the bidding up to thirty, and the pipe eventually sold for fifty.

During the course of the day he found the same thing happening with all the other items he had marked—the china eggs, the nineteenth-century Russian travel book, the little brass image of Kali the Destroyer. All of them went well over the estimates, the Russian book in particular making a hundred and forty pounds which led him to congratulate himself on his discriminating taste. In exasperation he made a bid for a fun object—an elephant's foot umbrella stand. It was his for fifteen pounds.

"Kitsch," he murmured to himself. He knew he could always dispose of it at the Dandelion Market, and if he kept it for a year or so he might make a good profit, since he could prove that it was from the Harmony Hall sale. Anything out of Harmony Hall would retain an interest value. Meanwhile he was buying for Michael again—an ornate pair of three light candelabra, a satinwood painted secretaire, a nineteenth-century bust of Shakespeare wearing a tasselled open-neck shirt and drapery over his shoulders.

Evening came, and before the crowds departed he managed to introduce Michael to Cousin Isabel, who treated him with a rudeness that was so subtle he mistook it for charm. He left reluctantly, still hoping for an invitation to dinner. The Boothroyds representatives all left too, having made their excuses and fled rather than face another Harmony Hall meal. In fact the dinner was lavish. Humoured by the prices, Cousin Isabel produced a slab of salmon from the deep freeze and Cousin Gerald sneaked a bottle of wine from the bin of rare vintages that was being sold the next day. Drury's enjoyment of these treats was tempered by the Sherlocks' repeated exclamations and cries of joy as Cousin Gerald added the approximate day's takings with the aid of a pocket calculator. They discussed how the medical cabinet with its dangerous-looking century-old bottles (which had been in general use in the household up to a week ago) had made enough to keep any nursing home going for a month, and how a book in which Cousin Isabel regularly used to press flowers went for three thousand pounds. They laughed when Drury mentioned that he had acquired the elephant's foot. The old man's face creased in a smile. (Now he could afford new false teeth.) "I can't say I ever admired that thing, but if you had let me know you wanted it, I'd have given it to you before the show started . . ."

Afterwards they went in similar procession as the previous night, accompanied by the security man and Mick Finnegan, who was in a hurry, since he, too, had made notes of the day's prices ("Isn't it great, Boss?") and was anxious to get away to his local to relay them to his cronies. They trotted through the house at a fair rate. No piece of furniture had been moved, but the atmosphere had changed completely by its mere transference into strangers' hands. The old place had been sold to an agricultural college, and soon it would be filled with manure-coloured metal cabinets and concertina files. Drury went off to be among the scarlet uniforms and to worry in case Michael abandoned him with the things he had bought on his behalf.

The following morning much of the glamour of the previous day had gone. There were fewer members of the nobility, film stars and newspaper reporters. However, all the dealers turned up, Michael among them, to Drury's relief.

"Listen, Jim, I've a buyer for that secretaire and a Yank will give me a profit on Willy Shakespeare. I'll have to work at them most of the day. Will you stick around? There's nothing I want except the copper pots in the basement. You can go up to eight hundred on them."

They were among the last things in the sale, so that Drury had to linger right through the afternoon with raucous locals bidding hundreds for sun-faded curtains and competing for laundry baskets and bedroom china. He invested another ten pounds of his own money on a pair of epaulettes from the same sort of fancy uniforms as the ones in the bedroom where he slept. They were silver and tinsel, embroidered with gold shamrocks and came in their own shabby tin box. Then the bidding housewives, joined by a number of dealers, descended lemming-like behind the auctioneer—not the smooth Boothroyds' man but a representative of the Irish partner—to the basement, where they spent some time competing for pudding basins. When the *batterie de cuisine* came up, the bidding for it was brisk and soon exceeded the limit defined by Michael. After that, interest flagged, and there were not very many people around when the auctioneer moved on.

"Number 917. Contents of housekeeper's room."

Drury had totally forgotten about the silver-coated garden statue that he had seen two days ago.

"Fifteen pounds!"

"Yours, sir!" A pencil stabbed in his direction as the porter peered to identify him and note down the purchase. A coup! He was delighted. He looked around to see what he had acquired in addition. A pair of sagging chairs, a stained carpet, a broken hair dryer and all the Gentleman's Relish and jam jars.

By five the hammer had come down on the last item of the sale. When Michael returned Drury proudly showed him the silver statue.

"What do you think?"

"You've got a bargain. Just shows, even the boys from London aren't perfect. They shouldn't have missed it. Do you want to put it into the ring?"

"What do you advise?"

"You might make a nice little profit."

Drury excused himself to the Sherlocks, who were so happy about the money they had made that they lent him the estate car. He followed Michael back to Ballyhack, to the Imperial Hotel which stood in the market square, a dour place whose illuminated sign stuck to essentials—the location of the bar. Not even on fair days had it seen such activity. The landlord sent away to Cork and Limerick for more crates of brandy and champagne. The continental buyers were behaving like the invading Bosch, shouting their orders and falling into rages if they were not immediately fulfilled. They waved at waiters and barmen with savage gesticulations. One small Moorish-looking dealer had the temerity to clap his hands when he wanted service.

Drury knew Michael's particular cronies, men who shared the same problems—the difficulty of finding quality goods in a rising market to replenish the things in their antique shops. Harmony Hall was like a thunderstorm during a drought. Like the Sherlocks they could talk about little else but prices as they settled down to dinner. Over the Scotch broth and roast chicken and ham the conversation provided a contrast to what he had listened to the evening before.

"What do you think of Brandt giving seven thousand for the Chinese table?"

"He'll get a hundred per cent profit on it back home."

"Even after paying all the import duties?"

"Those Germans are always moaning about import duties the way the English go on about VAT."

"Did you see how Morris went for the clock?"

"Hardly a Tompion."

"Go on you ignorant bastard. What's wrong with Henry Jones?"

"What's that fellow Higgins doing here at all? I thought he was in jail because of that business with the Turkish authorities."

"He bid for those Egyptian things."

"What did you think of the big O'Connor?"

"Not very saleable. A gallery piece. I preferred that portrait of the man in armour Du Moulin bought. He's very pleased with it. Thinks it may be a sleeper—one of those late Venetians, Strozzi or Benotti."

"It's not a Van Dyck at any rate."

"There you go again. There's other clock makers apart from Tompion, there's other artists apart from Van Dyck."

Another drink and Drury's long-held ambition revived, the one about

throwing up teaching and getting into the antique trade. He was quite
pleased with the modest purchases he had made—and yet, if only he
had more confidence and more knowledge . . . As he ate his tinned
fruit salad, he listened to the calls for champagne from all over the
room.

The hard business came after the meal, in the big lounge upstairs.
There must have been more than thirty dealers from all over Europe
sitting in groups around various tables. No-one coming unexpectedly
into the room could have suspected that in this convivial yet subdued
gathering with its relaxed atmosphere, muted conversation and plenti-
ful supply of drinks, hundreds of thousands of pounds were changing
hands. The book buyers were conducting one auction; the continental
ring with some gestures and displays of Teutonic and Gallic tempera-
ment were soon in the midst of their own; at a third table half a dozen
English dealers were dividing up their purchases.

Michael's group went over to a table marked RESERVED and settled down with cigars, brandy and catalogues. Gus, whom Michael and
Drury had encountered in the car park two days before, acted as chairman. Was it true he had started his career by ringing the handbell outside a seedy auction room on the Dublin quays?

"Now boys, we all know what was paid." A gold tooth gleamed.
"Let's have no messing."

Between them the five dealers had secured something over fifty lots.
The winning bidder would pay the ring the price that the resale would
make now. The total difference between the original price and the
resale would be divided up among them at the end. Listening to the
figures mount up Drury desperately wished that he was in the club. He
found yet another variation in auctioneering technique. The Boothroyds' auctioneer had moved along slowly with long pauses and modu-
lated time-sequences, when he regained his authority with thoughtful
sips from a tumbler of water. Gus conducted the resale with lightning
speed. Just the number and the price paid were called out, or rather
quietly spoken, almost *sotto voce*. After bids were softly and swiftly
made, another scribbled set of hieroglyphics was added to the catalogues. Prices were often raised to half as much again as had been paid
at the Boothroyds' auction. Drury tried to feel sorry for the Sherlocks.

When the bidding was just about completed he humbly mentioned
the contents of the housekeeper's room. Michael backed him up.

"Quite a decent little marble statue—should clean up nicely."

Drury said, "My great-aunt in Killiney has one very like it. Perhaps
they came from the same source, since she is related to Lady Sherlock."

"Male or female, the statue?"

"Oh, female." Weren't female statues more popular?

"Venus," Michael put in. "Maybe Grand Tour, but more likely a Victorian copy of some piece in the Vatican or some other Roman hot-spot."

There was a pause. "And broken? Antique breaks or what?"

"Eh?"

Gus explained patiently. "Is it a copy of a specific ancient statue? I mean if it was the Venus de Milo you'd expect the arms to be missing. Is this anything you would recognize?"

"Can't put a name to it off-hand," Michael said.

Gus grinned. "Off-hand seems to describe it." He looked round the table. The others all shook their heads. "I hardly think there's much point in putting it up if no-one has seen it apart from Michael."

"Tell you what, Jim." Michael turned to him. "I'll do a deal with you on the side. Nothing involving the other stuff. What say, lads?"

The lads, more interested in conjuring another round of drinks, agreed readily enough.

"I know a buyer, a fella in Castleknock who's looking for something distinctive to go in front of his neo-Georgian job. Smarten up the suburbs. Say seventy quid?"

Drury found that this round was his, and the tally was ten pounds. The statue might be worth rather more than seventy, but it was pretty damaged. He would have the problem of trying to divest it of its coat of silver, and then he would have to tote it around trying to find a buyer who would pay him more. He might be stuck with it for months, and in the neighbourhood where he lived there was a fair chance that it might be stolen or vandalized. He accepted Michael's offer.

The quiet deals were completed. Rolls of money were brought out and changed hands immediately. Gus produced his from a plastic carrier bag marked Clerys. There were denominations that Drury had scarcely ever seen. The Sherlocks may have made more than the quarter million that had been forecast, but here in the lounge of the Imperial they had lost almost as much again. Still, everyone was happy enough, Drury included. As he drove back he did his sums. Profit on the housekeeper's room was forty-five pounds, if he subtracted the round of drinks. Michael had paid for his dinner and in addition given him another fifty pounds for all the work he had done. Perhaps he should have bid up for the porcelain eggs? Mrs Duffy in Templeogue usually bought that sort of thing, but she was stingy and mightn't have liked the price, which he thought was high. The epaulettes and the elephant's foot, on the other hand, were purchases he could always get his money back on and more—just about the best things his limited budget could come up with.

Next morning when all the dealers turned up again at Harmony

Hall, and all the loaded pantechnicons and lorries with their precious burdens were sliding away, it was like the end of a race meeting. People waved their cheque books and shouted for their hired vans in the effort to keep up with the condition of sale that stated all lots had to be taken away by four-thirty that afternoon. As the house emptied, Cousin Gerald drove his cattle away further from the car park, while Cousin Isabel and Lord Skibbereen stood and smilingly watched the dismantling of the elegant rooms. The porters lugging tables and four-poster beds out onto the gravel looked disgruntled since it had not occurred to the Sherlocks to give them a tip.

Michael's ring had hired a big furniture van between them. They stood and watched their ornate purchases as they were hauled on board followed by the statue, which looked very grubby in the open air with its peeling silver paint and mutilated limbs. Some time in the past someone had dabbed at the mouth with red paint, making it look as if it was crudely lipsticked. Drury felt rather ashamed of having sold this battered object to Michael, the more so when it was followed out by his less glamorous purchases. A file of porters brought up the two broken chairs, the hair dryers and five large cardboard boxes containing the jars.

Michael said, "I'll tell the driver as soon as he gets out of here to slip down a quiet road and dump that stuff out on the side. Come on, we must get going before he's on his way."

"What's the rush?"

"He's going to stop off at that house you went into on the way down. I'll have a crack at buying the things you saw. If the old woman doesn't want an instant sale, well and good. If she agrees, this guy will be passing half an hour after and can collect straight away."

CHAPTER 4

"What was the problem?"

"Temperature and sore throat. I didn't actually call in a doctor."

"I wish you would when you don't feel well. If it's the start of an epidemic you owe it to us to let us know as soon as possible. Didn't you have a temperature and a sore throat last term?"

"That was when I was beginning flu."

"Heather called to see you on Wednesday, but couldn't get an answer."

Agnes would have been away at her part-time job in the shop that sold joss sticks. Trust Jaws. He wouldn't put it past her to question the neighbours. "I think that was when I was feeling really wretched. Agnes was out, and I didn't get up to answer the door at all that day." He wished he could allay the fluttering in his stomach over the fear of a reprimand. The fear increased during the summer term when a succession of people turned up at the school to be interviewed for jobs, all showing signs of enthusiastic desperation. It was not that he liked school teaching, and if he was dismissed he was entitled to the dole. Yet here he was humbly soothing Headmaster's ruffled feelings instead of giving him a Harvey Smith.

The exhilaration he felt over his comparative pecuniary success at Harmony Hall lasted for a week, after which the Morris developed a fault in the gear box which cost fifty pounds to repair. He could rationalize this; if he had not made that profit, he would not now be able to pay the bill. Still, he was depressed. On the following Sunday he decided to go and see his great-aunt. He visited her fairly regularly to steal from her and to ascertain if she was any nearer death. He tried to forget that his great-grandmother had lived to ninety-six. Aunt Hatta was not yet eighty; he could not bear it if she lived to ninety-six and he had to wait until middle age for his inheritance, if it was to be his inheritance. He liked to keep her sweet. Today, for instance, he would help her in the garden.

As he cycled towards Killiney he reflected how tired he was of the foibles of his relations and connections. Their parsimony in particular.

He had been to England a number of times and had come to believe
that the English vice was not homosexuality, but meanness. He was
sure Englishmen were meaner than Scots. This meanness had come
over to Ireland, taken root like the rhododendron and developed into a
healthy sub-species. It was the other side of the coin from the behaviour of eighteenth-century rakes. Dante put the spendthrifts and the av-
aricious into the same circle of Hell. As the Anglo-Irish diminished in
numbers, the spendthrifts became extinct, but the others survived.

In the days when Aunt Hatta possessed a car and Dempsey, the
chauffeur, drove her about, she used to save money on postage stamps
and deliver all letters and bills in the neighbourhood personally. Now
she had a roster of acquaintances organized to give her regular lifts
down to Dun Laoghaire and Dalkey, where she toured the shops and
supermarkets seeking out bargain offers of rotten fruit and vegetables,
half-spilled packets of sugar and dented tins of fruit. She looked a sad
old thing, and in times past people used to give her their Green Shield
stamps. She had been caught shoplifting, but up until now store managers had been sorry for her, or afraid of her, and had let her off. At
home the parchment of her lampshades was made out of old family
documents. In winter she used no heating, although the house was
fitted out with fat old radiators, their cold grilles clogged with dust like
fishbones. The damp fostered the arthritis that moulded her hands so
that they looked windblown, and pushed her figure into attitudes of
pain like the Burghers of Calais. She did not complain, but displayed
her diseased knuckles proudly like duelling scars.

Her house, Eagle's Nest, was another expression of nineteenth-century affluence with details that were positively Wagnerian. A large ter-
raced garden fell down towards the sea and the view was majestic. Visitors found the situation enchanting, but Drury thought it a gloomy old
place. A place for dying, he considered hopefully.

He got down at the gate lodge and peered through the bars at Dempsey, long demoted from chauffeur to gardener, who was sitting reading
the News of the World. He was deaf, and Drury had to throw gravel
against the window to rouse him to come and open up the gate. Aunt
Hatta insisted that it should be locked at all times, not with any con-
ventional bolt or chain and padlock, but with a bicycle lock she had
stolen from a hardware shop in Ballynoggin. Viewing her dark-clad
figure in her Wellingtons and ragged silk headscarf—the same she had
bought at Callaghan's stand at the Horse Show the year that Hitler in-
vaded Poland—he felt that the house would be more accurately christened Crow's Nest. Her dogs barked savagely. Some were big animals
of the Alsatian type such as macho men like to own. Others were small

and fluffy with fur hiding their eyes. All of them owed their comfortable existence to her life-saving expeditions to the dogs' home.

She greeted him with her usual ghoulish crop of disaster stories about the neighbourhood. Did he know of the Corporation's intention of building yet more houses for the masses? It would mean more vagrants, more burglaries. Had he heard about the latest break-in, the gang that had gagged and bound the guests at a dinner party and strangled the canary? How different from life when she was a child, when the lower classes had lived far away and there was respect for property and capital punishment.

Then she said, "You'll find a spade in the shed." Every year she opened her gardens to raise money for the nursing home cum cottage hospital that she patronized. For all her avarice, she dutifully gave a portion of her worldly goods to a motley of charities that sustained lifeboats, war graves, old soldiers, lepers, the blind, and a place in Egypt that ministered to worn-out beasts of burden. The scheme that helped the hospital had long been a favourite concern since it did not involve a cash outlay. People were invited into the garden on a summer's day to view the flowers and pay large sums for the privilege.

Preparing the garden for this annual event was a task that got more difficult with time. Dempsey was very old, Aunt Hatta only kept him on because he could not be evicted from the gate lodge. Otherwise she gardened herself. Someone working like that in the Third World would have harvested the rice crop of whole villages. She fought the weeds that thrived in the rich Killiney soil and flourished in the nitrogen of decay. She cleaned the flowerbeds beside the terrace and the flights of steps leading down to the lawns, kept a great herbaceous border under control, attended the azaleas and the rock garden, and thinned out the bulbs beside the woodland path. Dempsey mowed the grass, groaning. Drury had seen a photograph of him dating back to the thirties, using the same mower.

When Drury attacked a patch of nettles, his hands were soon blistered and his back ached from pushing a heavy wooden wheelbarrow. At last they went into the house for tea, through the basement. Past the closed door that rattled, outside which sat two dogs shivering and whining.

"Poor darling Florence, just coming into heat . . ."

Past the dark room that had once held potatoes, but now, since Aunt Hatta's reluctance to tip the refuse men and their subsequent refusal to remove her rubbish, contained heaps of egg shells and empty tins of dog food. Every now and again a mound of tins would move lightly, perhaps shifted by rats or mice? All seemed to be very clean. Past the maid's room where Drury glimpsed the walls furry with damp, the holy pictures, the iron bedstead, the full chamber pot. Past the room full of broken china, empty bottles, and old copies of the *RTE Guide*, the *Radio Times* and the *TV Times*, for Aunt Hatta might deprive herself of many things, but not of guides to programmes for her large colour television set. In due course they would be torn up for lavatory paper.

The kitchen was dark, lit by a single barred window. An old woman in a white cap sat at the deal table cleaving a cabbage, sending down green leaves and slugs to add to the filth on the floor. This was Angela, Aunt Hatta's maid, older than she was and more feeble—for many things Aunt Hatta had to wait on her. Between them they had to have a daily to help them with the chores. Mrs Keogh, who brought them all the neighbourhood gossip, was suspected of stealing which was why it took so long to prepare the tea. Things were hidden away, the tea caddy in the oven, the biscuits and cake no-one could remember where, until Angela thought of looking in the linen cupboard. However, Drury felt it was better to have tea here than lunch, when Aunt Hatta handed him over all her sausage skins to eat and tossed bits of bacon rind round the room for the dogs to seek out. He remembered a decomposing chicken whose insides were swabbed clean with a toothbrush before it was served up and a dessert that appeared to be decorated with sparse pieces of chocolate which turned out to be mouse droppings.

He took the tray upstairs, a hazardous journey, since he could not see ahead to avoid slipping on dogs' turds. In the drawing room two cats with prize-fighter's faces purred on stained silk cushions.

As always he could admire the silver teapot with the pineapple on the lid, and the sugar basin standing on little hooves. Aunt Hatta poured out pale tea made with a single teabag. The Worcester cup she offered him had a thick black crack where it had been mended with Seccotine.

"Your friend, the one who bought Castle Xanadu from Maud, called in here the other day."

He was very surprised. "Do you mean Michael Kenny?"

"I think that's his name."

"He's never been round here before, has he?"

"No, he rang up very politely and asked if he could come and see me."

"I thought you hated all antique dealers."

"Mr Kenny is rather different, isn't he? He's more a business man. And he's a neighbour. One should make an effort to know all the new people who come into Killiney—the respectable people, I mean. He wanted to talk about Bettyview, wondering if he could help in any way. He came round last year when the garden was opened and was very impressed. He's had some experience in charities of this sort, and he had one or two really useful ideas. About where to set up tables and that sort of thing."

"But you've been dealing with the Bettyview business for years."

"He offered to lend me his man for the day."

"That's Mooney who used to work for Mrs Willoughby. You remember how he used to mow down her cyclamens year after year and the time he burnt the tennis net."

"He could hardly get into that sort of trouble here. All he has to do is to help Dempsey keep an eye on things."

Drury was increasingly puzzled. "Is that all Michael came about?"

"We had a nice chat about this and that. He knows all about those people who wanted to buy up part of the golf course for housing. He told me about the time you took him to see the Hacketts. I think Hugh and Vera behaved rather shabbily. Everyone knows they're planning to move out." She had hated Mrs Hackett since the days they attended the same dancing class.

"Did he give you a contribution?"

"He was terribly generous—that was the really nice thing about him. Do you know he had his money tucked up in a big roll in his pocket? Does he always carry it about like that?" She added, "I took him for a little tour of the garden. He admired the terraces so much, and showed a real understanding of the problems of keeping a large garden in order. He was rather envious. Everything is so much better planned than Maud's place. The only thing he didn't like was the lily pond."

Drury leapt up, went to the bay window and peered down on the terrace below. There was the little silver-painted statue similar to the one he had bought in Harmony Hall. It had presided over the water lilies for as long as he could remember.

"Did he mention the statue at all?"

"My dear, do you know, he's actually bought it."

His heart went cold.

"He pointed out how shabby it was, and how it rather spoiled the pretty curve of the pond. Of course I told him that I always had a great affection for it because it had been Jack's." She lifted her eyes reverently towards the big tinted photograph of Drury's deceased great-uncle placed like an icon over the chimney piece. There were photographs of him everywhere, with different dogs, wearing old-fashioned skis, in sailing boats with uniformed crews, even standing by an old-fashioned diving suit. Since his death, Uncle Jack, much bullied in his lifetime, had assumed saintly characteristics. Like Queen Victoria, Aunt Hatta suffered badly from that condition that Drury had defined as the Albert Syndrome—the exaggerated reverence of widows for their husbands' memory.

"He said that it was quite unworthy of Jack."

"What does he know about Uncle Jack?"

"Oh he admires him very much. He's read *Through Kingstown to Bray* with great interest and likes it enormously." Drury was familiar with the look of the privately-printed guidebook Uncle Jack had written in his youth and illustrated with photographs he had taken himself.

"If he thinks it's so ugly, why does he want to buy it?"

"Oh he was so frank. He said he had heard that I considered antique dealers to be meat for the dogs. He could quite understand why I was suspicious of these people. He didn't particularly want this thing with its arms and legs broken off for himself. It was just that he knew someone who had one very like this one, and he thought it would be friendly if they got together at last. Wasn't that rather sweet?"

"What did he give you for it?"

"That's a very rude question, James. If you really want to know, he offered me three hundred pounds." Carefully gauged—not too little, not too much. "I was in two minds about accepting, but he said if I liked he could pop it into the hospital fund. Of course I laughed and said I'd better handle the transaction, since there might be a little commission in it for me."

He looked out of the window again. "Why is it still here?"

"I insisted it should stay until after next Saturday. You can imagine the mess it would make if it was taken away now. Men trampling flowerbeds and any amount of plants damaged. The garden's got to be looking its very best for the Bettyview day. He wanted to take it away at once but I said he could wait another few days. He even offered me a teeny bit more money, but I was firm."

Gazing down at the lily pond he had to admit that the torso perched above the goldfish was extraordinarily battered. All the limbs were broken off close to the trunk except for the stump of a leg. He remembered how annoyed his aunt had been the time he referred to it as the Thalidomide Victim. From here the peeling silver paint looked grey.

He'd better clarify one point. "I saw something very like this recently. At Harmony Hall."

"You mean when Isabel and Gerald sold up? How silly, I'd forgotten they had one too."

"Did you get this one from them, or did theirs come from here?"

"It was rather amusing. We had the two statues painted silver. "Jack"—again the reverent glance upwards—"thought it would be fun to give one to the Sherlocks for their silver wedding. We went down with it in the boot of the car." If she'd allowed one to be given away, she must have been convinced that the other was a dud.

"Michael Kenny's already bought that statue from Harmony Hall. That's the one he was talking about."

"I'm not really surprised. He must have terrible taste, poor little man."

"But he told you someone else had it."

"I should think he got rid of it as quickly as possible. How much did he pay for it?"

Drury hesitated. "Less than he offered you for this one."

"Gerald and Isabel had their things valued by Boothroyds, didn't they? I should think Boothroyds were pretty sniffy about Silver Sally."

When he got home he rang Michael immediately.

"I hear you've been to see my aunt."

There was a pause. "She's a wonderful old lady. Bright as a button for her age. Must be pushing eighty."

"Oh, well on in her eighties."

"And what a heap of fine stuff. I'd heard all the stories. Is it true she keeps firelighters in a K'ang Hsi tureen?"

"Only paper spills. She considers firelighters an expensive modern gimmick."

"You've been to see her yourself? I thought you only went the odd time—every few months or so."

"It's two months since I last saw her."

Another pause. "Bring anything out?"

He winced. "No." For once he had paid a visit without stealing anything. "She told me about the statue."

"I overpaid her for it, Jim. Is that what's worrying you? When you told me there was a pair to the one you sold me, I thought it would be nice to match them up. Like I told you I've got this man in Castleknock as a client. I swear I won't be making a penny profit after paying your aunt and her damned hospital fund. It's just a way of doing this guy a favour."

"What's his name?"

"Daly. He's in advertising."

Lies.

"Jim, God help me, there's not profit in it. If I do make anything I'll let you in on it. It won't be more than twenty quid at the outside."

He had to leave things at that, short of severing relations with Michael.

The following Wednesday he went into Dublin on various errands for Headmaster. He toured the city buying exercise books, thirty copies of Julius Caesar, ditto of David Copperfield and a box of cricket balls. He paid by cash carefully keeping the receipts that would be presented to the Department of Education. With some of the change he treated himself to a copy of the *Irish Times*. Carrying the big parcels, he went down Grafton Street and into Bewley's Oriental Cafe, full of the smells of roasting coffee, dark wall panelling and stained glass with Art Nouveau designs. He sat back on a red plush seat and ordered coffee and a cherry bun. He opened up the *Irish Times,* which was like an artichoke with everything of interest concentrated in the centre. The centre pages contained news about films, theatre and the arts, some strident articles by women journalists, and the usual abusive letters to the editor about divorce, contraception, rubbish and violence in the North, that had been sent in by bigots and madmen. A brief report about Harmony Hall caught his eye. The Sherlock wealth was now a matter of public knowledge. He was sorry for anyone who sent them begging letters.

"Hullo, Jim. That's great I've run into you." Maurice, the Museum man, smiled across the marble table. He had become one of the select band of people Drury would like to drop in boiling oil.

"Oh?"

"You remember those Benin bronzes we were talking about? Your family's donation to the Museum? We've got things straightened out now, and we're planning to present them to the Nigerian government."

"Oh."

"You're probably aware that since the sack of Benin in 1895 such bronzes have been dispersed all over the world. Naturally the Nigerians regard them as national treasures and are more than pleased to have them back. The Ambassador will accept them in his Embassy in Ailsbury Road. There will be a little reception. The Museum thought it would be a nice gesture to have a member of the original family present. Will I send you an invite?"

"No, thank you."

Maurice was taken aback. "Can you think of anyone else who might like to come along?"

He gave him Aunt Hatta's address. Her sombre clothes would contrast with robed and turbaned Africans and pale Museum officials. Very likely she would be furious about her family's bequests being given away and might show her anger.

Maurice said, "Michael made a killing at the Harmony Hall auction, didn't he?"

"A killing?"

"With the statue."

Drury felt like the unwary woodsman who has been hearing the crack of a falling tree for some time, and now it was on top of him.

"A marble statue. Clever of him to have spotted it. Apparently it was in the back of a kitchen cupboard filled with jam jars. The Boothroyds' people will be furious when they learn."

"Learn what?"

"What they missed. Pure carelessness on their part. This statue that Michael bought turns out to be very good. Greek from the best period. He called me in to have a look at it, also Tony Scully from the Gallery. Of course this wasn't quite in our line." Naturally since they wallowed in provincial ignorance. "We advised bringing in a man from London. Michael had an expert from the Museum flown over. Seemingly he's very excited. He wants a second opinion and other experts to look at it. Those people really passed up something. Just shows, you bring in the most experienced auctioneers in the world, and they let a thing like that go under their noses. Trust Michael to spot it. He's the sharp lad."

"It was covered over with silver paint."

"You saw it? The paint's off now, I can tell you. Well I must push. I'll send your aunt a line about the reception. Sure you won't change your mind?"

Drury left Bewley's in a daze of grief. Almost without knowing it his footsteps led to the street behind Stephen's Green where Michael's shop was located. This was an area that was becoming smart. Only a few years ago many of the buildings had been tenements or boarded up. Now, where children used to chalk out hopscotch diagrams in front of doorways with broken fanlights, there were restaurants, hair dressers, art galleries, ethnic shops selling bangles and brass, and antique shops. Michael's place was squeezed between a delicatessen and a shop displaying Chinese lanterns and personalized sweat shirts. Above the door perched a red alarm box, while the windows were barred and admission could only be obtained by ringing a bell. Michael's assistant led him in among the grandfather clocks, old chairs, suspiciously well-preserved mahogany tables and the chandeliers and mantelpieces that the new rich favoured. A Bossi fireplace conferred just the same touch of opulent vulgarity on its owner as the expensive car in his garage. Many marble mantelpieces were now imported from France, since Ireland had run out of them.

"Can I help you? Or would you just like to look round?" Another new assistant. Like all the others she looked well-groomed with her expensive clothes and blue eyeshadow. Her voice was refined Foxrock. She was not as young as she seemed, probably a bored housewife prepared to take up any boring job.

"Where's Michael?"

"He was in earlier for a few minutes. Who shall I say called?"

"I'm a friend. James Drury. I've got to see him."

"Oh, Mr Drury. I've heard about you."

"Where can I get hold of him?"

"I don't know. He has one of these mixed days."

"Where did he go?"

"He was taking the car to be serviced. Then he had a luncheon date at the Hibernian. It's a bit late, but you might get him there." She gave him an encouraging smile before her bored glance drifted towards the room at the back where she had been reading old copies of *Apollo*. Her eyes mocked him, like those of the young rake in the powdered wig, the stern judge, and the over-varnished ladies looking moustached and dirty who gazed down from the walls. Michael did a line in eighteenth-century portraits; they were for export, since Americans who were not particular about family connections bought them and passed them off as ancestors.

He picked up his parcels, which had been resting on a restored rent table, and departed. The door was shut and bolted behind him. To hell with trying the Hibernian, he'd go round to Castle Xanadu in the evening. He'd kill the bastard. Retracing his steps he struggled down Grafton Street, choked by traffic and the summer throng of tourists, and crossed the road, blown by wafts of hot coffee aromas from Bewley's. Down Nassau Street into Pearse Street, where a train was rumbling over the bridge across the road. He ran past a woman selling newspapers under the dirty archway of the station where some fanatical religion had erected an illuminated sign about saving yourself. He bounded up the moving staircase and struggled through the barrier designed to disembowel. The station's last remaining porter, a rose in his buttonhole, closed the gates.

The iron girders and the high glass canopy of the solid early Victorian station were ample enough for the dignity of columns of steam. As usual, the ugly diesel that squatted where real trains used to depart seemed a trivial substitute for the old ironclads. He climbed into the carriage bravely painted orange and black with the initials CIE, which, lengthened into Irish, proclaimed the national transport service. CIE had wasted little money on the interior of its carriages. The one where he found himself was austere to a point just short of penal. The red vinyl seats were torn, and the walls were covered with graffiti, Carmel loves, Up Arsenal, several fucks.

The train moved out past the gasworks and the old harbour to the Grand Canal towards the rugby grandstand at Landsdowne Road. This time of day there weren't many passengers: a woman with a shopping bag giving him a malevolent stare, a man deep in sleep. But at Landsdowne Road a group of Spanish schoolchildren rushed in like soldiers on the attack. Every summer Spanish children flocked into Dublin. They came from middle-class families with Fascist leanings, sent to holy Ireland because their parents imagined it to be a bastion of Catholicism. The girl who sat down beside him was dark, well made, but spotty. For a moment he thought of her in bed with him, wriggling under the sheets. She was talking to, or rather, screaming at a smaller girl with gold studs in her ears who could only be twelve or thirteen. Those Mediterranean types matured early and were prodigiously developed.

The suburbs and their back gardens gave way to the sea at Sandymount. The lines of wading birds, men digging for worms and the few clouds over the candy-striped chimney of the power station contributed to the same sort of view that had depressed Stephen Dedalus at much this time of year. Dedalus, too, had taught at a seedy preparatory school.

He thought about the second statue, the one that Michael had just bought from Aunt Hatta. No doubt it was a pair to the first one. Since so many things in her house were treasures, it was not surprising that the statue—torso, more accurately—was something of importance. Would he tell her of her folly? He thought of messengers executed for bringing bad news. Could she renege on the deal? No doubt Michael had proof of ownership in the form of a receipt, just as he had from Drury for the Harmony Hall statue. But his aunt had possession. She might have a case for keeping it. He would have to go round and enlighten her before tackling Michael.

The train rolled out of Blackrock, past the baths, past pink bodies lying on the grey beach trying to catch the sun. Despairingly he pulled out his cigarettes and found there was one left in the packet. He lit up.

"It's non-smoking," said the ugly old bitch opposite.

"I'm sorry." She glared at him again. A quiet smoke was now regarded as a social crime. He would either have to nip the cigarette out between his fingers or move on to finish smoking it. Or ignore her.

Lifting his parcels he waded through sweet papers to the next carriage which was crowded with gabbling Spanish children. He stood smoking, his parcels at his feet, since none of the shrill shrieking quarrelsome brats offered him a seat. Below him an office worker returning early was reading a book about yachts. Must be wishful thinking; he did not look the right type or rich enough to own one. The fellow beside him with the Trinity tie and the real leather briefcase might. At Dun Laoghaire they both got out, together with most of the Spanish mob. Drury was able to sit in comfort and watch the boats in the harbour, their sails catching the afternoon sun, the pillared yacht clubs designed to look like Russian country houses, the dreadful mailboat. As he gazed he caught the whiff of a familiar smell—cigar smoke. He glanced back along the carriage, now pleasantly silent, noting that there was only one other adult passenger sitting beside the far door absorbed in a newspaper. The man lowered it and he saw that it was Michael.

He felt no surprise. No Dubliner ever marvels about the innumerable daily coincidences involving meetings with acquaintances. The centre of the city is basically the same small intimate place where Yeats and George Moore kept running into each other. When Drury went into Dublin he wasted a good deal of time zig-zagging to and fro across streets to avoid undesirables. Today had been fairly typical. Although he could not help meeting Maurice in Bewley's, he had successfully evaded his old Trinity professor, the doctor who had delivered Kevin in Holles Street and been so scornful of the methods of Leboyer, Headmaster's accountant, the man who checked the fire-drill arrangements at Prospect, and poor old Mrs Fitzgerald, from whom he had to run away down Johnson's Court. And now here was Michael. If the Rolls was being serviced at his swanky Protestant garage, that would take twenty-four hours. It was natural for him to be coming home by train. Orla would be meeting him at Killiney station in the Porsche.

The fat pudgy face looked faintly surprised, then embarrassed.

"I didn't see you get on, Jim."

If Drury had been sensible he would have withheld his fire for the time being. But he was enraged.

"I heard about the statue."

Michael put out his cigar on the carriage floor. "Who told you?"

"Maurice."

He swore. "What did he tell you?"

"I gather it's worth a good deal of money. He told me the man from the British Museum was very excited."

"I'll murder that fucking Maurice. He's wrong as it happens."

"How wrong?"

"For God's sake, it's a nice little torso. I'll be honest with you, Jim. The thing may not be the very best, but it's a good little Hellenic piece. And they don't grow on trees."

"How good?"

"How the hell do I know until the boys have a proper look at it? And if I did know I wouldn't tell you."

"And the stablemate? The one that you got from my aunt?"

The smug grin changed to a look of alarm.

"She doesn't know yet how you swindled her."

"Swindle be damned. Sharp practice perhaps. You and the old girl were happy enough to take my money."

"I could understand about the statue that I bought. I was the fool. But the other one. You did the dirty. Used private information and then deceived a helpless old woman."

"Isn't that just life? Especially in the antique world? I'd hate to have to answer at the Day of Judgment for the number of old ladies from whom I've bought cheap. It's a hard tough cruel business, and I've told you that often enough."

The train stopped at Dalkey. The last of the twittering Spanish children got out, and now they were alone in the carriage. The station flowerbed was planted out with annuals. Like the yacht clubs, the pretty little building with its classical front suggested Russia. A setting for a story by Turgenev.

"I thought you'd be fair with me, Michael." He noted the whine in his voice.

"Fair! The trouble with you, Jim, is that you'll never make a business man."

"Business man! You mean crook! Liar! Swindler! Cheat! Thief!" In the empty carriage his voice sounded very loud.

The train was leaving Dalkey, passing through the granite cuttings covered with blousy pink, red and white valerian. It must have been Drury's rage that made Michael get up immediately, even though they had a tunnel to pass through and the curve of Killiney Bay to traverse before he reached his destination. He retreated to the space between the two carriages and stood beside the exit door.

"Take it easy, Jim. Don't get excited. Tell you what, I'll do a deal. Neither you nor your aunt can touch me, you know that. I've got the receipt for that statue and it'll stand up in any court of law. I don't give a damn what people think about the way I got hold of it. But since you've more or less acted as agent on this deal, I'll be generous and give you a commission for yourself. An ex gratia payment. Without prejudice. Shall we say five hundred pounds?"

Drury hit out. The blow caught Michael unexpectedly on the eye and he could feel the sting of his knuckles hitting skin. Michael made a grab at him and missed. They exchanged a few shouted obscenities before Drury managed to get in another blow. Michael was bigger, but out of condition, flabby, soft-muscled, and breathless from the cigars he smoked. His sports jacket smelt of them. But Drury was not an experienced fighter, and when he received a blow to the stomach and a blow to the jaw, he collapsed gasping to the ground.

With the harsh roar of the diesel the train entered the short tunnel. From that moment he could not remember anything that happened. Concussion wiped out several minutes of his life and he never recovered them. But like the faith that makes up the little gap between reason and belief, imagination filled in all the details of what precisely occurred after the train went through the tunnel. He saw the darkness yielding to a glimmer of light and the sudden full blast of sun with Sorrento Terrace and Dalkey Island showing against the summer-blue sea. He knew why they were so clear from the angle where he lay. They were clear because the door was open. All the time they were in the tunnel he was convinced that Michael had been fumbling with the difficult heavy passenger-proof door, putting his arm out of the window and swivelling the handle. The door was opened and the curve of the train kept it that way. His imagination told him that it was Michael's huge ham-like hands that made him slide inexorably out of the train. And he was always certain that it was not in imagination but in a sudden flash of memory that he glimpsed his aggressor as he flew through the air, and saw him smiling as if he were launching a liner.

CHAPTER 5

Perhaps it was not all that much of a miracle that he survived his fall. The train had been going very slowly. He was saved by *senecio cineraria,* the bushy silver yellow flowered perennial that is a feature of Killiney's sea cliffs. He was cushioned by a clump just under the railway wall where he had fallen.

He lay below the track semi-conscious, the grey matter of his brain stirred occasionally by the rattle of a train above his head. At times his memory gave a little jolt as total oblivion receded, a process that was not smooth but like a series of steps. At first the aching of his head and pulverized body took up every fibre of his consciousness. He lay poised between wakefulness and darkness for many hours until evening, when a little breeze started up making him feel cold and bringing him to some sort of life. Groaning he sat up and faced the magnificent view. Sunset was spilling orange light across the bay, illuminating the Sugarloaves and Bray Head. The first prick of lights appeared at Bray, one of the most unattractive seaside resorts in Europe, transforming it into a place of distant magical beauty, Camelot or Avalon.

The silence was broken by a power boat dragging a water skier in graceful arabesques towards Dalkey Sound. What a time to go water ski-ing. What time was it? He lifted his hand and looked dizzily at his Timex, finding after several minutes' concentration that it had stood up to its ordeal. (Could he make some money by writing a testimonial?) He got to his feet, hobbled a few steps, bent over and was sick. The rocks below were covered with lichen that was bright green against the smudgy brown of seaweed. Was it Katherine Mansfield who wrote of the Wa Wa sound of breaking waves? He'd have to sit again. Behind him under the cliff was a small cave with an ugly smear of litter on the ground in front, empty Coca Cola cans, Guinness bottles, wrapping paper, polythene bags and a couple of wrinkled contraceptives. A little way beyond some brave man had climbed up and scratched BRITS OUT on the railway wall. He kicked the cans out of the way and sat down again out of the wind.

His memory gave another lurch so that now he could remember almost everything that had happened to him that day until the moment he saw Michael sitting in the corner of the train. The gap was filled with a burning conviction that Michael had tried to murder him. In a life of mediocrity it was the first time he had experienced the passion of physical violence. The strange thing was that in spite of the fall, the bruises and the sickening shakiness of his limbs, he felt tremendously excited. The thought of having some sort of revenge on Michael was exhilarating. Had he meant to push him out? Of course he had—the door was opened, wasn't it, and that could only be done with effort. For interfering with his business affairs.

After half an hour and another spell of oblivion he remembered the statues. Two of them. They were good, very good. Worth ten thousand each? More? He groaned. He imagined what Michael would do with the windfall. Trade in his Rolls for a new Corniche or give a donation to his favourite political party or buy furs and jewellery for his current girlfriend or a yacht or polo ponies with his money and Aunt Hatta's . . .

A sliver of moon came up over the bay above the jagged rocks and the luminous pearl-covered sea. His limbs were getting stiff and all the bruises that made him feel a mob had been stoning him hurt in unison. From the cave it was only a few hundred yards to a very steep flight of steps which he had to climb on all fours. Up and across a metal bridge over the railway with a double line of tracks shining under the moon. Higher up lay the Vico Road. His progress was slow and gruelling, and his dizziness made him feel inebriated.

At last he was up on the road beside three grandstand seats overlooking the view. A train swept past. He sat down and closed his eyes. He recalled that Aunt Hatta's statue was not yet in Michael's possession.

"You okay, Mister?" A pair of lovers on the adjoining seat were staring in horror. Even by moonlight he must look bad.

"Quite all right, thank you."

They were silent. Then the youth said, "What happened?"

"I had a fall."

Another silence and some whispering. "You should have yourself attended to."

"I'm all right, I tell you."

More whispering, and now they were looking furtively up and down the road.

"You should go to the garda. We'll take you down into Dalkey if you like."

"Leave me alone."

Again they consulted together. "Look, Mister, the Special Branch might like to know. They could give you some protection, like." They had evidently taken him for an Englishman. His West British voice moulded by his tormented education in institutions like Prospect often made people mistake him for English. In this case they appeared to think he was an Englishman who had been roughed up by an illegal organization.

They changed tactics. "You should see a doctor. We'll drive you to hospital. We'll run you down to Dillon's Court."

"No, no, no, no!" If he went to hospital they'd keep him there for days in a noisy ward. They'd talk about being under observation and X-rays and hairline fractures and complete rest. And he must get home. He must get home and make plans. Make plans about what he had to do before Saturday. Preferably tomorrow.

The couple nodded intelligently. People who had accidents did not like to be taken to Dillon's Court whose poor reputation was very likely quite undeserved.

"We'll drive you to Loughlinstown, to St Michael's . . . or even into town to Vincents . . ."

"No. Goleen Park. Number 30." He had to shout at them again and again before they agreed to take him home. When the door of their little scarlet Datsun opened and the light went on, he saw that his shirt was torn. Many of the cuts on his face and hands had reopened and were spouting blood all over the phony wickerwork seats. He caught a glimpse of himself in the front mirror and noted that his eyes appeared to be surrounded by purple-blue skin like daisies planted in aubretia. He felt nausea again fighting with unconsciousness and struggled to keep awake. He screamed instructions about the route to his obscure suburb, fearful that they were still meaning to take him to hospital.

But the Samaritan couple did as he told them. When they reached Goleen Park they supported him one on each side up to the door.

"Jesus Christ!"

When Agnes opened up, he could see Kevin behind her on the stairs drop his plastic machine gun and burst into tears. He staggered into her arms, bleeding all over her ethnic clothes.

"What the hell have you done to him?" she bellowed at the kindly pair who did not stay to explain, but retreated rapidly to their car.

She watched him crawl up stairs which seemed as steep as the steps up to the Vico Road. She followed him. He gripped her by her arms.

"If Michael rings up for God's sake don't tell him I've come back! Don't tell him!"

He rolled into bed (which was unmade) and lapsed into unconsciousness.

Pain, chinks of light through the window, sounds of barking dogs, cars and people going to work. Pain. A train noise in the distance. This

woke him, and then came memories of Michael and money. Thousands? Millions? Agnes was in the room.

"What time is it?"

"Ten o'clock."

The fact that she had stayed away from work and the unnatural look
of solicitude on her face alarmed him.

"Did Michael call?"

"No. Headmaster did though."

"What did you tell him?"

"I said you had a slight car accident."

"How did he take it?"

"He was annoyed. He asked about David Copperfield. What do you
know about David Copperfield?"

"Oh hell. They'll be in CIE lost property by now."

"The he said it was Founder's Day."

"Blast Founder's Day."

"He hoped you'd make the effort. He said to remind you of jockeys
who climb back on their horses after they have fallen."

"He can't say good morning without making it sound like a threat."

"Would you like something to drink?"

"Not one of your loathsome infusions. Tea."

As she was going out of the door the phone rang. He shouted: "If
that's Michael I'm not here, I never got back last night." He could hear
the drone of her voice and the ping as the receiver was replaced.

"Was it him?"

"Right. Like you said, you're not back yet. I'm worried and annoyed."

"Good girl!"

He lay back and actually forgot about Michael for a few minutes,
luxuriating in the joy of not attending Founder's Day. He would be
missing the speeches, the prizes in the main hall, the address by the distinguished Old Prospectian. And, shock, Headmaster was due to make
his announcement that in the autumn a certain number of girls would
be admitted as a picturesque addition to the school, like a little bed of
flowers in a vegetable garden. He would spend the afternoon strutting
about in his scarlet Master's gown, while teachers like Drury would
don their humble BA gowns (Drury had never paid the ten pounds
necessary to buy an MA from Trinity) hooded with white rabbit skin,
and guide parents around unnaturally neat dormitories smelling of
Jeyes Fluid. Missing Founder's Day was almost worth being thrown
out of a train for.

Agnes brought his tea in a mug with his zodiac sign picked out in
gold. Gemini people were marked out for talent, power and success.

She sat on the edge of the bed rolling a cigarette. He had double vision, could see two of her.

"Are you going to tell me?"

"Not if you fill the room with that foul-smelling smoke."

"I've a right to know."

It was a great effort to talk, to put the narrative together. His words slurred as he told her what he could remember.

"How much are those statues worth?" Typical. You could always tell where Agnes's priorities lay.

"I don't know. Thousands obviously."

"You're a fool."

"What do you know about it? Even the best eighteenth-century marble copies of Roman statues don't fetch more than five or six hundred. How was I to know the one I bought was so special?"

She wouldn't believe Michael had tried to kill him.

"The door was open, right? You have this brawl. You fall out."

"How do you think it got open? CIE and other railway companies have passenger-proof doors which don't open at any old time by themselves. Michael first knocked me unconscious and then he put his arm through the open window and turned the handle."

"Why?"

"Because I was in the way."

"You don't kill someone just like that . . ."

"We were fighting, remember . . ." All the same it was a savage way of going on.

There was a sound of door chimes. Agnes went very pale and creeping over to the window, peeped out.

"Rolls," she mouthed. The chimes sounded again and again. After five minutes there were footsteps and the start of the much-glorified engine. Agnes came back to the bed, her eyes round.

"He only phoned twenty minutes ago."

"He wants to find out what happened to me. He wants to know if I'm alive."

"He must have thought the house empty."

"Couldn't he see the car?"

"There's something wrong with the distributor. It's at Hurley's."

He blessed it for not being in order. "He'll be round again. And for the time being you'll have to keep on saying I'm not here. Get Kevin out of the way. Otherwise there'll be 'Dadda's upstairs . . .' Where's he now?"

"Playgroup. Did Michael really try and kill you?"

"That's for sure."

"What are you going to do? Tell the garda?"

"No. Like you, they'll have trouble believing me. Can you imagine trying to explain how a person like Michael could start behaving like a homicidal maniac?"

"What about your aunt? You'll have to tell her about her statue and the fact she's lost a lot of money."

"The shock might kill her." He mused over this possible pleasing twist to his fortunes. "No. She's tough and capricious. The chances are that she'd make out the whole thing was all my fault."

"But if you tell her, she would still be able to hang onto the thing. She'd get in the lawyers."

"Old Peachey? He's useless." He knew Aunt Hatta better than Agnes did. Rather he knew that you never knew with her. She might well call in the lawyers and take the case all the way through the European courts. Or she might get a fit of honesty and insist that because Michael had bought the statue and paid for it, it was his, whatever it was worth. Either way she would blame Drury, because Drury and Michael had once been friends, and it was through him that Michael had learned about Eagle's Nest and what it contained. Besides, he wanted revenge, and revenge could be better secured without Aunt Hatta's participation.

"Go away," he said to Agnes. "Leave me alone." He was slipping into a doze. He slept and woke, slept and woke, pain and dizziness combating a sense of urgency that kept him very near wakefulness.

Late in the afternoon he came to his senses as fully as the limits of his condition allowed. He got out of bed stiffly and made his way to the bathroom where he buried his face in a cold sponge. He put on a dressing gown and tottered downstairs to the drawing room. Agnes laughed as much at his use of the word as he sneered at "lounge". She sat reading an astrology magazine and watching a violent film. He stood and watched too for a few minutes. The hero was being flung against a wall and rendered unconscious long enough for his opponent to get a head start and lead him a chase that encircled a used car lot and led to a warehouse with seven steel gantries, up which he sprinted before knocking the screaming villain down into a bed of old tyres. Television drama did not recognize concussion as a problem.

"Where's Kevin?"

"I left him at the Bradys' like you said to . . ." He was probably watching the same film and listening to the Tump! Tump! of fists striking flesh.

He switched off. "Did Michael call round again?"

"No, but he was on the phone."

"Very likely he's been going up and down on the train between Dalkey and Killiney looking out for my body."

"He sounded cheery enough. Saying you were probably with a blonde."

"He thinks he's killed me and I'm still stuck somewhere on the rocks below the train."

She was reading horoscopes. "Listen . . . this is yours. 'It would be foolhardy to pretend that your private life is easy at the moment . . . There is danger, particularly in the first week of the month when you appear to be accident prone . . .'"

"Very funny."

"It goes on 'However, this is the moment to capitalize on your abilities, enhance your prestige and grab opportunities with both hands.'"

He said, "I'm going to steal Aunt Hatta's statue."

She looked horrified. "No, Jim. You're not well. You've had a very bad knock. I think we should get in Dr Garland." It was a measure of her concern that she had gone so far as to mention a doctor, since the unformulated ranges of her philosophy included a distrust of medicine. (Psychiatry was different.) Kevin had faced a fierce period of childhood ailments without antibiotics, with no more equipment than that of threatened Victorian children facing a trip to Heaven before their time.

"I am going to. And you're going to help me."

"No way."

"And we have to do it quickly. It's never been in Michael's possession. It's still at Eagle's Nest."

"So what?"

"He hasn't had the time to show it to anyone or even take a photograph."

"How do you know?"

"There's a limit to Aunt Hatta's condescension. Oh, I don't know, he may have wormed his way in again. But one thing's certain, it will still be there for Saturday. If we took it, Aunt Hatta would never recognize it divested of its silver paint. We could keep it hidden for months, even years. And then we might return it . . . or sell it . . . in any case keep it out of Michael's clutches."

"Don't keep saying 'we' like that."

"Agnes, you must. If we manage to sell it . . . half would go straight into your little paw." She had her own bank account.

"How much is it worth?"

"At least a couple of thousand."

"It's not possible. Michael's collecting it tomorrow, isn't he?"

"We'll do it tonight . . ."

"No way."

"Do just one thing for me right away. It's heavy. We'll have to carry it. We'll need to get hold of some sort of trailer. Johnny Brady's got one, hasn't he?"

"You mean their burglary trailer?" The Brady brothers, whose mother looked after Kevin, specialized in funeral break-ins. They read the death notices in the newspapers and noted the times when funerals took place. Then when a whole mourning household were out burying the departed, they struck at the bereaved.

Amazingly, Agnes began to agree. Rather to his surprise she fell in with his plans. Perhaps it was the passion of his intentions. Or greed. There was no more talk of Dr Garland. It was she who rang up Johnny Brady and borrowed his trailer for the evening in exchange for a bottle of Jamieson.

After she put down the telephone he said, "We'll start a bit after midnight. We'll go to Eagle's Nest and park just outside the gate."

"How are you going to open it?"

He told her about the bicycle padlock with the numbered code. "Four numbers and the thing will only open when you get them in line."

"How are you going to obtain the numbers?"

"I know them. Aunt Hatta told me. She did not actually say she had stolen it, but she told me that when she saw it lying on a shelf in that help-yourself hardware place its code made it irresistible. It happened to be 1923, the year that she and Uncle Jack were married."

"What about the man in the gate lodge?"

"Dempsey's so deaf he wouldn't hear if the Valkyries came riding by. I don't think she's noticed his progressive decrepitude over the years. If by any chance he were to wake up, all I have to say is that I have an urgent message for Aunt Hatta."

"At one in the morning?"

He had been feverishly making plans all day. "I can act drunk. I'm not worried about Dempsey. Only the mildest of contingency plans have to be made about him. The main problem"—his head ached—"is the inner line of defence. The moat, the barbed wire and the electric fence have all proved to be unnecessary at Eagle's Nest. In sixty years Aunt Hatta has never been burgled. Except the one time during the war . . . and the poor fellow wanted to sue her for his lacerated leg."

"Dogs?"

"She has eight at present."

"And they are let loose in the grounds all night?"

"It's summer. In the winter they are generally inside in the warmth. But there's one good thing. Florence is on heat. That means most of the male dogs will be kept shut up, or they'll be sitting outside her prison howling. There are about five or six of them. That leaves only one or two females apart from the imprisoned Florence roaming around. And the howls of love will be indistinguishable from barks of warning."

"Are you sure?"

"Nothing's sure." The dogs would possibly recognize him if he called out their names. But he didn't know all their names. Rascal, Skelter, Florence. They could take some precautions. He told some soothing lies about this aspect of the expedition. He felt fearless, moved by rage. He moved on to another point. If they stole the statue and things went smoothly, where would they put it? They could hardly bring it to Goleen Park. She came up with a suggestion.

"What about Ballydevlin?"

"Where?"

"Eugene and Tony's place."

"I don't know anything about it."

"They have this cottage up in the mountains out towards Blessington."

"I never saw it." He did not go among her friends. He imagined a rainswept place occupied by her sort of people. "Who the hell are Eugene and Tony?"

"They're artists. Eugene's the painter we had that argument with in Davy Byrne's."

"How's that going to help us? When they see the thing either they'll report it or they'll sell it to the tinkers within the hour."

"But they're away for ten days. They've gone on that seminar on Massage and Meditation you were so horrible about."

"What's going to happen when they're back?"

"Nothing need happen at all. We could put it in one of the outhouses round their place. It would be quite safe there. The ground is too much covered with nettles even to go in for a slash. It's an ancient farmyard, there must be a half acre of nettles. They never go near them in summer. If we put it deep in there no-one would see it until winter came, by which time we'll have to have done something."

It was not very satisfactory. They discussed other possible hiding places. Could any of her friends be trusted? What about a garbage dump? They recalled how a consignment of stolen saddles had been hidden a few years back in the Enniskerry dump. Any place in a ditch by the side of the road? In a forestry plantation? Thinking of the number of people swarming over the Dublin mountains every weekend, he concluded that Eugene and Tony's place was as good as anywhere.

"You're sure they won't be back for a week?"

"Quite sure."

In a week there could be developments. The important thing was action now. Tonight.

She did the errands for him, since he felt shaky. She went off to the supermarket for two bottles of Jamieson, some ribsteak and marrow bones and a box of Black Magic. Then she visited the Bradys to blow a kiss to Kevin, who did not look up from the television, and collect the trailer and a coil of rope. They'd need a knife, a spade and their Wellingtons.

He stayed inside, curtains drawn, watching children's programmes and then *Crossroads*. He dozed. Once the telephone rang, but he did not answer it. Once he heard a car drive up, but it was only his neighbour returning from his insurance office. He'd need a wheelbarrow. What better than use Aunt Hatta's own, which was kept in the tool shed? His headache was worse. A hammer to break the padlock. Did he perhaps have a hairline crack in his skull? Agnes had agreed with his plans very readily. Not like her. She usually argued.

Her key turned in the lock. Normally she insisted that they never lock the front door since she had been told by the Bradys that locked doors invited intruders. He went outside with her to examine the trailer, which was coffin-sized and painted a discreet grey.

"It doesn't look very strong."

"Johnny says it's tough enough. It's taken things like television sets and car engines. And plenty of sheep." Drury knew that since the popularization of the deep freeze, going out into the Dublin mountains and rustling sheep had become a popular pastime among city people. After the Bradys had stolen a freezer—presumably transported in this trailer—they liked to keep it filled for their mother.

"What about their car?"

"He won't lend us that." The Bradys' car was also dull grey, and totally inconspicuous, a sort of non-car. Mrs Brady said that when she went shopping, it always took her several minutes to pick it out in the car park. "He's painted the Morris number on the trailer's back. It's good luck we already have the tow bar."

The tow bar was a sore point. When he had bought the Morris it had seemed a bargain, and only when it was too late did he realize that the tow bar, combined with the country registration, should have warned him that the vehicle had had a hard life dragging animals and tractor parts over long distances to farms and fairs. The last time he had the gear box stripped down, the mechanic had warned, "Watch out for the Big End!" He wondered how well the car would stand up to carrying a heavy weight. Would it collapse on Killiney Hill?

They left the house immediately in case Michael should decide to call again. They drove off, the trailer behind them, out of the neighbourhood towards Dun Laoghaire. They stopped at a pub that Agnes liked and he loathed. This was her part of the master plan, establishing an alibi. It had an illuminated sign outside proclaiming FOOD. Pretty crude, he thought, why not PEE? The food consisted mainly of sandwiches in cellophane, but he was able to get the barman to come up with toasted cheese. His appearance aroused staring and comment. He would have liked to keep a low profile, since he was nervous of a group of bearded acquaintances of Agnes's that he could see across the room. On a previous occasion he had got into a fight with them about H-blocks. They got annoyed when he said that if prisoners must have a hobby, throwing excrement about, although less dangerous than starving to death, was less worthwhile than studying for O-levels. He looked round and saw another man he knew. This terrible pub was frequented by so-called artists and writers. He recognized Roger, who had done a Gauguin and abandoned a wife and family and a job in public relations. For a time he had supported himself by forging Paul Henrys. Bad Paul Henrys (and in Drury's opinion, good ones) were easy to imitate, and easy to sell to affluent members of the middle classes. Then he had won some sort of phony prize, and after that his daubs were acclaimed. Here he was, surrounded by buddies and sycophants talking about truth and beauty and art values. Drury and Agnes sat apart listening to their noise until just before closing time, when they got up and joined them. He had to parry questions about his bruises—"a fall downstairs"—endure being called Seamus and pay for a round of drinks.

Roger and most of his companions were satisfactorily drunk when they were thrown out at closing time. Roger had got to the abusive stage. "You're all useless! What have any of you done in your lifetime? You might as well let the clay cover you now!" Drury felt he had successfully identified with them for the evening. If by bad luck he was caught in Aunt Hatta's garden, he could claim that he, too, was inebriated. (Would she disinherit him? He thought she might be lenient since Uncle Jack had been boozy.) He had never felt more sober. The expedition seemed madder than ever. He drove up to the Vico Road and sat waiting at a point overlooking the moonlit sea. Twice he got out to check the things they had brought with them. Once a police car came by, and they embraced, pretending to be lovers. The patrol slowed down and continued on its way.

He said, "Let's go home!"

"No. This is fun."

They were very near the place where he had climbed up the day before. There were too many garda around here altogether. When at a quarter to one they found themselves on the familiar twisty road made dark by walls and trees, they passed a whole group of them standing under a giant eucalyptus. These were guarding the Canadian Embassy, whose proximity to Eagle's Nest was unfortunate. He trundled by, wondering whether a sharp-eyed cop had noticed the trailer dragging behind a car which was not the sort of vehicle that normally wandered around the three-acre compounds of Killiney.

At the gate of Eagle's Nest they had to face the problem of Dempsey. They had decided that Agnes should stand outside the lodge making a lot of noise. If there was no stir, she would presume that Drury's estimate of his capacity for undisturbed sleep was accurate. She took the torch and stepped out. "Nineteen twenty-three," he whispered. As he drove off he could hear her harsh voice singing a ballad. If Dempsey could sleep through that they would be safe enough from him. He drove up the twisting leafy road and out over the sea again, right to Sorrento Terrace, turned in a lumbering sweep and came back. Perhaps Aunt Hatta had bought a new lock? Perhaps they could go home.

He slowed almost to a standstill as the gates of Eagle's Nest came into view in his headlights. Agnes signalled with the torch and swung them open. He manoeuvred the car and trailer through into crunching gravel, for this was one of the few drives in the area which was not tarmacadamed. Agnes shut the gates behind her, closing the flimsy trick lock by moving all the numbers at once, so that all she had to do to open them was to flick them back in unison.

The avenue curled up between banks of species rhododendron. He had to turn so that they would be able to make a quick getaway. This operation also proved easier than he had anticipated. Agnes ran up and unhitched the trailer, while he picked the spot where the avenue met the unkempt tennis court and did a difficult three point turn, ending up with the car wedged under a rhododendron facing the right way. The really difficult bit was hitching up the trailer again in the moonlight, trying to get it aligned to the tow bar.

They got back in the car and each took a swig of whiskey. This was for a two-fold purpose—to give them Dutch courage and an excuse if they were caught. Drunks were preferable to thieves. The box of Black Magic would be a thoughtful inebriated gift to his dear aunt. And if they were caught wheeling her wheelbarrow there was a chance that they could get away with an incoherent story that they had come to do midnight gardening in aid of his aunt's favourite hospital. A prank. And if the wheelbarrow had a silver statue in it, he could claim that he was wheeling it away to his dear friend, Michael.

"Listen!" he said as he screwed the cap back on the bottle. From the house above they could hear a wailing "Woo! Woo!" that sounded like Siberian wolves.

"My God!"

"Florence's courtiers!"

"They'll attack us."

"Whatever you do don't forget that meat." They walked up along the edge of the drive to where the moonlit trees opened out revealing the garden, the terrace below, and stretching to their left the distant moonlit view of the sea. With the foreknowledge of many afternoons spent gardening, he made his way easily to the tool shed. It wasn't even locked; there had been no need to bring the hammer he carried in his hand.

Holding the torch, he dislodged the wheelbarrow, an artefact that would have graced a folk museum. It had not been built for lightness but to be wheeled about my muscled under-gardeners who made easy work of its thick wooden frame and its solid wheels. As he heaved and cursed he heard new sounds. Not howls any more, but barks coming nearer. Warning barks, followed by a savage growl. Then more growls. Agnes shrieked.

"Shut up!" He flashed the torch and caught the gleam of many pairs of red eyes. One, two, three, four, five. Five? So much for his knowledge of dogs' mating habits. "Where's the sack? Give it here. Here boy, here Gussie! Good boy. Good Nero. Here, Tibby." He remembered some of those dogs had been named after Roman emperors. The growls and barks died down. Bringing the marrow bones was foresight, but the ribsteak proved wasted investment, swallowed down in seconds. And not quite enough bones. "Here, Rascal, Rascal, good dog!" Yap, yap, insistent. Damn the little brute, the smallest, but the noisiest. She yapped some more, dashing in towards him, nipping at his leg. It was as well he had worn boots. Yap yap! Aunt Hatta would wake. He picked up the spade which he had placed in the wheelbarrow, and struck out with a wild swinging motion. The dog lay still.

"Look what you've done!"

"Shut up!" He pushed the heavy wheelbarrow, threw in the gloves and rope, and after a moment's hesitation, the small corpse. If Aunt Hatta discovered it she would pursue the murderer to the ends of the earth. In any case there was bound to be a fuss. Better not to give her a focus for her grief, the consolation of the corpse.

Round about them came noises of bones being happily gnawed. He emerged onto the drive, where for fifty yards he was wholly exposed should Aunt Hatta peer out of her bedroom window. Agnes bent down and, hunched up, scurried through the undergrowth like a woodland animal. He crossed onto the terrace. The statue was brilliantly visible under the moon. He could see details of the truncated arms, the lifeless eyes lidded with paint, the curly marble hair that the paint could not obscure. It stood surrounded on three sides by trellis, much of which had broken under the weight of coils of wisteria. The pool it overlooked was so thick in waterlily leaves that it looked as if a little duck could waddle across it dry-foot.

He went up and gave the silver buttock a small push. No movement at all. The sawn-off legs were crudely cemented to the ivy-coated plinth on which it balanced. The cement clung, so that the statue seemed to be growing out of the base from which it would have to be dislodged. Beside him Agnes, waving the torch, was hissing, "Poor little dog. She'll have you hanged."

"Shut up." He went on heaving.

"Not in the best Protestant tradition."

"Give me a hand."

"Are you going to do that to all of them?"

"If they misbehave."

"If it doesn't budge I'm off." But she stayed and helped him pull. Even with her hefty efforts there was no result. He should have remembered the weight of the statue at Harmony Hall, which he had been unable to shift when it had lain in its cupboard. Sweating tears of exhaustion as well as rage, he thought of the money he would be losing after all these efforts. And of Michael's victory.

"You're wasting your time."

"Give me the rope."

He tied it round the waist and ordered her to help him pull. In vain. Then he noticed a tree behind the wisteria and wound the rope round it to get traction. More heaving.

"Give up!"

He had Michael in mind, which gave him the strength at last for producing the first small wobble, an almost imperceptible shudder. Now Agnes was pulling with all her strength and suddenly the statue keeled over and came crashing down in a bed of flowers. There was silence, apart from Agnes's panting. At the edge of the bed was some terracing of Lisdoonvarna stone. When he directed the torch on the fallen Greek he found that not only had the paving cracked like ice, but that the surviving bit of a stump on one of his legs had broken off some more. A further six inches of knee and thigh had become detached, so that now the poor creature was down to buttocks on both sides.

The task of heaving him into the wheelbarrow was almost as difficult as dislodging him from his pedestal. They threw in his broken knee—could it have some value as a separate piece of antique stone? By now many of the dogs had finished their bones and came running down towards them. But they were all on good terms, and it was easy enough to take no notice when barks were muted and tails were wagging. Pushing the wheelbarrow by the rockery path they avoided any exposure on the open terrace. Shrubberies had to be negotiated, then a bed of nettles.

"Look . . ." Above the terrace a light flicked on in the ground-floor room where Aunt Hatta slept. They crouched in the nettles under the accusing moonlight. Drury wished that when he came to help last week he had scythed with more enthusiasm. Around them friendly dogs whimpered and wagged their tails. Peering into the barrow he caught sight of the unruffled silvered features of his illegal acquisition, a handsome, curly haired, pansy-looking youth. Above them the light went out. They waited before moving on. The wheelbarrow had suddenly acquired a squeak, or had they not noticed it amid all the tension? No, it must be the result of the weight it carried, an accusing whine that accompanied them all the way down to where the car was parked. A last truly desperate effort was needed by both of them to lift the statue into the trailer. There was a noise of cracking timber.

"That's the end of it," Agnes said.

He directed the torch. "Not really. Just a little bit of damage to one of the boards."

"Won't it get worse as we drive?"

"I don't think so if we go slowly. Open the gate."

"The corpse. The dog's corpse!"

He had forgotten it. Oh God! The weight that had reposed on top had turned it into a nasty mess. He could not possibly leave it behind for Aunt Hatta to see. He scraped it up with the spade and threw it into the boot, sprinkling gravel on top of the bloodstains on the wheelbarrow. He remembered to retrieve the broken marble fragment before hurrying round into the driving seat. Agnes ran down, opened up the gate and held it open. He scraped the car against the gateposts as he drove through, and heard a thud as the trailer similarly hit a stone.

But they were away safely. He drove to Sorrento Terrace and then round and back, away from the sea towards the side roads that led across the Dublin Mountains towards the Blessington Road. Above Rathfarnham with a view of the city they stopped and had a drink to celebrate. The time was half-past two.

"Off we go."

The journey in the dawn light was made very difficult by the weight in the back that caused the trailer to sway at any speed. He felt increasingly dizzy and exhausted. He suspected that the adrenalin playing on the effects of his accident was affecting his driving judgment, which was the reason that he kept veering towards the ditch or wall or mountain slope or whatever else was on his right. Agnes might have done some of the driving, but she had fallen heavily asleep. He had to almost use blows to wake her when they turned off into the hills and he wanted directions. It took nearly two hours before they arrived at the gate of Eugene and Tony's property.

Dawn had come up to reveal that the cottages and the row of out-houses were all high up on the hill above them.

He nudged and prodded Agnes awake. "How the hell did you ever imagine we would be able to carry the thing up there?"

"I didn't think it would be a problem. How was I to know it would be so heavy?"

"Bloody fool." They quarrelled bitterly before he asked if Tony and Eugene had any sort of wheelbarrow. She didn't know, of course. He went up and wandered around the outhouses. She was quite wrong about them being neglected and unused. They were tidy as any well-run farmyard, and a horse peered out of a stable and neighed at him. A hell of a lot of good her help had been. There was nothing that could help him move the marble about. Grumbling he came down again to the car, and they started arguing whether to take the thing home to Goleen Park or to go and look for a lonely spot on a hillside or in a forestry plantation.

"We may as well bury it right here for the time being." Like a fool he accepted her advice yet again. The effort of moving on would be too much. The gate opened easily enough, but the rest of this stage of the operation required more effort than anything that had gone before. In addition to heaving and carrying, he had to dig a grave. He dug it in the ditch just to the right of the gate. After a very long time he made some smoothing gestures with the spade, but the site looked trampled and conspicuous. No-one after the briefest look would have a doubt that something had been put down there recently.

"I'll have to dig it up again."

"Wait. Get the trailer off the car." She turned the Morris and drove back some hundreds of yards to where the glitter and quiver of tins and plastic had earlier caught her eye. The inhabitants of Wicklow, who have unreliable refuse collections, often deal with the problem by dumping household refuse by the roadside. She found a number of black sacks which had been torn somewhat by foxes, so that rubbish protruded from their bulges like intestines out of corpses. But some were still portable. She drove back and scattered them and their foul contents over Drury's diggings with a skill that almost exactly accounted for the disturbance. She topped her arrangement with a piece of patterned carpet discarded by a wasteful householder.

"Won't our friends want to move all this and rebury it? Wouldn't they be ecology conscious?"

"They won't come back until next week, I tell you. You'll have to dig it up and move it before then."

He picked up Rascal's corpse by the tail and placed it on top. They drove back to Goleen Park in the dawn.

CHAPTER 6

He slept deeply and unnaturally, waking with a start to the chimes of the doorbell. The familiar tenor voice fluted through the hallway. "Michael!" Why had that bloody fool let him in? Then he heard Kevin's squeaky tones.

"Daddy's drunk."

He cursed the sudden surge of conscience that had induced Agnes to retrieve the child from the Bradys' at the same time they returned the trailer.

"Agnes!" That was Kevin's shouting. She encouraged him to be on first name terms with her. Now she was there, probably having come in from the garden, asking coolly:

"Would you like a cup of coffee?"

"Not at all, darling, I'm just going for my lunch. Could I have a word with Jim?"

"Daddy's drunk . . ."

He must make a real effort. He called out, "Come on up, Michael!"

The heavy steps on the bare boards of the staircase sounded menacing. "My God, you look a sight. What happened to you?" He himself had a fading black eye.

Drury curbed his fear and rage. "I'm not sure. I really don't know. I just got out of hospital. Dillon's Court."

"Oh, Dillon's Court."

"Last night." His double vision had returned and he could see two of Michael. He added quickly. "Do you know, I lost my memory."

"For heaven's sake."

"I must have had the hell of a fall. Seemingly I was found somewhere on Killiney beach. An early-morning bather ran into me. And I was brought in. I couldn't remember a thing about how I came to be there."

"Is that a fact?"

"I couldn't remember my name even. I had no identification on me at all so there was no way they could find out who I was."

There was a pause before Michael said, "What are you doing back home? Surely to God, man, you should still be in there under observation."

He answered glibly, "You know the way things are at Dillon's Court. They didn't even notice when I left. I just walked out. They wanted to keep me of course, but I left when no-one was looking. I couldn't stand the place another minute." It could sound convincing. The casual formalities of Dillon's Court were well known and so was the behaviour of patients, who were prone to miraculous cures.

Michael looked out of the window towards the view of Dublin Mountains struggling to rise above the suburbs. "What happened to you?"

"I don't know. I had a few drinks at lunch time on Thursday. I must have taken a lot more than I thought . . . and gone out and fallen. Or got beaten up . . ." He wished he knew more about concussion and memory. Very likely if he had such total amnesia, blocking out six or seven hours, he would be very seriously ill, struggling to speak in a thick lisp. He tried to make his voice feeble and a touch disorientated. Why should Michael know anything more about it than he did?

"Did the garda come in and question you?"

"I wasn't really in a fit state. I suppose they'll be coming round here in time."

"How did you get home?"

"Oh, I began to remember things. Some things. Enough to want to get out of there and back home."

"Memory back, eh?"

"Oh no, no, not at all. I mean parts of it. I mean I started off completely out of this world. And only gradually began piecing together fragments from the past. Who I was and so forth. The fact I should be in school. And then my telephone number. Almost as soon as I remembered that I staggered out of bed and rang Agnes and had her take me home." He recalled the time he had been in the hospital visiting Byrne when he broke his leg playing rugby. "They have the radio on very loudly all day in the public ward. And at night radio and television playing together. And the television is only visible to three patients at most and any others who have necks like ostriches. That noise must have done harm to plenty of concussion patients before now."

"Memory back, eh?"

"No. Nothing about the accident and nothing about the hours immediately before."

"It'll all come back to you."

"Oh no, apparently not. Just before I cleared out a doctor came in to examine me. He said the chances were I'd go for the rest of my life without knowing how I got to be lying on Killiney Strand." He should have said lying by the railway. Stuck to the truth. But perhaps the idea of erratic wandering or tumbling downhill was more convincing.

"Chinese, was he? Arab? Black with tribal scars?" The medical staff at Dillon's Court were often of exotic origin.

"Oh, no. He was called Dr Murphy. He said it was most unlikely I'd ever remember the events leading up to the moment I was concussed."

Another long terrifying silence. "Is that so? Well, Jim, you lie in bed . . . stay there . . ." Was he going? No threats, no menace? He was on his way out. He did not want to stay in the stuffy little bedroom with Agnes's underclothes lying on the floor. Downstairs he lingered, talking to her.

"Keep him in bed as long as possible, darling. You were mad to agree to taking him out of hospital. Do you know anything about the long-term effects of concussion? It can take seven years for a person to get back to normal."

Did he know he had been told a load of lies? Very likely. At least he had not tried to murder him again. After the door slammed Drury dozed another hour. The temptation was strong to lie back and do nothing. Perhaps for seven years. He seemed to have been as active as James Bond. He thought he should attend Aunt Hatta's garden opening. As usual. He had been there for many years, and it would look strange if he did not turn up this year as well. Even with his injuries? In the mirror the bruises were still very prominent. They had changed colour. Poor James. A fall downstairs? A car accident?

It took a superhuman effort to get up and go. He had to persuade Agnes to accompany him, and Kevin too, just as usual. He succeeded with great difficulty. When they arrived, a little early, Aunt Hatta stood on the terrace outside the house dressed in the clothes she had worn for the occasion for as long as he could remember. The tailored navy blue suit that vaguely suggested a matron's uniform was topped by a matching straw hat bouncing with artificial cherries. She walked very slowly leaning on a parasol. Two nursing sisters from the small private hospital she supported—which was not Dillon's Court—were with her, holding up her elbows and offering words of comfort.

"Oh James, how good to have you here in time of trouble!"

"What on earth's happened?"

"Poor little Rascal has disappeared!"

"She's probably wandered off on some little adventure," soothed the plumpest nurse.

"You know nothing whatever about dogs. Females don't stray. Rascal never left this garden in her life. Those horrible thieves have got her. Do you know, James, someone broke in last night and stole the statue that Mr Kenny bought!"

"Good heavens!"

"I haven't told him yet. I'll have to when he comes this afternoon." She took out a yellowed lace handkerchief and mopped her eyes. "The police were so nice. They agreed how awful things have become round here. One of them could remember the time when all the people in this area were gentry."

"Terrible!"

"That man thought I was a wee bit naughty just to have a bicycle chain on the gate. Of course I said I relied on having Dempsey sleeping right beside it in the lodge. And the funny thing was that the chain wasn't smashed at all. Somebody had decoded the lock. Wasn't that strange?"

"Good Lord!" He should have remembered to smash it before they drove away. That was panic. Agnes might have thought of it, too.

"Those coded locks only have a small range of numbers. Mine was 1923, so touching, remember me telling you how I chose it because it was 1923, the year Jack and I were married?" She had a tendency to repeat herself, exercising her stories relating to Uncle Jack fairly regularly.

"Dempsey knew the number?"

"Of course."

"Perhaps he mentioned it to one of his pals over a drink."

"That's what the sergeant seemed to think. Oh dear, I wonder if Dempsey isn't getting past it? I really think the time is coming for him to retire."

Agnes's unfortunate social worker instincts were aroused. "Don't you remember, Jim, telling all those people about the number on the lock of your aunt's gate?"

"When did I?" he shouted.

"Oh, it must have been some time in the Easter holidays. When we were in that coffee place in Blackrock with the big crowd. You said . . . how touching it was that your aunt's love for her husband should be expressed in this way. Anyone could have heard."

The cherries on Aunt Hatta's hat swung like flails. "I shall tell that nice detective sergeant, James, and he will look into your friends. What has happened to your face?"

"An accident . . ."

"It's high time you stopped frequenting public houses. Oh, poor sweet little Rascal . . ." Considering the number of curtains and shoes the dog had chewed, the shredded Carrickmacross table cloth, the books ripped to pieces and the constant diarrhoea, her grief was immoderate. The worst thing that Rascal ever did was to dig up her mother three months after the old dog had died, and eat her.

"Oh, poor little creature!"

Dempsey stumped up the avenue shouting with his deaf man's bellow. "They're waiting, Ma'am. Will I open up on them?"

"Of course! What on earth have you been doing all this time, you stupid man?" She was the last generation that dared to be rude to its inferiors. "Take Mr Drury down with you. And Sister Halligan, you go as well, and for goodness sake try and see things get done properly this time."

Kevin went over to the pond to look for frogs. If he drowned, Agnes wouldn't notice, for she was retiring to a patch of grass near the tool shed to settle and do some meditation. Drury went down to the gate, outside which a restless crowd was looking impatiently through the bars. There was a table laid with a money box and a roll of tickets, and a folding chair which, as happened every year, he had to offer Sister Halligan.

With Mooney in attendance (Michael had kept his promise about lending him), Dempsey unclicked the unfortunate bicycle lock and let in a hundred people from whom Drury and Miss Halligan extracted a pound a head, half price for children. More trickled in behind. When he had first started this chore as a schoolboy, the price of admission had been half-a-crown. The crowd was mixed. Since this was a Saturday afternoon, it consisted of a good many idlers who found weekends a hard time to fill up. Sometimes they packed into their cars and drove out to look at show houses on new building estates which they had no intention of buying. They might go to the amusement arcades in Bray or out to Enniskerry to view the black ruin of Powerscourt or join the queues of cars going down to Brittas Bay. Others would travel up to Glencree and Glencullen to listen to shrill racing commentaries on car radios. Paying to see someone else's garden was a pleasant alternative summer recreation. They wheeled in prams and folding pushchairs and panted up the steep drive. Empty crisp packets and sweet papers dropped down behind them.

He recognized a number of old schoolmates and others he had met in the past. They all appeared to have done well. Those unfortunate enough not to be established in hereditary positions in solicitors' offices or wine merchants had strayed into lucrative jobs in advertising or real estate. Others had promising careers in law where the government, to express its liberal attitudes, always had a proportion of high judicial positions open to Protestants in excess of their numbers. Politics offered golden opportunities as well, although few went into it. What was the reason for his own ill success? Was it an inherited tendency to failure, a weakening of tough Cromwellian stock? Or merely that families like his own whose members tended to choose unrewarding warrior activities or, God help them, go into the Church, always ended up poorer than these descendants of Dublin doctors, lawyers and tradesmen? They favoured Scottish names that suggested thrift and sobriety, Andrew, Duncan, Gordon, Ian. (His own name was Scottish, but less popular with this society, presumably because of King James. However it had been a family name before the Stuarts came into prominence.) Their wives had a busy earnest expression that suggested school committees and well-tended gardens. There was an air of affluent conservatism about them that was unmistakable. He was reminded of the fact that at an airport it is always possible to pick out a flight of sober Air Canada passengers from similar groups destined to board planes for America. "We are not a petty people," Yeats had said. Drury disagreed with him.

Handing out tickets was monotonous work as he smiled greetings at those he recognized, parried comments on his appearance and shouted to Dempsey to sort out the queues of cars. They were assisted by a young guard who may have been on the lookout for thieves. He would be doing a more useful job if he went round discouraging people from taking cuttings. Many of the old ladies walking through the gates carried large handbags with pockets and places to put knives which they would use to snip little pieces of Aunt Hatta's blooms. Tomorrow she would tour the garden mourning these neat amputations. (She herself was not above getting an acquaintance to drive her out to the Botanical Gardens where she would go into the greenhouse and take cuttings of rare and pretty plants.)

People still kept coming. He noticed a couple of antique dealers who hoped to peer through windows and note the contents of the house. Up on the front lawn a group of nurses were pouring tea from large tin teapots into cardboard mugs which they sold together with digestive biscuits and fruitcake. This annual event made a surprising amount of money. In other years, Drury had never hesitated to evade Nurse Halligan's watchful eye and pocket what he considered to be his just and fair commission for the afternoon's work. This skilful exercise needed sleight of hand and the ability to pick out the halfwitted from among those he admitted so that he could neglect to give them tickets. But today, even when Dempsey carried down a tray of spilt tea, and Nurse Halligan sat back relaxed and unnoticing, he was too preoccupied to practise any deception.

The guard outside the gate looked alert and guided a car into position just in front of Dempsey's lodge. Michael got out, locked the silent doors, slapped away small boys waiting to stroke the chrome, and strode towards the gate, greeting the guard by name. Drury excused himself to Nurse Halligan and retired into the rhododendron bushes. She must think he had a bladder problem; only ten minutes earlier he had made a similar retreat when Headmaster had ushered Jaws in through the gates.

Michael swept past Nurse Halligan without a glance, having assumed that as a patron of Aunt Hatta's he had no need to buy a ticket. Drury watched as he walked jauntily up the drive. From where he stood—he had come out of the bushes—he could see the scene above him with the clarity of an operagoer. He looked upwards towards the theatrical turreted profile of Eagle's Nest and Aunt Hatta and her entourage grouped on the terrace. Below and around them, paying visitors moved through the shrubberies like tea pickers. Michael strode upwards. Did his shoulders droop as Aunt Hatta greeted him and pointed with the ferrule of her parasol at a spot that Drury saw was the empty space beside the lily pond? Michael went down the steps and along the terrace to the place she indicated and peered about. Drury could not help giving a cackle of laughter that made Nurse Halligan look in his direction. Now Michael was going up to Aunt Hatta again, and his farewells appeared to be bad-tempered. He seemed to want to leave quickly, but Aunt Hatta accompanied him down the hill, with the two nurses behind, a slow navy blue flotilla. He had to reconcile his angry pace to Aunt Hatta's totter. They descended until they were within earshot.

"A battered old thing, Mr Kenny, which I don't think you or I will miss." They were close now, and even in the midst of her protestations Aunt Hatta could not help asking, "How much?"

"Better than last year, Mrs Good. But you remember how it rained right up until four o'clock?"

"Wasn't it wonderful the way the weather held today?" chirruped one of the escorts.

Aunt Hatta persisted, "Are you sure that includes all the children? They slip in so easily and there seemed to be more than usual."

"I suppose a few climbed over the wall in the usual way." Those who braved the barbed wire on hooked sticks that surrounded Aunt Hatta's property could be picked out by their torn clothes.

Drury had left it too late to make another retreat into the bushes. Michael was glaring at him.

"How's the memory?"

He smiled, trying to look concussed and stupid.

"I'll be seeing you, Jim . . ."

When Drury finally relinquished his post and went and collected his loved ones, he found Agnes asleep and Kevin with an improvised fishing net of black-currant netting that had caught a number of goldfish. He picked them up from where they lay on the grass and flung them far into the undergrowth. Up at the house the dogs were released from the basement and thundered through the garden attacking lingering visitors. Aunt Hatta's lamentations for the one that was missing still resounded as the Drurys said their goodbyes. They drove off, Kevin soaked and sullen in the back devouring melted Black Magic chocolates.

Agnes began grumbling. "God, that woman. Do you mean to tell me she makes the same sort of commotion every time one of those animals dies?"

"Especially if it is snatched betimes. An old white-muzzled companion's departure will be accepted with stoicism. They all get a decent burial—that's one of Dempsey's jobs. And a headstone." He had never told her about the cemetery. She wouldn't understand. Her peasant ancestors had no time for sentimentality towards animals. He remembered her scorn when his mother had bestowed anthropomorphic characteristics on a pitcher plant. ("The hungry darling! Ready for another little fly?") "The dogs are buried down at the bottom of the garden."

"A stone for each one?"

"Name, dates, and usually a text. Most of them have things like 'A Dear Old Friend' or 'Faithful and True'. There's one with a quote from Richard II. 'A jewel in a ten-times-barred-up chest Is a bold spirit in a loyal breast.'"

"I wonder what she'd have for that creature you killed? 'Rascal is in her grave. After life's fitful fever she sleeps well'?"

Snivelling in the back Kevin threw a dead frog, white belly upwards, into Drury's lap. He began to attack Agnes about her foolish defence of Dempsey. They were quarrelling by the time they got home. As they opened the front door, the telephone was ringing.

"Don't answer it." He swore as he tripped over the stone that lay in the hallway, a big fat oval of marble, the piece that had broken off the stolen statue like a slice off a Vienna roll. Kevin had scratched patterns on the side with felt pens and drawn a little face over the knee. The phone continued ringing as Agnes put on the kettle. It rang as they drank tea.

"Why not take it off the hook?" she shouted.

"He'd know we're here and be round like a shot."

"Sooner or later he'll be here in any case."

"I'm not prepared to talk to him now."

When the ringing stopped the relief brought him near to tears. It began again ten minutes later. After a dozen rings he got up and answered it, his hand trembling.

Headmaster's voice was honed to irritation. "Hello, James. We were glad to see you better." Jaws must have spotted him.

"I'm still pretty well under the weather. But I felt I should help my aunt. You see, it's been a long-standing arrangement."

"Founder's Day is also a long-standing arrangement."

"I'm really sorry . . . Yesterday I was under doctor's orders not to move. What? . . . much better now, thank you . . . a bit of a head-ache and some dizziness . . . Oh yes, certainly I'll be in on Monday . . . Do you want me to go down to the CIE? No? Berridge has al-ready? All right, I'll be in on Monday . . ."

He put down the receiver and almost immediately the telephone began ringing again. Why did they keep one at all? It cost so much and only caused anguish. Agnes insisted. She was too garrulous to do without it.

"Oh, hello, Michael. We just arrived back this minute."

"I've got to talk to you. Will you come to my place?"

"Not this evening."

"I'll be round to you, then."

"No. I feel like hell."

"You were alright this afternoon."

"I felt ill all the time."

"I've got to talk to you, Jim, like I said." The voice was cold and unfriendly and he felt a stirring in that part of the brain where his memory had been failing to function. But nothing followed. "When can you come round?"

An accident in the swimming pool was too easy to arrange. Not here either. Neutral ground. And he must get some rest. Not this evening. Not here or there. His voice became hysterical, Michael's soothing. It took them time to compromise in a way that was unsatisfactory to both, like delegates at a peace conference. Tomorrow evening at the Bold Shemalier.

He took the receiver off the hook—too late. Michael appeared to be certain he had stolen the statue. How did he know? Surely he couldn't have had the thing watched as it stood over the lily pond? Was it possi-ble that Dempsey had glimpsed Drury and Agnes through his dirty cur-tains, and had informed? But it seemed to Drury that Michael had known instantly that he was the thief, the minute that Aunt Hatta had informed him the statue was missing. He recalled the rage in his voice when he had said, "How's the memory?" Or was it merely strong suspicion? He'd have trouble to prove it. And he would hardly want to harm him until he got the statue back. Perhaps if he wanted it so badly a deal could be made. Michael had one statue already. He was a mil-lionaire, and here was Drury with one ewe lamb, so to speak. You'd think he'd rejoice at his old buddy showing some enterprise.

He went to bed, but in contrast to the heavy dozing of the last few days he now found he could not sleep at all. He tried relaxation techniques, lying with his limbs flopping around him, imagining he was on a quiet desert island prepared to sleep for days and nights together. What was the legal position about his aunt's statue with Michael having the receipt but not the goods? More and more he was convinced that he and Agnes had done the right thing. But he wished he had more confidence. From the beginning he had shown little sense. He knew Michael's track record, and it had been more than foolish to sell him the Harmony Hall statue without the slightest hesitation. It had been idleness, really. He should have made an effort first, spent a little money and had it valued and assessed. He had another vision of himself tumbling out of the train, big hands pushing him. He wished he could sleep. He got up and went over to the medicine chest where he found an old bottle of Mogodon with seven or eight left. He had weaned himself off them a year ago. To think his previous sleep problems had been initiated because a couple of boys failed Common Entrance in the subjects he taught. He drank down two pills with water from a glass which toothpaste had whitened like rime, and an hour later sleep came to him.

He spent Sunday in bed, something he hadn't done since he was a teenager. In the early days of their marriage he had been shocked by Agnes's habit of spending all day in bed on Sunday until six o'clock, when she got up to go to evening Mass. She was attentive now, bringing up meals, even tidying the bedroom. He had recovered somewhat by the time he dressed and drove down to the Bold Shemalier. He had made the date as late as possible, for half-past nine, and turned up half an hour late to demonstrate his independence.

He entered the hallway of another castellated Killiney house which had been converted into a luxury hotel. Casual guests were directed down a staircase covered with a purple carpet that sank to a sauna, and numerous crowded bars and restaurants. He passed the Grill Room, its function emphasized by curly gilded railings that cut off the padded cells where people were imprisoned with lumps of meat. The walls were hung with paintings, bright representations of currachs and bog cotton, their titles and prices punched out on tape and stuck to their frames. Like the hallway of Castle Xanadu, the floor carried a crested carpet; here the Kelly crest honoured Kelly, the boy from Killane, associated in balladry with the Bold Shemalier.

He went on to the bar where he had arranged to meet Michael. The walls were decorated with reproduction medieval armour, padlocks, and dark varnished pictures, sub-Salvator Rosa landscapes, cherubs, nymphs, saints and martyrs floating near the upside-down bottles of spirits adjusted to their measure. Michael was sitting up at the counter, holding a little briefcase like a travelling salesman, and talking to three cronies. There could hardly be a man in Killiney in the AB bracket with whom he did not have a jovial nodding acquaintance. He did not see Drury, who decided not to join the group and expose himself to the cost of a round. He wandered off and bought cigarettes from a machine —twenty, naturally, you could never buy ten in a place like this—and hung around for ten minutes, smoking and putting out the stub in a china vase full of sand.

When he returned Michael saw him at once, detached himself from his friends and bought two whiskeys. With a flick of his head he indicated that they should adjourn to a side table.

"Last drinks, gentlemen!" the barman called out.

Drury carried the whiskeys carefully across the floor, since Michael was nursing his briefcase.

"I want it back, Jim. Right away." He had to talk loudly, for the acoustics were complicated not only by the low ceilings of the basement, but by the noise that emanated from the nightclub right beside the bar, separated by a pair of padded doors. Every time they swung open they released a blast of ceilidh music or a burst of laughter from the end of a comedian's joke. The small room where the show was being held was packed tight with tourists who had been ferried here from hotels in the centre of the city to observe Dublin's night-life. In addition it contained numerous local people who were aware that this particular show continued until well after Sunday hours, and while it continued, drinks could be bought.

"Did you hear?"

"What are you talking about?" Drury watched a file of old yellowed American women wearing sparkling costume jewellery, escorted by two frail male survivors. Behind them a jig was playing, and there was a glimpse through the doors of girls in kilts, who appeared to be armless, jumping up and down.

"Look, I know you've got it. I saw part of it." Never commit a crime when you have concussion. "The piece of marble lying in your front hall."

Michael relieved his feelings with some inaudible obscenities as the padded doors opened again for uniformed waitresses bringing in drinks to the Irish part of the audience which was packed in the back of the room. He called for more whiskey to be brought to their table.

"Sorry, sir, bar's closed."

"I know the manager!" he shouted. "I'm a personal friend of his. Bring him here! Mr Sheehan! Tell him I'm the chairman of the local residents' committee . . ."

"Sorry, sir!" The barman brought the metal screen crashing down round the bar. Now the waitresses had to carry the drinks from far away, and the interior of the nightclub was the only place in the Bold Shemalier where non-residents could obtain drinks. That there was not a concerted rush towards it from all over the hotel was due to the £5 admission fee. Michael hesitated, not because he was unprepared to pay for both of them, but because it was obvious that once inside no conversation, menacing or otherwise, could be conducted. But he badly wanted a drink. He grabbed at a waitress and once again shouted that he knew the manager. She edged skilfully away and floated through the padded doors to drinkers now listening to a tenor singing about the Bard of Armagh.

"Come back to Castle Xanadu," Michael's voice was almost pleading. "We'll talk over brandy."

Delighted at his discomfiture, Drury refused; used to making drinks last, he had a reasonable amount left in his glass. In black mood Michael ordered coffee to be taken up, and motioned him to follow him up the purple stairway. They sat on yellow brocade sofas in the Marine Lounge where the curtains were tied back with rope swags and the prints on the walls featured leaning sailing boats with titles like *Decks Awash* or *A Following Wind*. Drury remembered Michael saying that his customers invariably preferred calm marine scenes. Storms and breakers were always more difficult to sell while representations of calm days at sea were soothing, like tanks of tropical fish in psychiatrists' consulting rooms. He stood up, sipping at his whiskey while he examined *In the Bay of Biscay*.

"Quit the messing," Michael snarled, pouring Nescafé from a silvered coffee pot. "I know all about it."

"The piece of marble that Kevin coloured came off the torso from Harmony Hall."

"It did not. That one was female. Remember the long hair, the boobs? And your aunt's statue is male. The bit you have in your house is a masculine knee. All muscle."

He tried another tack. "I can't understand why you're so greedy. You've got one statue already, the one you swindled me over. Is it really worth the trouble to get the pair? You're always telling me the trade is ruthless. Why can't you accept defeat just for once? You've lost out. You have no absolute proof I took Aunt Hatta's statue, and you can't prove anything about that fragment. If you call in the garda to search round my house, you'll only be laying yourself open to undesirable publicity. At the best it'll come out how you did the old girl down. You've always admitted it, but it won't look good in print: The Man Who Robbed Old Women."

"It wouldn't look quite so bad under the heading The Man Who

Robbed Rich Old Women. And right now, Jim, I've no need to call in any guard. It's quite enough to know in my own mind that you've got your hands on it." He sucked up a mouthful of coffee with distaste. "I want it back. And don't give me 'it's too far away' or you don't know where it is."

He wondered if he could get away with a story that he had sold it. But why not simply refuse to have anything more to do with Michael?

"To hell with you. There's nothing you can do about it. Not even throw me out of a train window." No response. "I've had just about enough." He got up and walked away over the Kelly crest.

"Come back."

"Fuck off," he called bravely.

"I've something to show you." Michael was brandishing the brief-case. Drury hesitated as the clasp was opened, revealing a mass of tissue paper. He came back to the sofa. He'd forgotten how pretty some of the things were. A Williamite toasting glass with a charming crude engraving of King Billy sitting on his horse. He'd been mad to let Michael have it for a mere forty pounds. A millefiore paperweight, chipped, it was true, but a lovely thing. A cameo showing a curly-headed Roman.

"I've got more."

"Do you mean to say you kept everything I sold you?"

"Not everything. It wasn't a matter of policy. Only the things that caught the eye."

He should have avoided temptation. Aunt Hatta was so very old. Poor old soul, tripping about wailing today in her mad grief. He had been putting his future in needless peril. The figures of his salary flashed in his mind. His mistake had been to go to Michael. His friend. Few other antique dealers in Dublin, avid for stock to sell and replace, would have asked him where the stuff came from. Old family things. That's what he had originally said to Michael. How had he found out? He must have wheedled it from him during a drinking session. (But he had always known at the back of his mind that Michael knew where the goods came from.) His friend. What made Drury more angry than anything was the miserable prices he had received over the years.

"I'm on good terms with Mrs Good. I went back this morning. I was most understanding. I said of course it was not her fault in any way. I refused to take back the money even that mean old bitch felt she owed me. She thought I was great. You go over and listen to her and you'll find her gushing away about that nice Mr Kenny. I remembered to offer my condolences over the disappearance of the dog."

Drury thought of the unbroken lock on the gate. A mistake, like leaving the marble fragment around for Michael to see.

"I could show her these any time, Jim."

"Oh, all right, you can have the bloody thing back."

There was a silence and Michael nodded. Packing up the paper-weight he changed the conversation. "You made an error or two in the stuff you picked out. I can understand you had to choose something small each time. Why didn't you take something really valuable? I saw she had some great porcelain . . ."

"Oh, I couldn't take any of her good pieces." Originally he had set himself a pecuniary limit of a hundred pounds, although later with inflation and rising values, that limit had been raised. "Does anyone else know? Maire for instance?" Maire and Michael had still been man and wife when Drury started pilfering. "Orla or any of the others?"

Michael grinned. "I'll leave you to worry about that." Drury thought it unlikely. Michael had a sheik's attitude towards the involvement of women in his business affairs. Then he asked where the statue was, and Drury explained about the cottage in West Wicklow. He wanted to go there right away, but Drury protested that he couldn't possibly find his way round the Wicklow Hills in the darkness. It had been bad enough with Agnes to guide him. For God's sake, it was now a quarter to twelve. Michael said it was later than that the other night when they had stolen the statue, but having wrested his main victory from Drury, he agreed to pick him up the following morning at eight. When Drury protested that he was supposed to be at school Michael didn't answer. A distant burst of applause filtered up the basement stairs from the cabaret.

Rage and a feeling of futility shook him as he drove home. In the hall he tripped over the piece of marble that had been the cause of his most recent problems. He picked it up and carried it into the kitchen where he pitched it into the garbage sack. It was too heavy, and tore a hole in the black plastic out of which spilled carrot peelings. He reached in, making his arm filthy, and retrieved it. He took it out into the back garden and heaved it over the wickerwork fence into next door. If Mr Gillespie happened to be outside, he would be struck on the head. Back in the kitchen he saw another object that inspired him with loathing. Beside the deal table, filled with curled copies of maga-zines, many cyclostyled with titles like *Earth* and *Muck* and *Horoscope* and *Divine Guidance*, was the elephant's foot that he had bought at Harmony Hall. How he hated the joke perpetrated on some great beast whose whitened bones mouldered in the African bush. Why should a remnant of nobility and a reminder of man's cruelty have to continue a jokey career? He found another black sack and carried it outside, maga-zines and all.

Agnes and Kevin were both in the sitting room asleep—she had not bothered to put him to bed. She lay on the sofa, a worn copy of the ghastly Tolkien beside her. He woke her and told her of Michael's threats and strategy. Her anger surprised him by its vehemence, soon reaching Force Eleven of her personal Beaufort Scale. She shouted reproaches at him for having taken up a career of crime in the first place. But she had known from the start about his thefts from Aunt Hatta, and had even suggested Michael to him as a fence. He shouted back a reminder that it was through her that he had met Michael in the first place; they both came from the same seedy midland town. He was stupid, unbelievably stupid, she yelled, not to have recognized the value of these marble pieces and all their work the other evening was wasted. He deserved, thoroughly deserved, the accident that had left the fading bruises on his face. She tried to add to them by throwing books at him. She woke Kevin with her shouting, and now he was crying. Drury could take no more that evening. He went upstairs to the hot untidy little bedroom, and took two sleeping pills.

He slept deeply until Michael's heavy hand on the doorbell woke him for the second time in three days. When the chimes repeated themselves, he had to go down in his pyjamas and let him in. Agnes must have gone off early, since it was not eight o'clock yet. He dressed and made Michael wait while he had breakfast.

Outside, the Rolls made the usual opulent contrast to the Morris, which looked more than usually dilapidated because it had a flat tyre. The weather had broken and soft summer rain was falling. He carried out the spade, still covered with mud, and threw it on the soft beige leather of the back seat. They made the Blessington road effortlessly and soon slid off right into hills and glens. Drury lost his way as they searched through mist among shivering newly-shorn sheep, and the big car had to back up several boreens. The lane to the cottage was tarmacadamed. Hardly a track in the whole of Ireland was without its coating of tar which provided regular work for the unemployed. Briar bushes closed in, scraping the car's sides. Here was the cottage above them, swirling in mist. Here was the gate. When they got out, the drizzle soaked them in a moment. Here was the horse giving a friendly whinny when it saw them. Grunting, Michael climbed over the gate.

"Where?"

Here was the spot, the garbage scattered all over the gorse bushes. The corpse of the dog, the worse for wear, its pelt gleaming with drops of rain, lay beside a large hole. Fox? Badger? The statue had been dug up, and had disappeared.

"You've been having me on."

"No, honestly." He pointed to poor Rascal. At least her remains demonstrated one thing—that someone had brought her up here from Killiney. Michael's curses expressed his opinion of Drury's stupidity in burying the statue in full view of those who lived in the cottage. It was typical of why he had never got on in life. "But there's no-one up there."

Michael strode up, followed by Drury. He broke the padlock on the top of the double door with the spade, unbolted the bottom half and went in. Odours of squalor greeted them. A rat had fallen into some drinking water in a plastic bucket and drowned. There were signs of artistic activity—spilled linseed oil and numerous little capless squeezed-out tubes of paint. Some had even coloured the telephone. It was typical of the way these people lived—no running water, but a telephone was a necessity. Eugene's daubs, hung on the damp walls, were representations of blue hills and thatched cottages, not unlike many of the pictures that hung for sale in the Bold Shemalier. Tony specialized in crude pen-and-ink sketches of people standing behind barbed wire or holding torches of freedom. Evidently he was politically motivated. Michael picked up a half-empty bottle of milk and sniffed.

"Fresh. They must have been here no later than last night."

"But they're not supposed to be here at all. They're in the west somewhere organizing a seminar."

"Who says?"

"Agnes."

"Friends of Agnes, these fellas?"

"That's how we got the idea of bringing the thing up here."

"Why didn't you just bury it in a bog?"

"It seemed safer to have a more definite hiding place. We didn't mean to bury it at all. Just to take it up to one of those outhouses and leave it for a couple of days until we decided what to do next. Then we found it was too heavy to carry up hill."

"These people were away you say? Friends of Agnes?" Michael seemed stunned, mute with amazement or anxiety. He left the cottage in silence and went down the hill in the mist. When he came to the dog's remains, he stirred them with his toe. Used to his wolfish bonhomie, Drury was alarmed, and began to think of his fall from the train. At last Michael said, "I can't believe I could be had that way a second time." He continued to stare down at Rascal, and Drury wondered if he were contemplating taking her home in the back of the car in one of those cartons filled with shavings he carried with him in case he made a delicate purchase in the course of his travels. He might put her in his deep freeze and keep her as evidence. But if those were his thoughts, he changed his mind at the last moment.

"Let's get out of here!"

CHAPTER 7

They drove down to the nearest village, a slate-roofed collection of cottages and dusty shops with nineteenth-century facades and the names of their proprietors in black and gilded lettering, mostly Byrnes and O'Tooles, since this was the heart of Wicklow. The picturesque appearance of the place was muted by the large new bungalows on its outskirts and by the refurbished pub standing in half an acre of black car park. The bar was scattered with leatherette chairs placed before low coffee tables supporting big glass ashtrays, and around the walls were machines with television screens showing little balls leaping eerily up and down. The place smelled of spilled beer and cold tobacco.

They were the only drinkers; Michael ordered Jamieson for both. "I take it one of them's a boyfriend of Agnes?"

"Actually they're queer."

"Oh." Michael drank down a couple of mouthfuls. "Did you tell anyone else last night what I told you? About wanting the statue back?"

"No, of course not. I didn't get home until after midnight."

"But you told Agnes? Christ, I should have thought of that!"

"Agnes?"

"She's the one . . ."

"What the hell are you talking about? What could she do in the early hours of the morning?"

"She could ring them, couldn't she?"

"Out to here?"

"No problem. This area's gone automatic."

"But they're away, I tell you. They're in Sligo."

"That's only what she said. They were back here last night, believe you me. I'll give you good money she rang them and told them to dig the thing up and remove it. And what's more she's cleared out."

"Cleared out?"

"Done a flit. Vanished. Left the family residence. Abandoned the protection of the marital roof. She does that from time to time doesn't she?"

"She didn't this morning. The car was there."

"It had a puncture. She went without it. The child wasn't there, was he? At eight in the morning."

"She's got this part time job . . ."

"Don't tell me she's out at work at that time."

"She may be back at home now. I bet she is . . ."

"Like hell . . ."

"I'll give her a ring." He took some coins out of Michael's change and went to the call box. There was no reply when he rang Goleen Park. On impulse he rang the woman who ran the gift shop where Agnes worked. She greeted him with "Hello, Jim" although he'd never met her. All Agnes's friends were on first name terms with everyone. They'd address the Pope as Karol. He asked if Agnes was there and if he could speak to her.

"No, Jim, she hasn't been in. She phoned earlier to say she was going away and wouldn't be in for the next week or so."

Drury went back to Michael and told him.

"Just what I thought. She's a clever girl. She found a way of getting back at me."

"Why should she want to get back at you?"

He leaned across the table so that Drury could smell his breath. "You knew about Agnes and me, didn't you?"

"Do you mean to say that you were lovers?"

He was not really surprised. If it was true, it explained a lot, certain insincere protestations of dislike, sheepish expressions and things like that. And that puzzling holiday to Greece which she said she had paid for out of horseshoe-nail lockets sold to souvenir shops. He knew some of her clothes were expensive—how expensive he had never liked to ask. Her gold necklace with the sign of Libra, was that a gift from Michael? What on earth could they have in common? A liking for variety, he thought sadly.

"I let her down one time," Michael was saying. Drury's stirrings of jealousy were mixed with admiration for her, if indeed she had managed this coup last night. Had there been a showdown at that party? He tried to recall details of her behaviour. She had been tight as usual. And some stupid row with him. Had Michael had time to quarrel with her that evening? With his vitality he had time for most things. So many rows one never knew which were the serious ones.

"You'll have to get hold of her." Michael's voice was nearly a shout.

"Me? It seems you're just as likely to know where she is."

"I'll be doing my best from my end, don't you worry about that. But it's your responsibility, Jim. You'll have to track her down from among her crazy friends. For starters, what about the child?"

Please to heaven she had taken Kevin with her to wherever she was, and not left him in playgroup or with the Bradys. "I imagine he's wherever she is."

"You'd better start asking around."

He felt exasperated. "Look, Michael, I'm tired of you playing the gangster. We had the gist of this conversation last night . . . all that bit about how you want the statue or you'll tell my aunt. Can't you see I've got to the stage where the thing I want most in the world is for you to take the damn thing off my hands. You threw me off the train"—he made no move to deny it—"you blackmail me, and now more threats. I don't know where Agnes is. I've no way of knowing where she is. She'll probably turn up at home this evening. You can't really know if she's arranged all this nonsense or not."

"Jim, I'll make it easy for you. I appreciate your difficulties. I'll give you a day or two to find her and to find the statue. After that, I'll be an angry man."

"What'll you do then? I tell you, I haven't the faintest idea of how to set about it any more than you. And it's only the wildest assumption of yours that she has anything to do with its disappearance."

"I'll still be the angry man, won't I?"

"Did you throw me off the train?"

"What kind of talk is that?"

"I can't understand why you are so concerned to get it back. I can appreciate it's good. But you've got one already, and it's not as if it's in all that good shape. Why is it so fantastically important to have the pair?"

"They are more than a pair. You remember the statue from Harmony Hall was of a little girl? You remember the way the silver paint ran thick on the leg? After the paint remover had done its job it left behind a pattern of leaves on the marble."

"Leaves?"

"I've had the top people over from England to have a look at them. Stylized leaves. Laurel leaves at their guess."

"I don't see the significance."

"Who's been teaching the classics to little West Brits all this time? Who's the lady most likely to have laurel leaves running up her legs?"

Drury was flustered.

"Ever hear of Daphne? Seems she didn't fancy Apollo but he wouldn't let her off the hook. He chased her and she got turned into a laurel bush rather than have him lay his hands on her? Guess who's been standing beside your aunt's pond all this time."

"Apollo?"

"That's it. They're not only a pair, those two statues; they are an in-

tegral part of the same group—they've come apart, but put them together again and they belong to each other. They're partners like Fred
Astaire and Ginger Rogers." He flicked his fingers and the lonely barman two hundred yards away took another order. One compensation to
be got out of this sorry business was that Michael bought the drinks.

"Even if it is a good group there seems to be very little of it left for
all this fuss to be made."

Michael leaned forward and talked with lowered voice. "Jim, the
Venus de Milo has no arms. The Apollo Belvedere likewise is short on
them. The Venus of Cyrenaica and the Victory of Samothrace have no
arms and no head. The only reason that the Laocoon has arms is that
someone stuck new ones on after he was dug up."

His stomach churned. "You're not suggesting that these things are as
important as the Venus de Milo?"

"Jim, you have no idea. I've had in the experts. They date those fragments to the fourth century BC, the great age of Greek sculpture.
Nothing to beat it since—the age of Polyclitus, Lysippus, Phidias . . ."
Most likely he had never heard of them until a couple of weeks ago. "I
first had in someone from one of those big London shops—a dealer. He
called in two more fellas, one from the Victoria and Albert and someone in the know from the Antiquities Department of the British Museum. Do you know, I didn't even have to pay their fares over?"

He was silent.

"They had a look at the fragment from Harmony Hall. Mind you,
this far all done by the eye. Very fine. Very fine indeed. Very possibly
an original. None of your Graeco-Roman copies." He grasped Drury's
forearm. "Did you ever hear of Praxiteles? Seemingly he was a sculptor
who did a number of nice pieces that got lost. But a lot of people believe that one of his statues survives in quite good shape. That's the
Hermes of Olympia. It's even got a complete arm. Plenty of art lovers
like it, and I wouldn't mind having it in my garden. Graceful, translu-
cent and majestic, and I quote. There happens to be some documentary
evidence to link the Hermes directly with Praxiteles. It's mentioned
in the diaries of a traveller called Pausanias who happened to see it a
few centuries after Praxiteles had passed on. However, not everyone
claims the Hermes of Olympia as an original—there are those who
think he's too pretty altogether."

"What's Hermes got to do with the fragments we found here?"

"Listen a moment. It appears Praxiteles also did a group of Apollo
and Daphne. All these experts like the look of my little piece from Harmony Hall, and a couple of them have suggested it was on the cards
that this might be one and the same. No-one could ever be a hundred
per cent sure of course, but even the likelihood puts these bits and pieces

into a very special category indeed. I remembered you said there was a similar bit of marble in your aunt's garden, and I knew that you and Mrs Good and the Sherlocks were part of an extended family."

With the ill luck that dogged Drury it was all perfectly possible. He began to look upon the current circumstances as an exaggerated version of the episode of the Benin bronzes. There was no need to ask how ancient Greek marbles had turned up in a cluttered house in Dalkey. Michael had evidently not done so yet; he was anxious to get them into his own hands first. Very likely Aunt Hatta had no idea where they came from. Any ancestor who did the Grand Tour could bring back anything. Implanted for ever in the minds of every art dealer in Europe was the story of the Guardi canvases found rolled up in a damp shed on the outskirts of Bantry. Guardi canvases or fragments by Praxiteles could reappear anywhere.

"You've told the garda?"

"I haven't all that faith in the guard. Too busy chasing after bank robbers. I haven't decided whether to ask them to put out an alert for Agnes and her buddies, if that's what you mean. I'd like to keep it in the family for the time being." Perhaps after all he felt sensitive about sharp practice and the stink of publicity if the story got known. Drury mused on the seventy pounds he had received for his statue in the first place, while Michael began babbling about the British Museum's intention of buying it and grants in aid, and contacts in New York and Washington who were showing interest, and how he would be in touch with Boothroyds the minute both pieces of statuary were together. Then he began to cajole. If Drury found Agnes and persuaded her to give it back he'd get a good commission. If not . . . Meanwhile he wouldn't leave the garda out of it altogether—he'd have them watch the cottage . . .

They drove back to Dublin in silence. The weather had cleared and they took the road over the Sally Gap in sunshine which instantly brought out a procession of holidaying cars. At the summit a man was selling pots of homemade jam, having chosen the windiest and most isolated spot to place his car with the opened boot. At Glencree they turned off round the sharp bend, nearly bumping into a minibus full of handicapped children taking the air. You wouldn't have known they were handicapped unless you read the fact lettered on the side of the vehicle, a curious exercise in advertisement. Below the road appeared the familiar cone of the Sugarloaf, Dublin's Mount Fuji. A peace gathering was taking place in the old reformatory where over-optimistic liberals arranged reasonable and futile assemblies to talk about peace and goodwill. Not long ago this wild mountain village had been isolated from the rest of the world. Not now; the steady growth of bungalows and weekend cottages round about had seen to that. Cottages were bought on sunny summer days when buyers were deluded into forgetting about the snows of winter. The Youth Hostel was full. Carloads of picnickers had evidently decided to eat al fresco beside the desolate German cemetery, dramatic as a setting for *Giselle*.

They flew on towards Kill-the-Horse Hill above Enniskerry and began the steep descent without slackening speed.

"Do the brakes ever fail?" he asked idly.

"Are you crazy? Power assisted."

Glancing sideways at the pudgy profile, Drury considered that if by a miracle the manufacturers of Rolls Royce had slipped up it would be an end to all his troubles. He and Michael would go sliding down faster and faster, past those two boys with rucksacks and that mad-looking tramp with his stained mackintosh and cudgel, down, down right to the large stone fountain in the middle of Enniskerry where they would die beside the vandalized telephone booth among the County Council roses. Better still, he thought, as they straightened up at the bottom like an aeroplane at the end of a dive, suppose the brakes failed at the top of a hill like that, or anywhere else, at a time when he wasn't in the car and Michael was driving by himself? He considered this possibility until they reached Goleen Park.

"Do your best, Jim. I'll be hearing from you." The tenor voice was as affable as it had ever been.

The Morris in the drive sagged where it had descended on top of the flattened tyre. Agnes had never been able to mend a puncture. He went inside calling her name. The house was deserted, the floor inside the dark hallways scattered with the usual windowed envelopes now issued in pastel shades since state organizations had started to cheer up their bills. Had she really done what Michael claimed, left in a hurry, creeping out before daybreak? What about Kevin? He rang the Bradys and listened to Mrs Brady's rich Dublin voice. No, Mrs Drury hadn't brought over the little fella today. No, she hadn't heard from her. That was one blessing at least.

He pondered Michael's elaborate surmise, wondering if there was anything in it. It was just as likely that she had merely walked out on him. She was always walking out on him, to return a week or two later. But when she had departed on previous occasions she had always left letters about her independence and her karma and so forth. And if she was going off with a lover, she would not have taken Kevin.

He changed the tyre and fried some eggs before deciding that the best thing he could do with the afternoon was to put in an appearance at Prospect. He arrived in time to supervise a group of juniors with dirty bath towels preparing to bathe in the small cold swimming pool. The afternoon passed, no more or less melancholy than the six hundred or so previous afternoons he had spent here. He confronted Headmaster and apologized for his absence during the morning, pleading a check-up at Dillon's Court. Headmaster was surprisingly affable, and enquired about his injuries. He introduced him to a confident-looking young graduate whom he had been interviewing for a job, a man with a history degree, a good Dip. Ed., a spell of Voluntary Service in a developing country, and distant relationship to Jaws. Another fool clamouring to put on chains and sit among the galley slaves. Was he after Drury's position?

When he drove back to Goleen Park, he found himself hoping Agnes would be there making some foul meal. But there was no sign of her. He began to believe that Michael could be right. After making some efforts to clean up, he got out her address book. The thoroughness with which she pursued acquaintance brought her in contact with countless people. Besides the usual artists and actors she had made a good many friends when she was doing social work. Did she keep up with them, barristers, drug addicts, religious of all types, ex-convicts, the twelve Christian brothers whom she had accompanied on a seminar, rich men, poor men and beggarmen? Over the years scores of her friends had intruded in his life—the sort who arrived for a meal only after the pubs closed and who snored the night away on his sofa. Flicking through the frayed pages he noted the people who had moved, the old addresses scored out and new ones written in illegibly. Several times he had suggested getting a new book, but the task of transliteration would be formidable. The pages were distorted and made knobbly by visiting cards—they mostly seemed to be cards of crackpot psychiatrists and family therapists—further addresses scribbled on fragments of newspaper, old wholefood recipes and a leaflet about a young fat Maharishi. He rang a few names he recognized. No-one had any idea where she was. Sorry, man. No way. We don't know, right? He gave up. He felt like that gormless woman in Grimms' Fairy Tales told off to go and spin straw into gold.

He found he was lonely. He missed Kevin's familiar whine, and even Agnes at her worst, sulky and dirty. In contrast to her he had few friends. There was no-one at Prospect whom he did not despise or hate, and outside school he had few acquaintances. If he thought about it, his only real friend had been Michael.

He drove over to a takeaway in Dun Laoghaire and brought a frankfurter and a bag of chips down to the pier. He found a seat and ate in the bright evening sunshine. There was no wind; the sea was a mirror reflecting the sails of numerous becalmed racing yachts filled with cursing crews. They drifted about on the water inside and outside the harbour, lying in the way of the mailboat with its box-like shape to pack in as many cars as possible, and its romantic name, *British Rail* 2. There was escape the old way—a ticket to England away from it all. He mused on ways he could get money on his overdrawn account. He might approach the bursar at Prospect—retired army, very old—and ask him to change a cheque. He could squeeze a hundred pounds out of him with luck. It would have to be Friday, oh, what a pity, the bank's closed . . . Then away to England. Like most Anglo-Irish he had relatives over there, distant cousins, more of them, retired and mouldering. He could live off them for a few weeks while he found his feet. A job. Not teaching. Never again. A job in an art gallery. Or better still . . .

He began the daydream he often indulged in. He would make a final visit to Eagle's Nest with some carrier bags and take a lot of china. (Forget about the problems of inheritance for the time being . . . it should be possible to choose valuable pieces from places where Aunt Hatta would not miss them.) Then he would go over to London and sell them quickly. (In which case he could hardly stay with relatives.) With the proceeds he would start a small antique shop in London with a specifically Irish slant. Whereabouts? Not in the very centre of things, but somewhere he could afford. Somewhere with plenty of Irishmen. Not in Kilburn, which he imagined to be populated entirely by emigrants and IRA men lounging on street corners waiting for pubs to open. Somewhere trendy and promising. Camden Town perhaps. Someone—was it Michael?—had told him that Camden Town had its own large Irish community and even a Gaelic shop. Selling Aran sweaters presumably. His shop would be different . . .

What would he call it? Hibernian Antiques? Celtic Antiques? No, not Celtic Antiques. Perhaps something whimsical like Ould Ireland? . . . He would have a wide assortment of stock, things that did not belong to any specific period, but would attract Irish Americans or successful emigrants thriving in Gerrard's Cross. Old Waterford glass would very likely be cheaper to buy over there than over here. Irish silver. Staffordshire figures of Daniel O'Connell and Parnell. Prints of the Virgin Mary surrounded by stars. Those big flat books of *Moore's Irish Melodies:* he could make a feature of them. Any Malton prints he could buy. He would go through old copies of *Punch* for pictures of Erin as a bad-tempered young woman, and threatening peasants with monkey faces and cudgels. He'd look out for *Freeman's Journals* and old photographs of evictions. There would be a section devoted to folk items, rushlight holders, bread rings, stone bottles. He had a few already. He also had the rosary and silver buttons he had found when he went searching near holy wells one Easter weekend. Perhaps he would at last recoup the seventeen-pound fee for hiring the metal detector.

At the back of the shop he would hang a banner (not for sale), perhaps several, of the sort they carried in Orange Day parades in the North. And perhaps a counter-banner showing Our Lady in clouds. (Where did they come from? He would have to find out.) His collection of souvenirs of the Papal visit to Ireland would find a modest place. There was no reason why a shop of this nature should not be a success. He saw himself living in a big modern flat. The girl who would share his life would be chic and beautiful, nothing like Agnes.

The mailboat moaned as it considered departure. The price of an Irish divorce, they said, was a ticket to England and oblivion. He made himself consider once again the obvious drawback to his daydream. Be realistic . . . it would mean abandoning your inheritance. The value of Eagle's Nest and its contents, however depleted by thefts, was immeasurable. Even if the statues were by *Praxiteles*, they would only be a fraction of its worth. Michael had always maintained that real money was only to be made by dealing in property. Antiques were merely a lucrative luxury. Michael was ruthless. He would stop short at nothing. He had tried to kill him.

From one of the yacht clubs came the sound of a gun as various yachts started out or slid over some unspecified finishing line. When the echo died away, a drifting idea settled in his mind as a floating baby barnacle sinks to a rock and attaches itself. Life would be simple if Michael were not around. There would be no threat to the smooth process of gaining his inheritance. He could continue his old way of life with one great advantage: if he could contact Agnes, he would still have Aunt Hatta's statue—that is, if Agnes knew where it was. He could sell it very quietly. He would not get the full price, but enough to allow him to give up teaching. And even if Agnes and the statue never reappeared, his problems would melt away without Michael and his vile blackmail. The bastard had tried to kill him, and had nearly succeeded. Two could play the same game.

The mailboat hooted again and lurched towards the mouth of the harbour making all the little yachts scatter. He rose and carried the greasy paper that had contained his dinner all along the pier. Upbringing and habit made it impossible for him to scatter litter. There were no bins available, so in the end the paper joined the mass of sweet papers, ice lolly wrappers and crisp papers that Kevin had left in the back of the car. The amount of junk food he managed to obtain was an affront to Agnes's theories on diet. As Drury opened the back door, he spotted the catapult he had confiscated from O'Brien ages ago. It had been last term, in the spring; O'Brien had been aiming at Jaws's bird table. He had taken it from him and thrown it into the back of the car, where it had lain forgotten for three months.

When he was back in Goleen Park, he picked it up and carried it inside under his coat, hidden from any peering neighbours. He switched on the light and examined it carefully. This was not the old-fashioned catapult of his childhood, the forked stick contraption that never did its duty when it was aimed at rabbit or rat. This was a formidable weapon of transatlantic origin made commercially. Among street gangs in deprived American cities similar catapults actually killed fighting boys. It had a strong handle moulded to fit the hand like the handle of a bicycle, covered with black latex or plastic, and scored with gashes to give the fingers tighter grip. Behind the steel frame, a powerful latticed steel and plastic brace fitted on the forearm to give strength and balance. The actual catapult mechanism consisted of an unusually tough plastic cradle held by elastic tubes of strong surgical rubber. Every boys' institution in the country lived in terror of weapons like this; the boys might as well be handling Armalite rifles. O'Brien had not asked for it back. He hadn't dared. He had left at the end of last term accompanying his parents to Rio de Janeiro.

Drury had also confiscated a bag of marbles from him. It had been the sight of the marbles that had made him suspect the existence of the catapult in the first place. As far as he knew the traditional schoolboy game was extinct, relegated to the era of *The Rover* and Billy Bunter. O'Brien had kept his friends entertained during the long boredom of weekends by killing pigeons. Marbles were perfect little missiles, and in America boys of rival gangs fell dead with pretty whorls and bullies penetrating their temples.

But marbles would not do for Drury's purpose. Stones, unobtrusive rounded stones were needed, the traditional missiles for catapults. Where from? When David set out to kill Goliath he had been lucky enough to be standing near a brook where he found the five smooth stones he needed for his sling. Drury looked feverishly round the house. Agnes collected natural objects from time to time, a revulsion to his enthusiasm for antiques. She had filled vases with dusty dried grasses and saucers with birds' skulls and broken sea urchin shells. A dish contained small pieces of sea-rolled glass covered with some stinking water which was supposed to enhance their colours. Far too small and, like the marbles, likely to arouse suspicion. What he needed was sea-rolled pebbles. He'd have to go down to the strand. It would be far too late for anything to happen tonight, and there was no hope that Michael would be out in the garden. Nevertheless he decided to check his escape routes.

He found a torch and the old Zeiss binoculars that had belonged to his father and had assisted the old boy in the futile pursuit of spotting winning race horses. He took the bicycle down to the strand, where

David's requisite for killing giants was found in a matter of minutes. The long summer evening had still not drawn to a close. Killiney, east facing, with the slope of the hill behind, was in deep shadow, although far out to sea the sun still cast its light. He left the bicycle at Killiney Station and began to walk upwards. Anyone could take a walk.

He went past the ruins of the ninth-century church whose dedication to the early Celtic saint Lenin gave rise to some local ironies. He walked up a steep narrow lane hemmed in by granite walls, the sweet compost of eucalyptus under his feet. The way led among a number of different sumptuous properties hidden away from prying eyes by these high granite walls; it was difficult to tell where one ended and another began. But Castle Xanadu was distinguished by the bright yellow chain fencing that Michael had placed on top of the wall and by the Gothic door with the rusty lock and waist-high weeds growing up against it so that it looked like the door in *The Light of the World*. In Mrs Willoughby's day Mooney had got hold of the pseudo-medieval iron key, and used to escape this way down to the Igo Inn. Drury turned the wrought iron handle and pushed. Not a movement; possibly Mooney had been obliged to change his habits since Michael had become his employer.

Higher up the hill, the wall and chain fencing gave way to a fence made of sun-faded board. Every stronghold has its weakness. Aunt Hatta's garden had been guarded by Dempsey and the bicycle chain. The vulnerable part of Michael's defences was the bungalow owned by Colonel and Mrs Hackett. Even after they had been burgled they had not tried to strengthen this fence, which had been aged when Drury was a boy. In those days he had pioneered the raids that now make life in the area so difficult. On several occasions he had stolen apples from the Colonel, taking pleasure in evading trip wires that sounded off the alarm in the kitchen of Darjeeling. Apples were all he stole. A later boyhood expedition had led to the discovery of the gap in the fence that separated Darjeeling from Castle Xanadu, allowing him to slip through and sample Mrs Willoughby's apples, keeping a look-out for Mooney, who used to patrol with a shillelagh. Her orchard had been cleared to make room for Michael's swimming pool.

It was only the end of June now, and the apple crop was not yet ready for electrified protection. Besides, he knew the Hacketts were away, a-chasing the wild deer and following the roe. The Colonel's polo trophies had been stolen during their last sojourn in the Highlands, but then, what could householders do, apart from never going on holiday? Some paid housesitters like babysitters to take care of their property while they were away. That was an expensive business. Others, like the Hacketts, trusted to luck and prayer, notified their neighbours and clamped a little red alarm box on the side of their homes that connected with the Garda Station in Dalkey. Drury had no intention of going near the house, whose drawing room light was kept on as camouflage. Was it possible the Hacketts had got a friend to stay? He made a lot of noise and listened for the old Labrador to bark. If it had, he would have gone home, but there was no sound. What about trip wires? They only connected with the house, so far as he knew. Silence. With the aid of his torch he went down to the corner of the orchard and found the gap in the hedge was just as easy to slip through as it had been twenty years ago. He stepped into the woodland of Castle Xanadu, a few briars creeping over wild garlic that mingled with the inevitable smell of eucalyptus.

The woods stopped suddenly beside some massive rhododendrons. Ahead was the castle. As he watched, it sprang into vision. Someone had switched on the spotlighting, not the whole range that had been lit on the night of the party, but the domestic spotlight kept for informal evenings.

He brought round the binoculars on the big window ahead which was opened, the Venetian blinds concertina'd upwards against the summer warmth. The room behind was lit by a chandelier. Every room, even the bathrooms, had chandeliers. The Zeiss was powerful, one thing his father had not hesitated to spend money on. He could pick out details of the library and almost, not quite, read the names on the spines of the books in the bookcase. He had often consulted Michael's collection of auctioneers' catalogues and the back numbers of *Apollo* and the *Connoisseur*. There were a good many Irish books too, since Michael considered they were a safe investment on the side. He had a good copy of the *Image of Ireland*, two *Post Chaise Companions*, a collection of nineteenth-century travel books, the usual early editions of Yeats and Shaw, and a signed first edition of *Ulysses* which he claimed was worth twenty thousand pounds. He had never read a word of any of them.

Drury stared at a Malton print on the wall, trying to make out which one it was. The Royal Hospital, perhaps. At first he regarded the moment when Michael stepped into his vision as a distraction. He had to adjust the binoculars in order to see the profile that seemed only a few inches from his own and needed a shave. Michael carried a cigar and a glass with yellow-brown liquid over to a rent table covered with silver-framed photographs of himself with well-known people—with the Taoiseach, with the Pope, with Princess Grace. He put down the glass and picked up a telephone receiver that had not been in Drury's vision—nor had he heard it ring. He talked silently, visibly giving his usual insincere guffaws, quite silent. He gestured like an Italian. He put down the cigar and picked up the glass and then reversed the process. If only Drury could lipread. If only he had a gun. But there was exhilaration in standing here watching him unseen, imagining him stopped in mid-speech. The conversation was long and jovial. Tomorrow he must come earlier. Not too early, for Michael worked hard for his money. Drury knew that, encouraged by American television, people thought that the rich spent most of their time driving big cars or stretched by swimming pools eating peeled grapes and laying pretty girls. But Michael was a typical rich man working a full weekday schedule. (He considered his attendance at auctions as part of his work.) However, he did make one millionaire's gesture: most evenings of the short summer he came home early and bathed in his heated swimming pool.

He put the phone down, picked up his glass and vanished beyond the framework of the window. The chandelier light was switched off. Drury made his way back to the gates of Darjeeling with difficulty, and nearly ran into a pair of lovers in the dark lane. On the way back he stopped at a pub and bought a quarter bottle of Paddy which he drank at home as he watched television. Sleep would be difficult. When he went to bed he took a couple of Mogodon, which did him no good at all. He spent most of the night planning. At five, just as daylight came, he got up and dressed. He bicycled down to the strand carrying the cat-apult in a supermarket bag. He walked along the beach towards Shan-kill and the old railway that had been abandoned when the cliff that supported the line had eroded. In the distance was a field scattered with rubbish by tinkers. At his feet the sea had given up its treasure, strewing the gravelly sand with plastic containers, shampoo bottles and the odd French longlife milk container. He reflected on the clean habits of sailors; over the years he had lived in Killiney he had found empty lavatory cleansers in seven languages. He stopped near the sew-age plant whose smell hung about the strand. The sewage bubbling into the sea attracted seagulls, but put off early morning bathers. He could practise unobserved, only stopping when the first suburban trains of the day roared past on the track that ran by the beach.

The technique of operating the gangland weapon was difficult, and he was pleased that he had this impulse to put in some practice. After half an hour of target shooting he managed to hit a tin at thirty feet, then at forty. It rang like a bell and folded in half. God, the catapult was powerful! The stones it discharged were supposed to go at the speed of a bullet. He speculated on the consequences of O'Brien aim-ing at a human target at Prospect and hit the can again. Michael bent double, no, it would have to be Michael struck on the head. Mystery. Victim of a vandal. He aimed at a gull and missed. The bird was flying high.

When he got back to the house he was in time for breakfast before going to school. Adrenalin masked the fatigue of his sleepless night. He was ravenous. There only seemed to be Muesli. He rummaged in the fridge. The frost round the frame of the freezing compartment had distended inwardly and the meat tray was stuck to it. He worked with a carving knife and found two pieces of bacon that had been buried in ice like mammoths. How old? He sniffed and fried them up together with bread from which he cut away pieces of mould with nail scissors. He enjoyed his breakfast, washed down with Nescafé. The phone rang just as he was setting out for school. He rushed for it, thinking it might be Agnes. Michael's voice.

"Thought I'd catch you. Any news?"

He said he was doing his best.

"As long as you have the matter in hand."

He put down the receiver, resolution stiffened. At school he spent his time shouting. Insofar as discipline went, the day was successful. Rage and sarcasm worked well in a combination that induced among the boys a docility rising from surprise. The secret of good teaching was to be as unpleasant as possible.

CHAPTER 8

As he drove home from Prospect it began to rain. His plans for the evening were a washout, since there was no way that Michael would be carrying out his hearty routine. There had been little rain that whole month, and it was cruel that it chose to fall this one afternoon. Calm. You are tired and trembling. Tomorrow will do, or even Thursday. Michael won't want to carry out his threats until there is no alternative.

Agnes had not written, not even a postcard. He remembered one from the past: "Guru delightful, radiating good influences." On other occasions she had written long letters full of nonsense, describing karmas, mantras, anima spirits, therapies, encounters and why oh why had he never tried to understand their importance in an age of materialism?

He bought a steak and mushrooms for his supper, and eggs and bacon for breakfast. He took the car out again and went to a cinema outside Dun Laoghaire full of screaming Spanish children, and watched a western where all the shootings and violent deaths were shown in slow motion. He came home and watched television for a time before taking two Mogodon which helped him get some sleep.

Michael woke him with a telephone call. "Any developments?" No anger or antagonism was apparent in his voice, only bonhomie. A reminder at the close of the conversation hinted at urgency.

"There's a big London sale of Greek antiquities in the autumn, Jim. Christies or Boothroyds, I can't remember." So likely. "It would be good to have things straightened out before then, you understand."

The sun shone all during school hours and the day was still fine as he drove away from school at five. Michael would be back home around five-thirty, unless he was distracted. There was a good chance that even now he was sitting in a bar. Drury put on shorts and jogged from Goleen Park, the catapult in his shirt bulky as a chicken's breastbone. At St Lenin's he became cautious. The other night the time had been late, but now commuters from the station might well be using this route as a short cut. It was too steep for a comfortable stroll and he panted as he ascended at a jogging pace. The path was deserted when he looked up and down beside the gates of Darjeeling before boldly climbing in. Through the orchard and the wood he got to the edge of Michael's garden. The Rolls was at home, parked on the tarmac beside the lofty flight of front steps. He edged slowly uphill among rhododendron bushes, making for a slope above the swimming pool. If he were caught, he was merely coming to see Michael. I have some news about Agnes . . . This catapult? Confiscated from one of the boys, little devil. The shorts? Oh, to hell with it.

He was nervous of dogs. Michael had imitated his neighbours. His dogs were of the usual breeds that emphasized the aggressive spirit of their owners, but the Alsatian was inbred and its hind quarters were paralysed, while the Doberman was a curiosity, as friendly as a cocker spaniel. It was their bark he feared, not their bite. And the cry of the peacock, although that was rather too good a guardian, with its tendency to cry out at anything at all.

The vantage point he selected was among rhododendron and holly that made a small prickly closet from which he could peer out. It was a position that gave him a clear view of the swimming pool two hundred feet below him. The water looked inviting, turquoise blue with no more ripple than a veined tremor. In former privileged days he had bathed in it, and had attended parties conducted round its edge. There was no-one there now, and always a chance, a good chance, that no-one would come.

He heard whistling and the clop-clop of wooden therapeutic sandals on stone. Michael came into view wearing a striped bathrobe and carrying a towel. It seemed he would bathe from the springboard end. Would he be diving in? He took off the robe by the laddered steps linking the water to the tiled sundeck and lawn. His stomach protruded over his togs, and when he turned he exposed the black bear's pelt that covered his back. A fly must have landed on his shoulder for it was given a crisp slap. Drury could see the mark that briefly showed red.

His ideas were similiar to those of David's, who did not kill Goliath with the pebble from his sling shot, but merely knocked him out. Only afterwards did he borrow the giant's own sharp sword to cut off his head. If Drury struck Michael hard enough with a stone from the catapult, he would fall forward into the water and drown in his own pool. Drury fired and missed the big fat stationary target, when yesterday he had been hitting empty tins on Killiney Strand. He was so wide of the mark that Michael did not even notice the missile, which must have sunk into the water beyond him.

He plopped into the pool, not from the springboard but from the edge, and swam sluggishly, thrashing through the water. It was not a very joyful swim, just up and down the requisite number of lengths in a clumsy crawl. Now he was gasping for breath. His lungs were clotted with cigar smoke. Now he leapt out and trotted round and up on the springboard from where, after some grunts, he dived in once more. He was treading water, swimming over to the side to regain his breath. Drury, who had experience of supervising water sports, knew that few pastimes were duller than watching other people swim, even if one were waiting to kill a swimmer. Michael never seemed to stop, not for a moment, except when his head presented itself at the side of the pool where he chose to rest. It was not big enough to be certain of hitting.

The swim lasted for ten minutes before his dripping body emerged up the ladder for the last time. He picked up his bath towel, big enough for a shroud, and wrapped himself in it. Never would there be a broader base to aim at. Drury flexed his arm and picked up a second stone. He had practised. Missed again. A near miss, because Michael had noticed something go by or had heard a gentle thud as the pebble buried itself in the turf behind him. He had given a small jerk of the head before continuing to rub himself down. Drury would have to make another shot good, since the active part of Michael's brain would come into play with another miss.

Clop-clip, clop-clip, bloody hell. Here came a woman, also wearing wooden sandals, carrying a tray of drinks. Not Orla, evidently a new lady. Michael's girls changed about as often as the season. This one was older than Orla; he recognized the shop assistant he had seen the day Michael threw him off the train. Her bikini was brief, and in the modern way made no attempt to conceal the scars on her stomach. Gall bladder? Appendix? Hysterectomy? They were slashed on her skin like the patterns on the glasses she carried. She poured out drinks and added ice. Her golden tan must have been obtained abroad. She wore diamond rings. She was not bad-looking, slim as only a woman who looked after herself could be; very likely a masseuse pummelled her regularly. Agnes could learn from her and not let herself go to seed. Why couldn't she dye her hair blond like this? Agnes wasn't even thirty yet, and her hair was already going grey. Why didn't she realize that nothing was madder looking or more witchlike than long grey Afro hair?

Michael and his girl were sitting side by side on slatted wooden chaise longues covered with turquoise cushions. The girl was oiling herself, then oiling him. Why don't you go in and cook a meal or something, you idle rich bitch? He heard muttered conversation without making out any words. The pair of them lay soaking up the late afternoon sun. Did he think before that Michael was a hard worker? They had more drinks. Michael consumed another cigar, the smoke spiralling above his head. At the end of half an hour he got up and dived into the pool and swam two lengths. Then he got out and dried himself again, the great white target presenting itself to Drury's aim once more. Another ten minutes went by before the woman picked up the tray and followed behind Michael back into the castle.

Drury waited for yet more time to pass before edging towards the shrubbery in the direction of Darjeeling. He crept through the vegetable garden of Darjeeling and the thick shrubbery without a glance up at the bungalow, and climbed the gate without taking precautions. He did not have the inclination to pretend to jog. The feeling of let-down was total. He was like an athlete who had undergone rigorous training, putting everything he had into one particular moment, the hundred yard sprint say, and then losing everything. He supposed he could come back tomorrow, but the edge of energy had gone.

He lay awake in the night. If he were a mechanic he might disengage the brakes of the Rolls. Explosives . . . probably several of the young men on the housing estate opposite knew the basic means of making a letter bomb. Likewise they knew about firearms. He was not on the sort of terms with the Bradys that he could go and seek their advice. He had no access to guns. Knives, though, he had in plenty. It was extraordinary how persistently the boys brought knives into school. They did it over and over again, undiscouraged by confiscation and punishment, hoarding their penknives, flick knives and those daggers divers used when they wished to cut themselves loose from octopi. He had samples of them all. But he did not think he could use a knife for murderous purposes.

Michael rang again the morning, less affable. He had been working at his end to try and locate Agnes. He had contacted a friend in Dublin Castle—he had friends everywhere—who told him that the drug squad was interested in some of Agnes's friends. This was no news to Drury. Did he know that the drug people had their eye on Agnes as well, and seemingly were in two minds about whether to bring in the whole lot of them? I'm warning you, Jim. You get hold of her and tell her to quit messing. And get that thing back. I'm beginning to lose patience. I'm in two minds about getting in touch with your aunt. Any progress? I'm getting a bit hassled, Jim.

He trembled as he put down the receiver. Would he have another go? Try the same plan? More of the waiting game. Today was a half-day at school and he got home around four, far too early. He thought of private eyes and chauffeurs and others doomed to hang around. He walked down to the beach, where the coarse sand was strewn with people. He sat down within sight of a couple of pleasant-looking girls, to have his view of them blocked out by a red-skinned man setting up a striped windbreak. Children threw sand at each other. A troop of ponies from a local riding school came by, all out of control and lunging at

screaming babies. The last animal in the string let loose a pile of steam-
ing turds very near him. There was something to be said for Michael's
private way of enjoying the summer weather. He wondered how many
of those swimmers out there knew about the warm sewage that made
the seagulls scream with delight. He got up, lit a cigarette and walked
northward along the beach among dogs, bathers drying off, a few men
fishing, and boats pulled up on the sand. Above the beach was a collection of derelict huts, one of which was marked TEAS in bright red letters. Several decades must have gone by since teas were last served
there. He remembered looking through a book of old photographs of
Dublin and at one particular print that had been taken from just about
here. About a hundred years ago. A group of soldiers and their girls or
wives—stylish braided uniforms and wide skirts—stood clustered round
much the same sort of rowing boats that he could see now; one soldier
had been holding up an oar. No transistors then. He thought that the
Ayatollah in Iran had the right idea when he banned the broadcasting
of pop music and only allowed religious music to go out on the air. If
people on beaches had to have noise, how much pleasanter it would be
for them to listen to Palestrina's Mass or "Eternal Father Strong to
Save" than the bloody awful racket that he could hear coming from
every direction. Bodies were thinning out the farther he walked away
from the steps down to the beach. People wouldn't walk more than
fifty yards or so and liked staying huddled up together like seals. He
reached the very end of the beach where a shelf of rocks terminated the
sand. Only then did he realize that the spot directly above him was
where he had landed from the train after Michael had thrown him out.
(His memory still betrayed him.) It seemed a very long time ago now.
He could see a pair of lovers squatting outside the cave to which he
had crawled so laboriously. Killiney was full of lovers, or were they the
same ones he had seen in the lane outside Darjeeling? He directed the
Zeiss on them. Ha! Was it for that priests banned crossroads dancing?
There was the high granite embankment supporting the railway track.
The sight of it fuelled his hatred for Michael and stiffened his resolu-
tion to try again.

He walked back the roundabout way to the station and took the
route up past St Lenin's. The gate of Darjeeling was open. An old man
with a white moustache was wheeling a barrow full of compost. An old
woman in an apron made of sacking was weeding. An old dog barked.
The Hacketts were back from their Caledonian holiday, and he could
not get past them into the garden of Castle Xanadu. Suddenly there
seemed to be no further purpose to life. He supposed he might try and
contact Agnes again. Did she have the statue in her possession? Had
she sold it perhaps? She could have ignored its potential value just to

get back at Michael. Had she had a lovers' quarrel? He remembered
her final row with Number Two Lover, the time she helped him run
his delicatessen, Les Cuisses de Grenouille. During the fight she had
hurled stock from the shelves and the floor grew slippery with coleslaw
and crunchy with coffee beans. He tried to remember what he had told
her about the statue. She did not know the Praxiteles theory, but she
knew that it was ancient and valuable. Would greed outweigh her
anger? Or was it possible that she had nothing at all to do with its disappearance from Eugene and Tony's cottage?

When he got home he looked through the address book and started
to ring around with an energy he had not previously shown. He made
a dozen calls before giving up. Either her friends knew nothing, or they
were telling him nothing. No-one had suggestions to offer, and he
thought he heard sniggers. Poor old Jim, cuckolded again. His mind
filled with hatred towards her and Michael. Had he really dreamed of
murder and gone so far as planning it? He felt an overwhelming relief
that he had not been able to complete his intention. Except that
Michael was still poised to ruin his life.

At school next day he could not keep order. The atmosphere of rebel-
lion was not like the usual unruliness that pervaded his classes, but
something that went a stage further. In every class he taught that
morning the boys tasted blood, and from now on until the end of term
they would give him no peace. Whose class is that noise coming from?
Mr Drury's, sir. Amid the paperthrowing and bedlam of Upper Third
two prospective parents walked in with Headmaster, wearing a gown
and looking wise.

After school he was driven to accepting a date for a drink with Trimble, the Science Master. He arranged to meet him at nine. Meanwhile
he would have some pork ribs at a Chinese restaurant in Dun Laoghaire. Like many Dublin citizens, he had never felt quite at ease in a
Chinese restaurant since the Abbey Street fracas when rival oriental
gangs had set upon each other with butcher's cleavers and knives. But
he liked pork ribs. Tomorrow he would make plans and assume that
Michael would carry out his threat to go to Aunt Hatta and tell her everything. Perhaps he had gone today? Should he go and see her now,
this instant, and steal the most expensive thing he could lay his hands
on? What about seizing her jewel case which she kept in her ground-
floor bedroom, instead of his usual furtive inspection of the Miss Havi-
sham interiors upstairs? Grab it and run, forget about his inheritance,
his wife and child, and flee to England? What about Kevin? Wasn't
that rather sad, leaving him behind? It occurred to him that even if his
aunt disinherited him she might make a settlement on Kevin. But look

how she disapproved of Agnes. Those charities she supported still beck-
oned, and Cousin Jeremy did as well.

At the top of the hill he saw the Rolls. A Silver Shadow, finished in
white with a tan roof, magnolia hide and white wall tyres. 1978 Dublin registration. Unmistakably Michael's. It was parked below the
steps of Victoria Hill Park between inferior suburban cars, its grille
grinning like an alligator among frogs. Where was Michael? Was he
drinking in the Druid's Chair which was located down to the left? In
that case, would he have parked this far up? Unlikely as it seemed, he
appeared to be taking a stroll in the park.

He'd have a word with him. He must sort things out once and for
all, convincing him that he was helpless in the matter of locating Agnes
and the statue. He must sort this out. He had no bad intentions at all.
The long foolish episode involving the catapult was finished. But a
showdown was needed. He parked the Morris well down the hill outside the Druid's Chair, walked up and entered the park gates. A plaque
painted Republican green commemorated its opening in June 1887,
when Prince Albert Victor of Wales did the honours, celebrating the
fiftieth year of his grandmother's reign. No-one now remembered the
Queen's Memorial Association that had provided for this park to grace
a lively suburb.

He took the steep path up to the Mapas Obelisk, built in 1742 at the
instigation of John Mapas in order to provide work for victims of the
famine that had raged that winter. The graffiti lads had been hard at
work on its crumbling sides. IRA RULES. BRITAIN MUST GOE. A follower
of Hugh O'Neill might have written that. SID VICIOUS. STRANGLERS.
BOOMTOWN RATS. LIVERPOOL. QUEEN VICTORIA IS—crossed out—WAS
SHIT. Old ladies led dogs and children played hide and seek among
veronica bushes. Beside the monument the crowds thickened. Some
looked at the view, which even on this grey moody evening was superb.
To the north a vista of suburbs, their sprawl limited by the contours of
the Dublin Mountains, led into the city. He could make out the Liffey
like an arrow to the bow of Dublin Bay. Southward was the line of
Wicklow Hills that ended at Bray Head, a falsetto magnificence. But
most people weren't bothering about the view. They were mobbing a
couple of fools with hang gliders who were preparing to throw themselves off the cliff beside the monument, and swoop down to the spit of
sand on the beach below.

He could not see Michael. Most probably he had gone on along the
welltrodden path that led down through landscaped woods. He hurried
down. Why? It was unlikely that he would catch him up, since here
among the bare brown paths beneath oak and pine was a junction, one
path leading over the knobbly heights of Killiney, the lower one mean-

dering down towards the Vico Road. Which way? Upwards at a guess. There was plenty of time before his engagement with Trimble. If it got too late for a Chinese meal, he could catch up with a toasted cheese sandwich. Trimble wasn't important.

A notice read: "Persons entering should exercise due care, children should not be permitted to wander unattended." Steep clifftops and the quarry invited accidents. He walked down, along and then up the landscaped terrace path towards the spot where there would be another view, east facing, of Dun Laoghaire seen over the quarry. The quarry was the result of granite being gouged out first to build St Patrick's cathedral a thousand odd years ago, and later to construct the piers of what was then Kingstown Harbour.

Suddenly he caught sight of Michael ahead of him near the top of the path. A dog was bounding beside him, the Doberman pinscher. Incredibly, he was exercising the brute. He must have decided to forgo his evening swim and bring the animal out here. He did not have his Alsatian with him because its infirmities had crippled it so that it crawled about with the movement of a toad. By contrast, the Doberman was frisky. He did not have it on the lead, but threw sticks for it. A woman leading a small mongrel crept by on her way down. He turned round to look at her. He appeared to be swaying. He didn't recognize Drury, although he was looking directly down on him. Was it merely because he saw him out of context?

Drury prepared to wave, to call out, to run up to him and begin an urgent angry talk. Then, just as he was about to lift his hand, he changed his mind. He watched Michael turn and make his way upwards again, wearing a Tyrolean hat of all things for a warm summer evening. He was staggering just a little. He was drunk; footless. Drury had known him to be drunk at this time of day on several previous occasions following business lunches. He regularly attended boozy meals where the economic state of the nation was determined. Sometimes, like today evidently, they were prolonged. His passion for exercise brought him out here to walk off the fumes, since he realized that rather than plunge into his pool and drown he had better do the rounds of the park in an uphill loop.

Drury decided that he would get in front of him and the dog, and wait in the proximity of the quarry. Quarry in every sense of the word. It was easy; he just had to go straight off the path through some low-growing briars, firs and newly emerging heather. He did not go with much speed, but he would get to his vantage point well before Michael, who was going very slowly indeed. He reached the second high bare ridge overlooking the bay, a spur covered with weedy grass and occasional grey knuckles of granite boulders. At the end was an old sig-

nal tower and the antenna of an aircraft safety aid. Then a low wall
skirted the quarry.

He could see no sign of Michael. In fact no-one was here at all.
Strollers were returning home to tea and there were always fewer people on this side of the park, since the route from the entrance was too
far and too up-and-down for all but the most enthusiastic strollers. Most
of them congregated near the Mapas monument. It was possible that
when Michael came down by the quarry, whose walls were rather low
for safety, there might be an accident. Drury ran over to where the wall
curved and contemplated climbing over and squatting on a ledge on the
far side. He peered over. He knew exactly where the ledge was, because scouting had condemned him to a certain amount of rock climbing. This quarry was popular among inexperienced climbers, and at
Headmaster's insistence he had spent several hours of horror with some
senior boys and a madman named Hudson, clambering up rock faces.

Beneath him the rock fell precipitously, cut out in giant bites. Below
and beyond were grey and red roofs of houses that lapped down to the
harbour and the sea. Ahead lay all of Dublin. Just below him—talk of
the devil! There was the very man, Hudson, on the ridge, his Bruin-
like figure hung about with nylon ropes, pitons, irons and wedges. The
boys called him Nadia. He had two learners with him from the
Upper Sixth, whose insane parents had given consent that they should
put their lives at risk in this absurd way. They had not seen him. He
moved off quickly. You can't throw bodies down on the heads of un-
suspecting schoolboys.

But all he wanted was a confrontation. Looking back he could see
Michael and his dog weaving in his direction. It seemed that he was in
no state for a coherent talk, and perhaps it would be better just to
sneak off without being recognized. The signal tower offered sanctuary.
If he could run to there Michael would pass without knowing that he
had been anywhere near. Drury ran for the shelter of its austere stone
rooms, evil-smelling and made hideous by graffiti and litter. The dog,
which was off the lead, might pick up his scent and follow him in here.
But why should it? In any case it was a stupid dog. He could hear a familiar voice.

"Rex, Rex, come here, Rex." He even smelt cigar smoke. If by any
chance Michael followed him in here, Drury would look a terrible fool.
There was an empty bottle lying beside him which he picked up and
held by the neck. He waited for some time, five minutes, perhaps
longer, before peering out. The hilltop was deserted. If anyone,
stranger or otherwise, had appeared, of course he would have gone
straight back to the car.

The game involved no-one seeing him. Where had Michael gone?

Towards the quarry path and the low wall. Would he have had time? He had vanished, together with the dog. What about the other way? Drury heard a faint bark. Yes, he must have taken that path leading straight down towards the Vico Road. It was very steep and offered yet another view, this time Dalkey Island with its ruined church and Martello tower. Further off were the Mutland rocks, to which they used to chain pirates and leave the rising tide to drown them. He ran down very fast, stopping abruptly when he caught sight of Michael trying to recall the dog, which appeared to have run off. His voice was convulsed with anger as he alternately callled and gave a series of whistles, preceded by drunken hiccups. Strangely enough he was standing—and swaying—in view of that place. The spot where he had thrown Drury off the train. Of course he was a very long way above it, high above the Vico Road and the railway. And what was stranger, was that just then a train went by underneath, a dirty black and orange diesel stringing five carriages behind. And there was the wall Drury had toppled over, and below it rocks and seaweed.

What did Michael remember? He was still calling out, "Here Rex! Here Rex!" The yapping of the disobedient dog made him stand facing the sea, his back to Drury, the Tyrolean hat and feather showing in perky silhouette. The evening light was fading and the pall of clouds filtered gold as the sun tried to break through. The dark green vegetation seemed to be oppressive and tropical. There was no-one about. Michael was standing there, facing the sea, in a very dangerous place. Just ahead of him was a monument, a broken stem of a cross with a surround of iron railings which was a memorial to a man called Thomas Chippendale Higgin. It was an extraordinarily dangerous place. The dog was still barking, so that Michael did not hear as Drury came up quietly behind him. The drop was not all that high, and there was no guarantee that he would be fatally injured if he fell there. Drury had fallen further from the train and survived. Now he pushed, one big strong push. Michael tottered, tried to regain his balance and descended about two hundred feet below. He lay very still far below.

Drury looked down on him from where he stood beside the monument which had an inscription: "Dust thou art to dust returnest was not spoken of the soul." He had been very foolish and foolhardy. He had not made one final check to see if anyone was watching. The sea was dotted with small sailing boats and someone might have binoculars and might be using them, looking upwards along the ridge. On a terrace of one of the houses on the Vico Road he could see a woman watering flowers who might have glanced up and seen him. And he noticed a hang glider with great coloured wings like a dragonfly hovering far out from the Mapas monument. He was fairly confident that the pilot was too occupied with the hazards of his lunatic occupation to notice Michael's fall. But what about strollers, strangers and lovers?

He couldn't wait to check if Michael were dead or badly hurt. Perhaps as an irony he might be concussed. He turned quickly and walked back the way he came, up the same faintly marked path towards the signal tower. He did not look back, but walked with big rapid strides uphill. He must not run. He remembered feeling rather this way when, as a student, he had stolen a sweater from Dunne's Stores and as he walked out into Grafton Street it had seemed to him that his back grew physically hot. Never run but walk calmly, calmly. If anyone had seen him they would have shouted, cried out. He heard a pattering behind him. My God! He turned in horror, one arm thrust up before his face.

Michael's dog pounded up at full speed, its teeth bared in a wolf-like expression. His arm went down to his throat in a gesture of self-protection. The dog stopped and its sleek black body undulated like a Chinese dragon at a festival. It uttered a couple of barks which to his immense relief he interpreted as playful.

"D . . . d . . . down! N . . . no!" He was stuttering. He must go on, keep on striding up the hill. The dog bounded ahead, waiting with more barks for him to catch up. "B . . . back . . . Go back!" He must not call it Rex. Someone might overhear, and to call a dog by its name was to give it positive encouragement. He must get out of the park as quickly as possible. The best way was down the quarry footpath, round and past Shaw's cottage. It meant a long walk back to the car by the Vico Road, but he must get out of here. "Get away!" Rex had run ahead of him again, squeezing past his feet, and now he was peeling off towards a distant objective. To his horror he saw an old lady by the signal tower leading a blue roan cocker in a harness. What the hell was she doing up here so late in the evening? Rex ran towards her and she cringed in terror when she saw the monster come to eat up her pet. Rex's tongue lolled out as he dropped on his forepaws in an attitude of play. Bloody fool animal. Not mine, madam, not mine. He turned quickly and walked away towards the quarry path. Surely he was too far away for her to identify him should the matter arise?

By the steps he saw a warning notice about "Precipitous slopes", hardly in the right place. It was a comfort, or at least a point in his favour, that authority—very likely as long ago as the days of the Queen's Memorial Association—considered the slopes of Killiney Hill Park to be dangerous. Had others fallen? For that matter, what had been the fate of Thomas Chippendale Higgin?

Past banks of ivy this path debouched into a lane and a line of quiet villas. One of them was Torca Cottage where George Bernard Shaw had stayed as a youth. The fledgling dramatist had been impressed by

the view, particularly by the clouds in the heaving Dublin skies. Trees
and undergrowth must have grown up since his time. Last spring
Drury had brought up a panting Lower Fifth to see the place as a prel-
ude to going to the National Gallery and viewing pictures donated by
the Shaw Fund. It was doubtful they would ever read a line of Shaw's
plays. They were even too young to be familiar with *My Fair Lady*.
There was a plaque on Torca Cottage: "The men of Ireland are mortal
and temporal, but the hills are eternal."

The path split and a sign pointed towards the Green Road. That
would lead back to Michael, since he had come almost in a circle.
Downwards, reached by a precipitous path, was the Vico Road, where
lights suddenly rippled on. It must be nearly time for the park to close.
He must hurry to avoid keepers—he had never in his life seen a
keeper here, but presumably they existed. Anyone who walked along
the Green Road and looked in the right direction could catch sight of
Michael. Or perhaps not. He recalled the case of some woman who had
gone aloft from this park a year or two ago; her mortal remains had not
been found for months.

He went down the steps of the Cat's Ladder, counting. There were
supposed to be two hundred and thirty; the boys had counted when
they climbed up that time. As he went down he suddenly heard a noise
that had become familiar, a pattering like a squally shower. Hound of
hell. It pushed past, almost dislodging him and sending him the way of
its master. Then it stood waiting for him below, its tail wagging. It
gave a yap and a half-yawn and whine the way a puppy does. His only
course was to ignore it as if it was a persistent oriental beggar and to
continue as fast as he could back to the car. Unfortunately the car was
quite a distance. He could reach it by going the long route—indeed, he
had the choice of two long routes. He could go round the head of Sorrento Terrace and round, which would take hours. Or down to the station and up the whole length of Killiney Hill Road. That would be
prudent, but he would be late for his drink with Trimble. He would
like a drink. And as a matter of fact, it would be just as well to meet up
with him and show coolness. In that case he had better get back
quickly. But the shortest and most obvious route led him past Eagle's
Nest and also past the Canadian Embassy. He decided to take it. There
were plenty of strollers on this warm evening on the Vico Road, many
more than in the park, because they could park their cars and not move
more than a couple of steps away. He would not be inviting attention
to himself by walking briskly back to the Druid's Chair. Except for
the dog. He was down on the flat now. He crossed the road to the pavement overlooking the sea. A star had come out. Motorists sat in their
cars, their radios turned on. He strode as fast as he could, trying not to

behave like a competitor on a walking race. Rex bounded ahead of him,
sniffed a stranger, then raced back to him with a little submissive
tremor of recognition. Master!

"Bugger off!" he roared and the dog cringed and trotted on, frequently turning with a wriggling movement to look back. Perhaps the
animal was showing intelligence. This might be its way of seeking help
for Michael. When Michael fell he should have stayed a moment
longer to see what had actually happened. The road turned in from the
sea. There were no pedestrians here, and the dog still accompanied
him. Every now and then it ran off the pavement into the middle of
the road; twice it got in the way of an oncoming car, and one hooted
and braked to avoid a collision. He looked sternly ahead. He walked by
Eagle's Nest with his head down, and past the Embassy on the other
side of the road without checking if anyone watched him. Up ahead
the dog bounded towards the little pseudocastle that made a landmark
just near the entrance to the park. Here was Michael's car once again.
He turned down abruptly towards the Druid's Chair. Looking back he
saw to his great relief that the dog had abandoned him and was sitting
beside the Rolls waiting for someone to open the door and allow it to
jump inside.

His control of himself had been steady up to this point, but now he
wanted to run as fast as he could. He made himself walk the last fifty
yards to the car. A Morris Minor was conspicuous, almost as conspicuous as a Rolls. He should have parked elsewhere. But when he had
jumped out and followed, he had no plans. Just a vague wish for a
showdown, not for an accident. He was trembling as he backed, scraping the sides of the Volvo that had been badly parked beside him. No
sign of the driver who, no doubt, was guzzling inside the Druid's
Chair. The Volvo had acquired a long straight gash. Would its owner
recall the little vehicle huddled beside it? He reversed shakily and
pointed the round nose down the hill. Glancing in the mirror he could
see the Rolls very far away and the dog looking like an insect.

He drove the three miles to Bray as rapidly as he could, for he was
late and Trimble had a Protestant attitude towards punctuality. They
had arranged to meet in a hotel along the sea front. Trimble lived only
a few yards behind in a road full of nursing homes, but was too mean
to make a rendezvous that involved him in excessive driving.

At the pub, cars from the North of Ireland were lined up outside.
How terrible conditions in the North must be if coming to Bray from
there was considered to be a holiday. He got out shakily and looked at
the back bumper of the Morris, which had a new set of scratches as if
someone had scraped a comb over it, another blemish to add to the
browned rust marks. Resisting the impulse to cover it with a rug, he

went into the main bar crowded with Friday-night drinkers. He was actually glad to be meeting Trimble; it would have been bad to have had nowhere to go after all that.

"You're late."

"Sorry, I had a puncture."

"What'll you have?" Trimble's face fell when Drury made the mistake of ordering whiskey. In the dismal circles in which he moved, stout or pale brown beer was the accepted pub drink. Spirits belonged to a higher plateau of gracious living. He would have to stand Trimble whiskey in due course. Had he enough money? Usually when he went out drinking he only took a small amount of cash on the theory that the less you had the less you spent. But before that impulse outside Victoria Hill Park he had been planning his Chinese meal. So he had plenty. He felt hungry. He could get sandwiches if he wanted, but it would look a little funny. Cigarettes blunted the edge of appetite, and he shouted after the barman to bring him ten Carrolls. He was trembling.

Even before the drinks came, Trimble launched into a tale of woe. The claustrophobia of preparatory school life incubated his paranoia. The boys called him Happy.

Drury had to restrain himself from swallowing his whiskey in one gulp.

"What's so funny?" Trimble asked.

He jumped. He had not realized that he was smiling. He decided not to wait, and ordered another Paddy at once. Did Trimble look surprised? The Guinness in front of him emptied with hourglass slowness.

"It's rather serious, Jim. Did you receive a salary increase at the beginning of term?" He spoke in the same tones as the boys with their endless "It isn't fair!" In fact he had nothing to worry about because he was quite well off. He had no family, lived at home with his mother, traded in his car every two years and last year had gone to Kenya on a safari tour. Drury sipped his drink and changed the subject, keeping the conversation going with skill, like whipping a top. The right bit of encouragement made Trimble bring out all the usual dreary Common Room subjects—Olympics, rugby and politics, inflation, Margaret Thatcher, South Africa, Lord Mountbatten. When Lord Mountbatten died, he had been the sole topic of the Common Room for weeks. Drury had tried to enliven the boredom of those endless exclamatory discussions. On one occasion he suggested that the IRA had destroyed a father figure. Irishmen loved their mothers, those suffering martyred women in the heroic mould who kept the family together in times of historic misery and deprivation. They hated their fathers. Fathers were betrayers who represented authoritarian evil. Look at the plot of *Play-*

boy of the Western World. Lord Mountbatten, and for that matter, the British Ambassador who was killed a couple of years before, were personifications of authority. Their deaths were greeted with tacit approval by those who wished subconsciously to avenge their mothers. Drury's other theory, which Headmaster had disliked even more, was that the murder was the contemporary equivalent of blowing up a monument. In the sixties Republican patriots had been content with Nelson's pillar. A violent decade later his Lordship had been exploded instead.

Here was Trimble getting round to precisely this subject, not for any sort of political comment, but merely to grumble about the effect the murder had on school life. Lord Mountbatten's death happened some weeks before the beginning of term, but that had not prevented Headmaster from imposing three meatless Sundays—mourning combined with economy. Trimble imitated his rich sorrowful tones. "This is a black day for civilization . . . I think you will all agree that we should make a small sacrifice in order to remember the more worthy one made by a great soldier and statesman . . . Hymn Four hundred and forty-three. For all the Saints."

Drury laughed, hearing hysteria in his voice. With shaking hands he lit a cigarette from the butt of the last. When he treated Trimble to another whiskey he muttered, "You're in funds, Jim!" Was there any note of suspicion in his voice? Since the day when he had broken down weeping in class and had been led away from the delighted boys to a regime of tranquillizers and basket-making, no-one had taken him seriously. He reappeared serenely a couple of terms later. Headmaster had difficulties in finding another master willing to teach physics and mathematics at the salary Trimble accepted and grumbled about.

As the hours passed Drury ate peanuts, which was all the food available, and drank a lot. The frenzy of closing time approached, Trimble still howling out his stories and complaints.

"You on duty this weekend?" he asked as they came out at last and made their way through bedlam to the car park.

"Yes, worse luck." For once he was glad. It would keep his mind occupied while things happened offstage so to speak. He must wait to learn the results of the accident. He was drunk, just a little drunk. Thank God Agnes wasn't at home. He turned into the main street of Bray without looking, and the Morris was very nearly sheared in half by a madman who really was inebriated. The ironies that his death would create at this particular juncture made him laugh out loud. He felt happy. A great load was lifted from his mind. As he staggered under the Moorish porch of his house, he was happy as Larry. He drank a pint of milk that had been standing on the doorstep all day and

was a little sour. He climbed upstairs, singing. Soon, soon to faithful
warriors comes their rest.

"Agnes! Agnes!" It wasn't too often that he had erotic thoughts about
her, which were usually the accompaniment of alcohol in the accepted
Irish way. And she wasn't here. Not a sign of her. She was gone from
the land where her young hero slept. To hell with her. He had managed something pretty well today, and she was one lover the less this
evening. He went into the bathroom and was sick. Gave what Australians call a technicolour yawn. What James Joyce called mulberry coloured multicoloured multitudinous vomit. He returned to the bedroom,
flung himself on top of the withered bedclothes and passed out.

He woke in terror. Dawn sunlight shining through the tight-shut
windows enabled him to see the time on the electric clock surrounded
with white iron scrolls that had been a wedding present from Agnes's
relations. Ten to three it said; that meant the time was actually around
five, since it had not been adjusted after the last power cut.

So what should he do? He considered the techniques of easy sleep, of
relaxation that began with the face muscles and worked down slowly
bit by bit to the toes. Turn your eyes up as if you were looking into
your brain. Think of some peaceful situation, a sunny bank by a
stream, a beach and the soft sound of waves, lying in a hammock. Had
he really killed Michael? He saw his face with great clarity, not dead or
anything, but animated—the big almost aquiline nose, the side
whiskers, the narrowed, faintly Mongolian eyes, the mouth clamped
round the cigar. Nothing had been premeditated. Perhaps he wasn't
dead. Very likely he wasn't dead. (In which case, unless he got concussion the same way that Drury had, he would remember that he had
been pushed.) The park was dangerous. All those warning notices said
it was. Michael had always been careful of his well-being. He had
made his money dishonestly. The sun wormed its way in between the
slats of the Venetian blinds. Lo, there breaks a yet more glorious day. It
was too late to try taking a Mogodon.

He got up, had a pee and went downstairs to make tea with a
teabag in a mug decorated with a vintage car. He felt in his jacket
pocket. Thank God, some cigarettes. He must have bought a second
packet just at the end of the evening. He went upstairs again and lay
in bed smoking. He was very frightened. All that waiting in Michael's
garden near the swimming pool had been make-believe. And then, look
what had happened. Had anyone seen them, two men against the hori-
zon, one of them slipping? It was not premeditated. The Rolls must
still be there, parked beside the entrance to the park, and no doubt the
dog sat nearby. Had anyone noticed him with the animal? Now that

the pubs were long closed, some passing squad car must have taken notice. The mick that owns that can't still be in the booze. But of course they'd recognize it. That's Mr Kenny's car. With less than two hundred Rolls Royces in the whole of Ireland they were bound to know each individual vehicle. Maybe he's attending a party. When would an inquiry start? Would his new girl ring up and say he was missing? Hardly, unless she wanted to be the laughing stock of the suburbs. Probably they had a dinner date last night, since Michael was invited to some orgiastic function most weekends. Who were the first people who went into Victoria Hill Park when it opened up in the morning? Joggers, people who kept to paths. Agnes had taken away the transistor so that he could not listen to the news. Not that an accident to Michael was likely to loom large among items about economic gloom and the fall of governments.

On the way to school he called in at a newsagent and bought the *Irish Times*. He sat alone in the big parking lot outside the supermarket going carefully through the fat Saturday issue. Nothing, and nothing on the back where late news was printed in red. He found himself running his eye down the death column, just as his mother used to do every day, even before her regular glance at tumbling stocks and shares. No name of Kenny. How could there be, any more than among the In Memoriam notices? There was a big weepy batch today— Always Remembered, Called Home, Peace Perfect Peace, R.I.P., Sadly Missed, Masses Offered, With Christ which is Far Better, Absent in the Body, Present in the Lord. It was stupid to feel relief because of a postponement. Like feeling relief because the bus bringing the firing squad had been delayed by a mechanical fault. Perhaps Michael would not be found for days, weeks, even months. Perhaps he had got up and walked home.

After Drury's recent failure to keep order, he knew the boys were out to get him. But he howled at them and they became docile, while the session of prep he took just before lunch was comparatively peaceful after he had beaten Switzer. (There was none of that trendy nonsense in Prospect about obtaining written permission for a beating.) The restless silence was uniform, the big room, chilly even in summer, dominated by the scratching sound of pens. Headmaster forbade biros, and nibs squeaked to a background medley of muttered sh . . . sh . . . ing, pellets of paper flying around back rows, cribs passing, girlie magazines exchanged with rustling noises, and the steady tick of the kitchen clock over his head. They were comforting rhythms, varied occasionally by the gnawing of a penknife carving initials in a desk top. As he corrected exercises, he felt Prospect to be a refuge.

CHAPTER 9

There was a reek of onions, or was it body odour? A maid with wild white hair dumped a cracked tureen in front of him and he doled out soup, a shallow dip covering each willow pattern. He glanced up at the High Table where Headmaster and Jaws sat with privileged boys—Henderson who had miraculously passed Common Entrance into Harrow, Grattan-Vere whose father was a lord. They seemed like the subjects of a medieval Italian painting, princely patrons looking down benevolently on their people.

After lunch he had a further escape from reality when he drove the swimming team in the minibus to a neighbouring school. Behind him some boys fought, some lit cigarettes, others took out penknives to mutilate the seats, all sang obscene songs. The school they went to was a Catholic replica of Prospect and the same cooking smells greeted them when they stepped inside. They were led down a linoleum-covered passage painted in litmus colours of pink and blue, and lined with pictures of past headmasters just as the main assembly hall at Prospect was. The headmasters here were all clerical men, evidently of strong and holy nature, since their portraits, in the Italianate style, were touched with much the same mystical light as the representation of Jesus showing His heart. The boys were quiet as they turned into another corridor containing a statue of His mother preserved in a glass case. Their feelings of awe may have affected their swimming, as they were invited to plunge into a lavish indoor heated pool, very different from the slimy little outdoor puddle they were accustomed to. Swimming frog-like, on their backs, flailing their arms, gasping, they lost every race. Helping to record these defeats on squared paper, Drury thought of Michael's pool and Michael lounging beside it. Then he was busy again, too busy to think, shepherding the boys into the unaccustomed luxury of the shower room. They frolicked for hours until the water cooled in the taps while the home team, still modestly attired in bathing suits, waited its turn. Later they ate a substantial tea served in an assembly hall dominated by pictures of Pope John Paul II, big as a sunflower.

On the drive home the boys sat quietly, subdued by defeat and incipient colds. He suddenly lusted for news. He stopped at a newsagent where he went in and spent two pounds on ice creams in addition to the *Evening Press*. While the boys devoured his gift with amazed apathy, he looked at the front page. Headlines in evening papers were always enormous, whether they dealt with a world war or a suburban gas leak. Today's full headline treatment was reserved for a waffling politician. Underneath . . . there it was. A report on Michael's death. Strong startled paragraphs. Man Found Identified. Prominent in business circles. Popular socialite.

He was dead, then. Drury did not feel fear, although he knew he should. He should be afraid that he had actually managed to kill him. He should be afraid that the body had been found so soon. If it had lain neglected and hidden for months, any suspicion of foul play would have been harder to substantiate. He did not feel any relief that Michael was no longer here to threaten and blackmail him. He felt remorse. He recalled old times when Michael had made his life interesting and amusing, when he had taken him out to meals or on long wild pub crawls, or had invited him to parties. Over the years before this ghastly summer he had enjoyed knowing him.

He was rather pleased that his response to the news should be so civilized. When his mother died he had been ashamed of his relief that the poor old thing had departed. Now he was prey to something very like grief, demonstrating a fundamental decency. He felt a truly gentlemanly regret. He luxuriated in his sadness as he showed the Saturday evening film in the gymnasium, listening to the wheezing of the hired projector. He followed the story, which was of the bland Walt Disney type full of boys and girls in homespun clothes climbing down off covered wagons. Two bad men were cleanly disposed of. He went home, took his Mogodon and woke up eight hours later, having slept like a lamb.

Thank God Sunday was also a working morning. Amazingly, the last Sunday in term had come round, a day when church service took on an embarrassing air of thanksgiving. The church was big, and the school added nicely to the two or three already gathered there. The walls were covered with memorials varying from Georgian testimonials of virtue written under funeral urns and statements relating to nineteenth-century Empire-builders, to more recent deaths recorded on misted brass. He thought about Michael's demise and the dangers to himself which could not now be averted, as he listened to the choir drawn from the school. It was singing an anthem, exchanging the same pieces of information chorally several times over with varying degrees of emphasis. He stood and sat and stood again and committed to memory the statement on the wall above him, that William Bowers had died from the

results of a fall from his horse in 1840 in British Upper Burmah. Statements and petitions to God in the bland officialese that had taken the
place of the robust prayers in the Book of Common Prayer led up to
the sermon. Headmaster in his gown, looking more than ever like Dun
Scotus on the five pound note, preached thanksgiving and farewell.
The boys fidgeted in their pews, fighting silently with their neighbours,
examining the contents of their pockets—string, knives and pocket cal-
culators. He brooded on Michael and danger and felt a wave of fear.
He stood and put thirty pence on the plate. Lead us, heavenly Father,
lead us. There was chicken for lunch and an afternoon supervising carpentry class. The boys liked carpentry. On the whole they showed a
surprising degree of contentment. Some, who came from broken
homes, actually regarded this fearsome place as home. Others endured;
their middle-class parents, goaded by affluence, clamoured to get them
into the school. There was even a waiting list.

After tea he drove back to Goleen Park. The small figure on the
doorstep seemed to be an intruder.

"Hello, Daddy." He'd almost forgotten Kevin's existence.

"Where's Agnes?"

"Inside."

"Where have you been all this time?"

"In Tallaght."

Agnes was in the kitchen watering the cannabis plants. "You nearly
let them die."

"Where have you been? Kevin said Tallaght."

"That's right. We were at Liam's place."

"I thought Liam and Nora had gone to live in Mayo?"

"They're up for his show. Paintings of wild flowers."

A few years ago all her artist friends painted abstracts. Having
scorned drawing lessons during their years at art school, they now
struggled with crude realism.

"I suppose if you want to hide, Tallaght is as good a place as any."
He recalled the wide spaces of that tormented suburban stretch. "But
why in God's name didn't you let me know? A phone call, anything? I
was frantic."

"Why?"

"You know very well why."

"If I want to go off on my own, I don't have any obligation to tell
you. Right?"

"You've always written or something before." His voice was almost
pleading.

"This was different."

"Why? Not even a postcard." But he knew why. For once she did not feel guilty. There was no need for explanations. He sighed. "And what about Kevin? It would have been a courtesy to let me know where he was."

"You only stress your parenthood when you want a row."

"I suppose he had a delightful time in Tallaght?"

"He did, as a matter of fact. There's a beautiful spirit among those kids in working-class communities. I can assure you that your absence in his life doesn't injure him."

"Thanks very much. What have you done with that statue?"

"Statue?"

"My god, if you knew the difficulties . . ."

She burst into tears. "Michael dead, and that's all you can think of . . ."

Careful. "Why did you come back?"

"If you must know, I outstayed my welcome." People who stressed harmony and communal living usually ended up fighting. "And I read the news about Michael." She sobbed. He'd like to shake her. He'd put up with a lot from her, and Michael was the last straw. Suddenly he felt positive satisfaction for that moment on Friday in Victoria Hill Park.

"Where's the statue?"

She was crying and shook her head.

"I've got to know. Do you realize another day or two and he'd have done what he threatened and told Aunt Hatta?"

"He's dead, right? So your troubles are over."

"Listen . . ." Careful. "Agnes . . . please . . . You've no idea of the mess you left me in."

"I don't know where the statue is."

"What do you mean, you don't know?"

"It's gone from Eugene and Tony's."

"I know that, for God's sake. I felt a fine fool when I took Michael up there. He said it must have been you who arranged its removal."

"He said that, did he? Not you?"

"Agnes, did you do it?"

She sat down at the kitchen table and lit a cigarette. "I got angry the night you came back and told me Michael would go to your aunt if he didn't get the statue back. It was so typical of him. He was a sadist. Blackmail was too much. He always got things his own way." More tears. It was in her interest to keep Aunt Hatta from disinheriting him. He wondered how much of his inheritance would be legally hers if they separated. She'd hang on, though, one way or the other, as long as Aunt Hatta was alive. "I phoned Eugene and Tony and told them to dig it up and take it away."

"But they weren't there. They were in Sligo. Organizing massage and meditation, you said."

"That wasn't quite true."

"They weren't in Sligo?"

"They were. But they came back. A bit sooner than I said."

"When?"

"The day we hid the statue up there."

"And you knew they were there?" He felt like beating her. "Michael was right then?"

"I suppose he was."

"Why did you lie to me?"

She hesitated. "Jim, so many things go wrong for you, right? I knew you wouldn't go through with this business properly, and something would happen. Like Michael bullying you into giving things back. And when I heard from the first—after your accident—that the statue was valuable, I thought it would be a good idea to bring Eugene and Tony into it. They're good friends . . ."

"They were good friends."

"I don't believe they'll double cross me. They're gentle people. Not like Michael. It's just some sort of temporary setback."

"All the time we were up there burying that statue you knew they'd be back in a few hours?" She'd been suspiciously eager to help him in the first place when he was concussed and acting not quite himself. He should have left well alone at that stage. Bitten the bullet. Accepted Michael had got the better of him.

"Why did you leave here and go off to Tallaght?"

"I got thinking. If I left without telling you, Michael would guess that it had been me who had the thing removed."

"But Agnes, what's the logic in that?"

"Did he or did he not think of me first thing when you got up there?" He'd like to shake the truth out of her about her and Michael. "I thought if I was out of the way for a time, and he thought it was me, then he wouldn't threaten you and blame you."

Au contraire. She looked shifty. "You haven't explained where the statue is now."

She was crying again. "I honestly don't know, Jim. I can't get in touch with either Tony or Eugene. There's no answer when I ring them. They had to keep out of the way for a bit because I hinted that Michael or you might get in touch with the police. But they should be back now. I didn't have the car to go out to see."

"Do you think they're going to hang on to it?"

"Oh, no, they wouldn't do a thing like that."

"But you can't raise them on the telephone. Don't give me that. You came back here when you realized your friends were double crossing you. You always come back. Because you know one way or the other if things work out when Aunt Hatta shuffles off the mortal coil I'll be a rich man. And you'll be·a rich lady."

"I came back because I read about Michael's death."

"You did, did you? Well, let me tell you something else. You know that statue's priceless? Worth a mint. A fortune. Michael found out it's by some sculptor named Praxiteles, and it's unique. A couple of hundred thousand. More maybe. Your good friends are robbing you—and me—in a fairly big way."

More tears, that really made her sad.

The door bell chimed. "You answer it." "No way." Visitors, like people on the end of the phone, complicated life. Was it a guard, a detective sergeant? He saw himself being led away with gyves upon his wrists.

In the end he went and opened up. Dempsey stood on the doorstep. "The missus would like a word."

His bicycle was parked behind him. Aunt Hatta had saved the price of a phone call by sending him along, assuming that he would combine message carrying with a visit to the pub.

Drury could phone or call on her. He felt he'd like to get out of the house and leave Agnes to her own mournful thoughts. Dempsey refused to part with the key of the new lock on the gate. In the end Drury had to drive him back up the hill, watch as the new elaborate lock and chain were undone for his benefit, and then give him a tip.

Aunt Hatta was in the kitchen feeding the animals. Normally each received a slice of stale bread with a little pink processed dog food spread on it like paté. She made one tin do for the whole lot, including the cats. Today, however, the butcher had called. The dogs watched her, salivating and shivering. Some were old, with white muzzles and a squirming gaiety that endured with age—old, old puppies. The two mewing cats wandered among them, tails high. Aunt Hatta dug in the saucepan with a blackened silver ladle and pulled out a sheep's skull that appeared to have been hit with a mallet from the way it sagged. Head meat peeled off the cheekbones in gelatinous strips, dripping gravy over the bread that had been doled out on plates. A sieve caught bone fragments. The eyes remained after the meat had been torn away round them, gazing up, blue-black, reproachful. When they were plucked out of their sockets and placed in the cats' dish, they continued staring like St Lucy's eyes.

As Angela arranged the plates on the floor far apart, he noticed one with a gilded edge and a view of Naples, and another patterned with flowers and butterflies which were revealed by a dog's eagerly working tongue. Another dog was eating out of a chamber pot. He watched a cat bite through an eye as neatly as if it were a little apple.

"You heard about poor Mr Kenny?"

"Very sad."

"He was a good friend of yours, wasn't he?" There was a new dog gobbling up food from a blue Lambeth dish, a big black animal whose truncated tail wriggled with pleasure when Aunt Hatta spilled out more gravy for it.

"You'll be going to the funeral, won't you? I'd like you to take me along as well."

"It won't be for some time, will it? There's bound to be an inquiry—an inquest. And what about an autopsy?"

"That's taking place in a day or two, I understand, and will not interfere with the funeral arrangements." He was always amazed how much neighbourhood gossip she knew. Some of her information came from Angela, standing there now peeling potatoes that went into the pot with her fingerprints visible on their exposed surface. More was garnered from Mrs Keogh, who did two afternoons here each week and was also part of a group of women collected daily in a minibus to go up and clean Castle Xanadu.

He didn't trust himself to speak as the black dog finished its meal and came over to him with a joyous bound.

"Smack him, James, smack him."

"Isn't that Michael Kenny's Doberman?"

"Yes, the naughty boy. Quite untrained, of course. It seems Mr Kenny took him up on Victoria Hill and got pushed when he was playing with him. Down, Rex, push him down, James. He's very strong, and must have knocked his master over, the silly fellow. Do you know, they found him sitting right beside his car."

"What's he doing here?" It was like one of Edgar Allan Poe's tales of nemesis.

"I phoned Mrs Kenny as soon as I heard what had happened. I was so afraid they might have him put down. So unfair, not the dog's fault at all when no-one tried to train him."

"Mrs Kenny?"

"Yes, she's moved back into Castle Xanadu."

"Playing the widow, that's what." Angela spoke from among potato peelings. It must be five years since Maire Kenny had moved out after the most almighty row that had shaken suburban society. There had been rumours of a court case over marital disagreements, but perhaps it was merely the law's delays that had not brought it about as yet.

He stroked the silky cartilages of Rex's ears. "Of course Agnes and I will take you. Give us a buzz as soon as you find out for sure what day it is."

"Look out for the death notices." She dug within the skull for brains. "Angela thinks removal of the remains on Tuesday and the funeral the day after, isn't that right, Angela?"

"Yes ma'am."

He left shortly afterwards. Had it all been so easy? A post mortem would reveal plenty of drink taken. Would there be some way in which the vertebrae were laid out or the skull was cracked that would reveal Michael had been given a push by a firm human hand and not by a stupid dog? How had he died? Had his neck been broken? Those stupid antics stalking him with a catapult had been a terrible mistake in view of what had happened subsequently. Had he been seen? He realized one thing now, too late. An accident such as he had brought about should never be a matter of planning. It should be a matter of opportunity swiftly seized.

What about motive? Had Michael confided either to one of his girls or to a group of comrades over drinks—perhaps even the same drinks that had sent him reeling round Victoria Hill? Something he had never thought of, all those nights he had lain awake planning the worst for Michael. It was possible. He seldom mentioned his business affairs, but there were times when the whiskey was flowing when Drury had heard some startling revelations about well-known prominent figures. A bit too late for thoughts like that.

Perhaps he should get in touch with a solicitor. No, leave it until trouble came. And certainly not old Tom Peachey, his family solicitor, whose firm so earnestly endeavoured to prove that the old ways were the best ways. Talking about the law's delays, four years after his mother's death he was still waiting for some pittance she had left him. His aunt also employed Peachey and Keane, which did not promise well when it came to the time for him to inherit. Americans thought the name a good joke; it had appeared in the *New Yorker* to Tom Peachey's distress. Much good he would prove if Drury were questioned by tough policemen under harsh lights. Would the guard already be round to interview him? "Anyone call?" he dared to ask Agnes, sunk in meditation or sulks in the kitchen. She shook her head.

They both wished to avoid confrontation. For the next few days their relationship entered a familiar rugged phase of truce. They were more wary than usual. He did not wish to provoke argument, and she was frantically in the wrong. Presumably she spent the time when he was at school ringing round her friends trying to get information. She took the car up to Eugene and Tony's place, to find that it was still abandoned. Often he felt a dull regret about the statue's disappearance, but it was overlaid by all his other worries.

The blessed end-of-term routine required his attendance all day at Prospect until late in the evening. Last Lessons. *Julius Caesar* read in class. Discuss. Stoop, Romans, stoop. Up to the elbows in blood. Why, he that cuts off twenty years of life, cuts off so many years of fearing death. The final bustle of the last morning when the boys departed. Headmaster had a confidential talk and Drury found that he would still be in employment next term. Very likely all those applicants he had feared so much would not take his job because they demanded more money.

No enquiries, no unexpected phone calls, no cars arriving at his door disgorging detectives. The death notice said: "Suddenly, following an accident." His eyes lingered hungrily on the word accident. An obituary appreciation appeared in the *Irish Times* with the initials A.R. which were those of Gus Riordan. A great loss to the community. A man with a wide circle of friends. On impulse he picked up the phone and dialed the number of Castle Xanadu which he knew by heart. The engaged signal nagged back. Seemingly Maire Kenny had not hesitated for a moment to take up her role of tragic widow. A speedy drive over from the flat where she had lived apart from Michael all these years and there she was, ready to enact her tragic role, surrounded by friends. He rang a couple more times. Always engaged. He decided to write a letter of condolence on Agnes's recycled writing paper. He had to do a number of drafts. We were horrified. How much he will be missed. The world is a sadder place.

The morning of the funeral was sunny, a fact he observed from the moment the sun came up around half-past four. His sleeping problems had become worse and he took three, sometimes four Mogodons a night. (Once he went as far as taking seven.) They knocked him out all right, but the penalty was this early morning wakefulness which he was helpless to prevent. He lay awake listening to Agnes's heavy breathing from the spare room at the other side of the cardboard-thin wall.

Many hours later he put on his only suit, a pinstripe, and found his black tie buried at the back of a drawer filled with socks that were unwashed, widowed and heelless. How could it be so filthy when he had only worn it a few times? He sponged it and waited for Agnes to put on the dress she had once worn to juvenile courts which made her look ordinary and smart. They left Kevin at the Bradys, Mrs Brady assuring them that her boys would not take advantage of the fact they were away at a funeral. That was what friends were for. They picked up Aunt Hatta who was greatly looking forward to the outing.

In the church, the congregation appeared to include everyone who had ever been seen at Michael's parties, plus a good many more business associates, neighbours, barmen, minor celebrities, politicians, and most of his girls seated inconspicuously here and there. A bishop was helping out with the ceremony. They found a place right at the back. As Drury turned into the pew he glimpsed the tented black of Maire Kenny and the massive coffin with its heavy brass handles.

Here were the Hacketts huddled into the same pew as themselves, struggling not to fidget and show restlessness like horses in a burning stable. One of the more positive results of ecumenism was the regular attendance of members of one religious denomination at the funerals of another. The Colonel carried a bowler, which he considered correct for these occasions. Top hats were too old-fashioned, although Drury could remember a couple at his mother's country funeral five years before. He recalled the difficulty of getting her transported across Ireland from Dublin to the family vault. Waist-high grass had to be mowed specially in the churchyard, and the runinous church opened up for the first time in decades. (When he died, similar efforts would be made for him.) Colonel Hackett had been there too, along with other old military men with bowlers and white moustaches.

The priest's voice raced, the bishop contributed, a bell tinkled and soon they reached the stage where members of the congregation turned and shook hands with their neighbours. The people in his pew imitated this action self-consciously; he touched Mrs Hackett's limp hand. After Mass was finished, men in black overcoats, although the day was hot, brought in a steel trolley and shifted the coffin. The church's vaulted interior echoed with a crackle of cellophane as one glum figure went off carrying family flowers. When the trolley rolled away to the side, it came into Drury's vision for a moment, and he glimpsed the polished plate of silver or brass, he wasn't sure, which presumably bore Michael's name in copperplate. He felt a new curiosity about the departed, and an odd twinge of satisfaction that he had been responsible for these splendid obsequies. He was a cold fish, no doubt about it. Then his primary emotions reverted to their static blend of fatigue and fear. Beside him Agnes was weeping. The chief mourners, the widow and relatives, some black-clad and smart, some dishevelled country folk, were going up the aisle towards the door. Agnes gave a sad smile to a woman she recognized. Interminable time passed before they could make their slow exit and join the queue to sign the book. They crowded round Maire.

"We were shocked."

"I'm sorry," he murmured as others pressed round. Was there a cold stare in reply?

"Let's get out of here."

"We can't until the hearse leaves," Agnes hissed. She had wanted to go along all the way to Dean's Grange. Aunt Hatta, who knew that going to the graveside was unnecessary, wished to get back to watch show jumping on television. She tapped her umbrella on the tarmac as attendants bundled flowers into nooks and crannies around the coffin. Drury had sent rosebuds: "With fond love—Jim and Agnes" he had written with the florist's borrowed biro, on a plain card she had found with difficulty in her stock of cards with black edgings and pretty decorations. In the thatch of wreaths and sheaves Aunt Hatta's offering from her own garden was distinguishable by its garish, unexpectedly beautiful circus colours. The Hacketts' tribute was similarly flamboyant.

The back door of the hearse was slammed quickly as if it shut on an overcrowded wardrobe. After Michael was moved off, his relatives followed in big black cars. Other mourners in their own cars waited to join in and creep in the procession that would stretch the length of the Clonkeen Road. There was a new bustle as others made their way to where their vehicles snaked along the pavement. Listening to the crump of slammed doors and the start of motors, Drury shepherded Aunt Hatta and Agnes walking ahead of him. He did not want to talk to anyone. From time to time he caught the eye of an acquaintance and gave a grim nod.

Across the road a teenage youth stood outside a tobacconist's. He came across, making his way between the cars. He came straight towards Drury.

"Hey, mister!"

He was walking by his side, now. The creature had a crew cut, wore heavy boots and a dirty brown suit over a filthy T-shirt inscribed with "University of Texas." "Mister, will ya listen . . ." He spoke low, his voice hoarse from smoking. He smelt of buses on a wet day. He seized Drury by the elbow.

"Clear off!"

He clutched again, seizing a fold of pinstripe material.

"Will ya fuckin' well listen . . . I seen ya up on the hill." Agnes was turning round. Drury wrenched his arm free and turned away. Behind him the voice was saying, "I'm tellin' ya . . . I seen ya in the park with Mr Kenny . . ." The road was full of cars moving very slowly. Drury walked out between two of them so that they hooted with annoyance. He did not run nor look back. He reached the pavement on the other side which was a lot less crowded. He glanced back and glimpsed the youth, the bright brown of his suit standing out against funeral clothes.

He was about to cross. He waved at Drury, but did not shout. Thank God, no-one was turning to look.

Drury hurried away, in and out of pedestrians, weaving with big strides. He came to the edge of the pavement again with a vague notion of recrossing the road as if he planned to seek sanctuary in the cathedral-sized church opposite. The youth was still following some way behind. He strode on again; he must not run. What about a bus? There was usually a troop of buses outside the church, and the stop was right here. But nothing when it was needed. Far up in the direction he had come he could see the high brows of one coming along at a funeral pace. Hopeless. The youth was running his way.

In the road, part of the procession stopped before a set of pedestrian traffic lights. A grey BMW stood stationary just beside him, packed with people whose faces were composed and sad. The front window was rolled down and a dark-suited elbow stuck out. He recognized the face behind it.

"I say, Gus."

"Hello, Jim."

"Look, I'd rather like to get to Dean's Grange, but my car's developed a puncture. Any chance of a lift?"

"Room for a small one."

He squeezed into the back, keeping his face averted from the window. The car was painfully slow to move on, and he waited to hear the hoarse shrill voice crying out behind him. The creature could trot beside the car all the way to the cemetery gates if he really wanted to keep up.

He was with a group of antique dealers and their wives, whose scent filled the choking atmosphere. Dan Mahoney, wearing a velvet-collared jacket and pearl-pinned black tie was driving, Duffy, who dealt in china, sat beside him. Smith, a small man squeezed in among the women, smiled craftily as usual. He was one of the few dealers Drury knew who had really good taste; his shop was full of pieces of restrained elegance that suggested Georgian thrift. The trio always moved about together in a pack. They huddled at the back of auctions apparently unable to say two sentences running without winks and innuendos and meaningful smiles, talking nonstop through the bidding, occasionally signalling to the auctioneer with gestures like brushing flies away.

The remarks they made now were callous.

"I wonder what she'll do with the castle?"

"Too big for one person."

"Worth a packet."

"She'll find consolation soon enough."

"Sure, she's had it already . . ."

"What sort of stock did Mike have before he went?"

"Will she sell it off?"

"Surely. There's no-one to take over the business."

"She might take to running it herself."

"She'd never have the flair. Old Michael was no fool . . ."

"Except at the end . . ." They sniggered in a subdued way.

"What possessed him?" asked Mahoney as they turned towards Kill Avenue.

"He was drunk out of his mind," said Smith.

"Go on . . ." said one of the wives.

"I know for a fact. Rooney saw him leaving the Shelbourne around five."

"Oh really . . . he wasn't a real drinking man."

"You never saw him after a long lunch. Always the worse for wear," Smith persisted. "And always the bit about I'm going to walk the dog. Safer than taking a swim, ha ha." Business lunches were a side of Michael's life in which Drury had never participated.

"It won't come out at the inquest," Mahoney said.

"Of course it will," said another wife.

"I'll give you good money it won't. He wasn't involved in a traffic accident. He wouldn't have been contravening the law by walking dead drunk all over Dalkey and Killiney. They'll keep it quiet not to cause distress, the way they do with suicides. Not to hurt the widow . . ."

The women beside Drury giggled and fell to discussing Maire's new role as tragically bereaved. The procession had picked up a little speed, and Drury was reminded of Shaw's description of funeral horses racing to the cemetery. Now they all had to slow down again. He turned his head and looked through the rear window. Nothing to be seen, just half a dozen cars that were part of the cortège, interspersed by some stray housewives trying to get to the big supermarket at the crossroads. He felt a lump in his pocket and shifted to feel the key of the Morris. Agnes and Aunt Hatta would be unable to use it to return home.

About a hundred people went on the long walk over smooth tarmac, through the shaped evergreens out into the open far corner and the patch of lush and poisonous grasses where Michael was to be laid. Drury walked with them, lingering to read inscriptions on headstones. He stood well back from the proceedings with rope and earth, occasionally looking all round for the youth in brown. Had he lost him? He must have had a close look at him when he was circling Victoria Hill Park behind Michael. And then he was somewhere on the Green Path and had seen what had happened. What had he seen? Everything? He knew Michael's name. What was it Michael used to say? "I make a point of keeping friendly with these people . . ." He knew them, Connors, Cashes, Plunketts and many more, dealers like he was. This youth might have approached Drury then and there on Victoria Hill. But he was very likely afraid, having just seen a man pushed sharply so that he fell over a cliff and broke his neck. He could have screamed or could have come up, but not if he were afraid. Drury wouldn't have harmed him. But he had gone home to his humpey or trailer or tigeen, no doubt to his wife and scores of kids, and thought about what he had seen. He had not gone to the police because people like that did not have voluntary contact with the police. But he must have worked out that there was a chance that the man who had pushed Mr Kenny and had caused the accident would be at Mr Kenny's funeral. Blackmail, of course. Could Drury buy him off with say, twenty pounds? No chance. Even if he paid a lot more, no doubt the first time the creature became drunk he'd be talking about it to his fellow itinerants. Was there a chance he could find his home address? Was he here in the graveyard now? Drury looked round again, sweating and feeling sick. He might be waiting outside the gates. The ceremony appeared to be over now, and the crowd was breaking up. He hesitated. What was to stop him wandering around inside Dean's Grange for the rest of the day?

A gloved hand softly touched his arm. "Thank you, Jim." Maire had sought him out to thank him for his gesture of accompanying the corpse all the way, an effort not expected from a Protestant. "Michael always liked you." He nodded, unable to speak. Tears slipped from her eyes.

"Like a lift back to your car?" Mahoney asked.

"Oh, no thanks. I left Agnes with the problem of the puncture. I've got to get into town." He clung to the group as they walked towards the gates, keeping his head down. A bus was approaching the cemetery stop, and he could catch it easily. "I'll go after that . . . thanks a million, Dan." He climbed to the top and waited for the bus to move. It was ahead of schedule, and stood parked for minutes, its doors yawning open. He was no more vulnerable in here than he had been out there. From his high seat he could look out over the wall into the graveyard where he had just been. Who was that distant figure in reddish brown? Not possible to tell from here. It was easy enough to get lost in there among the tombstones. Bus employees standing about smoking thought of no-one but themselves. He stared hard; he could not decide for sure about that man who had disappeared behind cypresses. The doors closed with a pneumatic sigh. It was terrible to have to rely on public transport.

When the bus reached Stephen's Green he disembarked and made his way blindly past busloads of American tourists into the park. He mingled with the girls in summer dresses and the old men feeding ducks. He made for grass, took off his jacket, lay down and closed his eyes, listening to the rustle of leaves over his head and feeling the beam of weak summer sunshine. He dozed off for a time to be woken by the noise of a transistor. He started, looking round in terror. Was he going to have to look out like this for the rest of his life?

He would go away for a time. There would be little difficulty, since term was over. Generally he hated summer and the fact that he had never been able to afford a proper holiday, just a few days crouching in a tent in the rain with Kevin in nappies, or that week in a cottage in Kerry lent by Jaws's brother-in-law when the rain had been like monsoon. For the last two summers he had stayed at home. Last year he had toyed with the idea of putting together a best-seller; he would research a handbook about car licence numbers around the world. The days had passed away, and nothing had been achieved apart from a little pin money earned looking after Michael's shop. (What would become of that now?) This year he had to get away. Not for good. At least, not yet. He recalled his dream of going to London, but that was not on just now. But a week or two would clear the air. It was easy to panic now, but if he thought about it rationally, as long as he managed to keep clear of that youth it was extremely unlikely that someone of that type would go to the police. He would never be able to go walking in Victoria Hill Park again, not that he had the inclination. He would take his August salary. Agnes would have to manage on her own. Why not? He thought of her seminars, working weekends, conferences, group meetings, charismatic gatherings, therapy sessions and dirty weekends. It was his turn.

Where would he go? Nowhere in Ireland. He would go abroad to a place in the sun. His passport was up to date after that terrible Easter trip to Brussels. The whole of Europe and its traditions to choose from, and all the combined schools could offer fifty twelve-year-old boys was memories of the pissing mannikin. He set off towards Grafton Street, looking round every so often with a movement that had suddenly become second nature. He collected a selection of garish brochures from unhelpful travel agents. This was the crowded time of year and he should have booked weeks and months ago. Very few vacancies were left. The cheapest place to visit and the easiest was Lourdes. He considered spending a week there. It was a thriving French town, presumably with numerous little cafés serving delicious meals. The countryside around must be rather pleasant; wasn't the place at the foot of the Pyrenees? He might hike or something, and escape all the religious junketings.

Or could he? He could not endure any more religious fervour after the Papal visit. He had gone to see Pope John Paul II in Phoenix Park along with all the rest. He had to deliver selected members of the scout troop delegated to make themselves useful. They took a train from Bray, arriving near the Park at five in the morning. Even then a great mass of people was pouring in from all directions. In the dark the great robing tent, all lit up, was like an enormous glow-worm, while the illuminated cross behind the stepped altar sparkled in the distance.

He had delivered his charges to Mr Byrne, the troop leader, and retreated into his designated wooden corral facing the altar which was a quarter of a mile away. He waited five hours as the misty sun rose over the trees, and the crowds thickened, and then listened to the roars as the Papal plane with its fighter escort flew over their heads. He barely survived being trampled by four tough women from Belfast and their children who formed a vociferous group in his enclosure. When the Pope landed in his helicopter, the rest of the day was spent trying to make out what the distant small figure happened to be doing now. The words of his long sermon borne by the loudspeaker were blown about in the wind. The Host he held up, as big as a ping-pong bat, was a symbol of purity, of the ideal. Wholesome pop music and band music streamed towards the Liffey. When the Popemobile came by the northerners pushed past him. "Children in front!" was the cry, but the harridans blocking his view were all past their first youth. After he caught the briefest glimpse of the smiling, plump, pleasant pontiff, benign yet stern, the personification of God the Father, orchestrating the waves of cheering, he felt forlorn. He reflected how his forebears, many of whom had been clergymen and who all thought of themselves as Irish, would have despaired if they had foreseen the million people gathered here. He had spent the rest of that weary weekend in front of the television watching the visit; to Limerick, to Maynooth and to Knock which was like Benares, identifying the clerics, politicians and other Papal groupies who turned up at every ceremony. Agnes was ecstatic, the house burgeoned with Papal flags, and she took Kevin off in the darkness to Maynooth. The Pope waved at Kevin, Kevin waved at the Pope. It was the man, not the message Agnes liked; his views on the proper status of women were unappealing.

No, not Lourdes. There was a cheap seat available on a flight to Minorca the next day. A cancellation, you're lucky sir. A week—in any case it was all he could afford. He booked, paid, and hurried round to the bank for traveller's cheques. Usually he hated the bank and the menace it offered; always the irrational fear of the figure of the manager coming out of his office ("Could I have a word with you, Mr Drury?"), the locking of the office door for security purposes, the fiddling with the computerized television before it proclaimed his overdraft. Today he appreciated the mahogany fittings and thick carpeting as he overdrew his account once more, not enough for immediate comment.

What to do for the next twenty-four hours? He had to go home, since his passport was at Goleen Park and he had to collect some clothes. He went to the Shelbourne to telephone Agnes in comfort. Calls cost more from there, but it was a small worthwhile luxury.

"What the hell happened to you?"

"I felt upset all of a sudden." She didn't reply. "You know . . . Michael's death. I couldn't take it."

"I was more upset than you were. Where did you go?"

"I went to the graveside."

"I wanted to go . . . you said it wasn't necessary . . ."

"I'm sorry. I acted on impulse. How did you get back?"

"It was terrible. Neither your aunt nor I had any money."

"You ought to have more sense. She hardly ever carries money."

"She got home by her beggar technique." He remembered how Aunt Hatta liked to stand at a traffic light waiting until the lights went red. Then she would totter over to the first stationary driver and tap at the window. "Might an old lady beg for a lift?" She invariably got one.

"I had to walk," Agnes wailed.

"I'm really sorry. Try and understand." She didn't reply. He continued, trying desperately hard to keep his voice casual, "Anyone call round this afternoon?"

There was a pause, a long pause, damn it. "Who'd be calling?"

"I just asked."

"Collect the car will you now. I have to have it before eight o'clock." He remembered she was going to a pop concert.

He queued for the bus and endured the movement of evening traffic, which was slower than the pace of the hearse he had followed that morning. Around half past six he got to the spot beside the church where the Morris was parked. He prepared to descend from the top when a lucky impulse made him glance out of the window and see the youth in brown lounging beside the church railings, near to where the Morris stood.

It was horrible. He crouched down where he stood at the top and the bus went on. The creature was left behind, so that his walk home from the terminus could be made without the fearful look around.

"Where's the car?" Agnes asked immediately.

"There's something wrong with it. I couldn't get it to start."

"Blast. What the hell am I going to do? I'm late." Considering she was always late, her panic was exaggerated. The last thing he wanted was an evening talking to her when she was in this mood.

"I'll treat you to a taxi."

"A taxi?" She sounded surprised, as if he had offered her a chariot of crystal with wheels of beryl and throne of sapphire.

"I messed you about today. I'd like to make up for it."

She said nothing as she took the money he offered her. She had washed her hair and switched on the hair dryer, so he couldn't talk to her above the whine.

"How'll I get back?" she asked before she left.

"Get a lift. Or another taxi." He handed her another two pounds and she looked at him enigmatically.

After she had gone he spent the evening quite happily with Kevin, playing cards—twenty-one—and watching television. He stayed up long after the child went to bed and then followed. Another nearly sleepless night; people went mad with as little sleep as this. What could he do about the Morris? He didn't dare send Agnes for it in case the youth in brown was still there. He imagined him going up and tugging at her sleeve. And if he left the keys at a garage and asked for it to be collected, some other link between the car and Goleen Park might be forged.

He got up early and boarded a bus full of sleepy roadmen. Would the creature have stayed out all night on the watch? Before getting out he looked up and down in every direction. He could not be sure. He got off and ran towards the car with his head bent as if he were moving through a shower of rain. The engine started without trouble and he got away.

He would not return to Goleen Park until Agnes had gone to work and deposited Kevin for the day. (He was never fully cognisant of the playgroups and baby-minders that looked after him.) Meanwhile he would drive into the Dublin Mountains and take a long walk in the early morning sunshine.

CHAPTER 10

The plane did not depart until midnight, so that the day was very long. He broke it up by going to the cinema, buying a number of thrillers and reading one as he prolonged the cafeteria meal at the airport. He slept a little, reclining on a black chair, and woke at eleven. Package tours from Dublin often departed at unfriendly hours because the planes that took passengers to London and Manchester by day were used for transporting holiday-makers at night. The lounge was crowded with yawning people in wheelchairs waiting for the Lourdes flight. He was glad he was not going to Lourdes. Surely it could not be good for all these invalids to be up so late?

His plane landed at Mahon a little before daybreak, and the passengers alighted to the scent of flowers massed in troughs around the airport buildings. Feeling pleased at the unaccustomed warmth in the air, he climbed into a bus to take him to his hotel. As dawn came up he gazed out at limestone walls surrounding stony fields and thought how the landscape resembled Connemara. It began to drizzle. He rested a couple of hours before breakfast, which consisted of weak coffee, bread, a foil-wrapped pat of butter and a small plastic container of jam. Feeling hungry, he reached over to the vacant place behind him to help himself to a second pat of butter. The head waiter came up immediately and scolded him, because that was not included in his package deal.

The rain stopped by the afternoon, but the weather had a tendency to cloud that took the edge off the pleasure of lying beside blue water. He was entitled to bread and breakfast and attendance at a party given by the travel agent, at which free glasses of sangria were distributed. The hotel only merited one star because of a shortage of bathrooms. Some Spanish teenagers in the charge of nuns were staying there for a week. Indistinguishable from those who infested Dublin, they spent much of their holiday playing slot machines. Their perpetual shrill voices were punctuated by the guffaws of prosperous Germans. The English sat in sad groups, penny-wise. The Irishmen in his party abandoned their wives for bars where they drank local beer.

By day he lay out on his strip of hotel towel among Germans oiling each other and paddle boats for hire. By night, sounds of slot machines, disco music and German laughter kept him awake. By the fourth day he longed to leave. Was there any alternative to returning to Ireland and his terrible problems? He observed the enterprising artists, tough middle-aged divorcees, homosexuals and other expatriates who chose to live in Minorca and run restaurants and antique and souvenir shops. What about opening an antique shop in Mahon? It must be miserable in winter with rain, wind and empty hotels.

At the end of the week he was down to his last few pesetas. He had to vacate his room by three o'clock in the afternoon, eight hours before his flight departed. The plane was further delayed by engine trouble and did not take off until well after midnight. The passengers had been promised a good Irish breakfast, and he waited for it as they flew over the Pyrenees. But something had gone wrong with the distribution, so that there were only enough servings for people in the first seventeen rows of seats. The rest—he was seated in row twenty-two—received a Spanish doughnut and lukewarm coffee from smiling apologetic hostesses. Dawn came up, babies cried. When they reached home he looked down at Dublin Bay, the jaws of death, the mouth of hell. The airport was full of the same wheelchair invalids he had seen the week before.

He had to wait another two hours before the first bus into the city. From the bus station he walked along the Liffey to Westmoreland Street and into the branch of Bewley's there, where he ordered a proper breakfast. Wonderful. The newspaper he read had nothing in it that interested him. He hoped that the inquest had taken place while he was away and that he would never have to hear anything about it. His initial remorse now evaded him; the relief tempered by regret that governed his emotions was a constant gentle sadness.

Until he walked out of Bewley's he had forgotten about the terror of being on the lookout for a figure in brown. When he crossed the road opposite Trinity a hand tapping him on the shoulder gave him a bad fright. Hello, Jim. Been away? Lovely tan you've got there. Only Joe Hethrington, who had escaped school teaching and gone into television. Life in Dublin was going to be intolerable.

On the train out to Killiney he slept deeply, waking with a start in time to see the train slide out of Dalkey tunnel and the spot where Michael had pushed him all that time ago. A bit more than a month. From the station he walked to Goleen Park and let himself in by the back door. Agnes sat at the kitchen table hammering copper, Kevin beside her crayonning violently. He jumped up when he caught sight of his father.

"Present, present!"

Drury opened his little suitcase and handed him a grey model of an armoured car. The four cannabis plants had grown during his absence, their spiked brilliant green filling the room with a jungly sort of light. Agnes made tea and handed him the Libra mug. He lit a cigarette from the duty-free carton he had brought home.

"I want to talk to you."

It was an opening that had heralded the worst moments of their lives together. "Not now, for God's sake. I've been up the whole night. I haven't had a wink of sleep. Do you know Aer Lingus has things arranged so that people going on package holidays invariably come back in the middle of the night? Nothing like feeling really refreshed and relaxed after your time in the sun."

"I want to go away."

"What do you mean? You're always going away."

"I want to go away for a long time." She reached over and took one of his cigarettes. "What I really want to say is that our marriage is finished."

He drank his tea. In spite of all the comings and goings, she had never before suggested actually ending their union. He had always considered himself cynical in attributing the reasons to his expectations. Strangely the regrets were immediate. He thought about the years together, the shared interests that had shifted direction so soon, the warmth that had gone cold. "Do you mean that you're thinking of a divorce?"

"Don't be silly." Couples who got married in Ireland did not talk about the impossible. Several of Agnes's cold-blooded friends journeyed over to England for their weddings, so that if their marriages did not work out, they could get divorced more easily. For him and Agnes a legal separation would mean a long spell on the other side of the water. He thought fleetingly about an annulment. The church had made their union so difficult . . . would it ease things now?

"A separation?"

"Right."

They looked at each other in silence. "What would you do?"

"I thought I might go to Galway and join Jody and Elizabeth."

"Surely to God that must be the last commune in Ireland? I thought communes went out with the oil crisis."

"Jody's all right, he's rich and the place is really lovely. They sell their batiks to America, oh, everywhere in the world. Or there's a chance I might go to India with Katey Burke. She wants to see an Ashram in Poona where the guru offers a choice of every single kind of therapy that you might want and you seek out exactly what your need is." Poona's image had changed since Colonel Hackett used to visit it.

"What about Kevin?"

"I'd take him of course. The experience would do him nothing but good."

"Perhaps I should come to Poona as well?"

Silence. "I want to be alone, I tell you."

"What's the difference between going away now and all the other times you've gone away?"

"This time I really want it to be for good."

He sighed. "Look, I'm tired. I've been up all night. I don't want to hear more now."

"I want things settled now. I want you to agree."

"Oh, I agree. I agree. Now can I go to bed?"

"Let's settle things first."

"They're settled!" he bellowed and left the kitchen. She made no attempt to follow him as he pounded upstairs, nor did she lose her temper and yell up at him. He managed to catnap for a few hours. When he woke and went down again he found she had cooked him a good meal and dispatched Kevin somewhere. He resigned himself to discussion. They began with an informal warm-up. He enjoyed the steak and asked for news about what had been going on while he was away. The inquest? He slipped in a question about that casually. Yes, it took place at the beginning of the week. Accidental death. Her eyes were averted.

He could think of only one way to change the conversation. "You really want to leave?"

"Right." She lit a cigarette.

"Why now? We've had our ups and downs before." She did not answer. "Give me one good reason why you should go off taking my child out of my life."

"I don't want to talk about it."

"Which is why you began the minute I had stepped in the door, knowing I had been travelling all night . . ."

"I just want to get things straight."

"Go on, get them straight. Tell me. There's another man."

"No."

"What then?" Like a fool he went on badgering her.

"I just think we've gone on long enough . . ." Suddenly he recognized the particular quality in her voice. Her hands were trembling. But he couldn't leave her alone. He was shouting, "You want to leave, you tell me why."

She shouted back. "I don't want to live with a murderer!" She burst into tears. "Oh, I didn't mean that, I didn't mean that!"

"What the hell are you talking about?" For an instant his indignation was genuine. There must be a certain amount of false witness that is the result of a suspension of truth. A totally different thing from ordinary falsehood.

"Nothing." Still trembling she lit a cigarette from the butt of the last. It was grotesque that she should be so afraid. She stammered. "It seems to me . . . that Michael's death makes things easier . . ."

There was a long heavy silence. He actually cleared his throat before saying, "What do you mean?"

"What were you doing around the time?"

"What time?"

"When Michael died?"

"Are you implying that I had something to do with that?" His voice sounded falsetto.

She must be a brave girl if she felt so afraid and still persisted.

"At the funeral. The man who came up and talked to you. What did he want?"

"What man?"

"That tinker."

"Oh, him. He wanted a touch."

"I heard what he said."

"What did he say?"

"He said, 'I saw you in the park.'"

"He certainly didn't. How could 'Please mister, could you spare us fifty pee' or whatever it was, turn into anything like that?"

"And then you ran away."

"He didn't say that. It's meaningless."

"He did."

"I can't remember what he said exactly. It wasn't that. It's over a week ago and I've been away. Suppose just for argument's sake he did say that, what would it mean in any case?"

"That you were in the park."

"What park?"

"Michael died in the park . . ."

"There are dozens of parks. Herbert Park, People's Park, Phoenix Park."

"You were in the park. And this man saw you near Michael . . . and then afterwards he didn't follow you. Right? Maybe he was afraid, maybe he lost you. And then he thought he'd turn up at the funeral and wait, hoping to see you." She burst into another torrent of tears. "The dog, Jim. I saw what you did to your aunt's dog with the spade . . ."

"Oh, for God's sake." He went and found the half bottle of duty-free whiskey he had bought at the airport and poured two drinks. "You worked out that I pushed Michael? Or something? From that one little phrase you didn't even hear properly?"

"Why did you run away outside the church?"

"I told you. I hate bloody funerals. A fine thing for you to come up with. You think I followed him and pushed him over the cliff so that he fell and broke his neck? Charming. Charming thing to have your wife believe. Look, if it makes you feel better, I'll deny it. I didn't kill him. Scout's honour." He made the three finger salute and she smiled wanly. "As a matter of fact, I miss him." He nearly added, "It was an accident." "You string along a ghastly suspicion like that just from mishearing a begging tinker, and it fits in very nicely with what you want to do. You want to go off with someone. Like you wanted to set up with that fat bartender who was trying to get into film making."

"I haven't anyone. Why did he go up to you and not to someone else."

"I haven't a clue."

"Oh, let's leave the argument."

"Just like that. 'Let's leave the argument.' You come up with a monstrous suggestion like that, and then you say quite calmly 'Let's leave the argument.'"

"I'm sorry."

"You really think I killed him?"

"I don't know . . . No. Jim, I want to go. Not for that. I just want to go."

"Go. Leave. Goodbye."

"We've got to settle things first. We've got to talk about money."

"Ah!" That was why she hadn't left him already, so that he would have come back to an empty house. Even though she was afraid of him, she had stayed and waited to face him.

"I've got to live, right?"

"Live. I don't give a damn. Take everything I have. Such a lot. I take it you're not waiting around for Aunt Hatta's demise?"

"We might sell the house and divide up the proceeds."

He had never thought of that before. "We wouldn't get much after paying off the mortgage. About two thousand each if we were lucky."

"And you'd go on paying a bit towards Kevin's keep?"

"He's not to go to Poona." She'd bleed him to death, while he joined that sad phenomenon of modern times, the weekend fathers, the holiday dads. "I know absolutely nothing about separation and divorce and what it involves financially. I'm not prepared to discuss it now. We'll go and see Peachey as soon as you like."

"There's one other thing about money. Your aunt's statue. I think I can get it back."

He poured out more whiskey.

"I managed to get in touch with Tony and Eugene while you were away. They've got it hidden safely. They haven't sold it or anything."

"Did they say where?"

"No, of course not. In some arms dump or other, I suppose."

"Arms dump?"

"It appears that they get involved in a wee bit of arms smuggling from time to time."

"Arms smuggling? For whom?"

"Up to the North of course. For people there."

"I thought they were queer."

"Why shouldn't gays be involved in the Republican movement?" There was respectable historic precedent although "gay" seemed an inappropriate description of certain martyred patriots. "Seemingly they dug it up the same morning, right after I told them where it was. Before you and Michael drove out. And Tony says they had a good laugh."

"I'll bet."

"Eugene wondered why I didn't use the stump to display my bracelets."

"What did they do with it?"

"They went and hid it. In their horse box."

"They don't sound horsy types to me."

"Of course they aren't. But they use the horse box in their work like the Bradys use their trailer in theirs. Tony and Eugene are careful. Did you see the horse they keep up at their cottage? When they want to transport things secretly they put the guns and stuff under the floorboards of the horse box. Then they put the horse in on top all dolled up with its mane and tail plaited, and they dress up in riding breeches and jackets and pretend they're going to a show or a hunt. That way they can drive anywhere with anything and no-one has any suspicion. They go all over the six counties."

"They took the statue away?"

"Right. But Jim, I might get it back." He was silent. "Is it really worth a great deal of money?"

He hesitated. "It's very hard to say. According to Michael it was part of a group and the one that I bought in Harmony Hall was the other half of it. He seemed to be convinced that they were priceless both together. But the one we took away is only the half of it. And it's stolen property—certainly for as long as Aunt Hatta is alive."

"Stolen property gets sold."

"Only for a fraction of its worth. And it isn't as if this was easy to dispose of like a diamond necklace. The problem is that Aunt Hatta could always identify it."

"How could she? I bet she never looked at it properly. You could break off some more of its leg. If it's sold in England or Europe or sent to America, even with the paint stripped off she's not likely to hear of it."

"Perhaps not." There was that dealer, Higgins, whom he had seen at Harmony Hall who specialized in sending smuggled antiquities from the Middle East to North and South America. He might be happy to dispose of Aunt Hatta's statue. Plenty of museums might be interested in adding it to their collections, although they might be unhappy if they found themselves buyers of stolen property. "The difficulty would be to give it a plausible provenance."

"That's easy. You've one advantage coming from a family with all those absurd large houses. You can say that it came from your old home, the one the Land Commission pulled down. You can say it came from the back of a cupboard."

"Another cupboard?"

"Why not? Or the attic. Or the woodshed. You might even sell it on the open market and ignore everything that's happened so far. You could say that you had it in your possession all this time and only realized its worth when Michael told you about the worth of the Harmony Hall statue. And he's dead."

"You mean pretend it's yet another statue? A third one?"

"There could be half a dozen if you wanted. Some ancestor of yours come back from the Grand Tour with a load of junk which got distributed round the poor relations."

It was true that anything could come out of an old family house. He recalled Major Percival, who found a gold torque in a bog while out shooting and sent it over to Sothebys the week after, forestalling any official delays and talk about treasure trove by saying that it had been lying around his place for centuries, its worth unrecognized.

But Maire Kenny, who now owned the Harmony Hall statue and must soon learn about Michael's negotiations with English experts would get suspicious. It would be better to wait for a year or longer before making any move to dispose of it. And what were the risks in trying to get the statue back from Eugene and Tony in the first place?

"How much is it worth?" Agnes asked again.

"I don't know. I refuse to believe the bit about Praxiteles. It could never be proved. You can't go round looking for a signature."

"Why not? Michaelangelo wrote his name across Our Lady's chest."

"That was after the period of high art in ancient Greece. I don't

know though . . ." He thought of the little piece of first-century glass
from the Constable Maxwell collection sold at auction a year or so ago.
It had a signature, "Aristeas the Cypriot made it." Two and a half
inches high, it had gone for something like £70,000. He remembered
Michael's excitement. He must have been thinking in terms of hundreds of thousands, although that was for both fragments put together.

"Why can't Tony and Eugene dispose of the thing themselves?"

"In the first place they've no idea of its worth. And it's a bit trouble-
some when they know it's stolen, and you know yourself it's not very
nice looking. When I hinted at buying it back for five hundred
pounds, Tony appeared to be quite pleased."

"How the hell can we raise five hundred pounds?"

"We'll think of something . . ." Her fear of him appeared to have
evaporated somewhat. He might remind her of how large a proportion
of all murder is domestic, a matter of disagreement between husbands
and wives. Suddenly she was all action. She rang Eugene and Tony,
using a number written on a scrap of newspaper in her address book.
They were ex-directory. He remembered the incongruous paint-spat-
tered telephone in their squalid cottage. She got through to one or
other of them, and had an inconclusive conversation. Not now, sweetheart. Things are a bit tricky right this moment. We'll be in touch.
Don't call us, we'll call you.

In the ensuing atmosphere of gloom and argument they decided to
put up the house in Goleen Park for sale right away. The whole family
went into Dublin on the train the next day, Drury catnapping in a
corner seat and waking up in alarm at each station. Loading Kevin
with sweets, they went into a real estate office near Stephen's Green.
The interior was hung with pictures of lavish houses and estates that
had been sold recently. Harmony Hall figured large, with several studies of the pillared portico and plastered ceilings.

When Drury gave his address the young man who dealt with him
looked grave. He knew about the Corporation Estate opposite. Three
bedrooms? There was very little demand for houses with three bedrooms. Didn't they know about difficulties in getting mortgages? Loans?
How the recession had dealt a blow to the property market? Very well,
they would take a lower price than the house was worth. The agent
looked unhappy. It was not a question of settling for less, but of selling
the property at all. There were scores of estate houses all over the country waiting for buyers.

Of course Drury was aware of the recession. When the subject came
up in the Common Room at Prospect there were people prepared to
bang their heads against the wall in despair. However, in the circles in
which Michael moved he had seen little evidence of it. *Au contraire.*

The agent droned on. There was no point in putting the house on the market during August when house purchasers tended to be away on holiday. He suggested they begin advertising at the beginning of September. They discussed the merits of auction, when the house would be advertised three clear weeks beforehand, like banns being called before marriage. But such a dismal property would be unlikely to sell at auction and a private sale would be a better idea in his considered opinion. Don't be in too much of a hurry. These things take time.

They came out into the sunshine of Stephen's Green, Drury carrying the cheese, apples and grape juice that Agnes decreed would be their lunch. All the way in on the train Kevin had been shouting about the playground. He regarded this stretch of scarred asphalt as a corner of paradise, and so did half the children in Dublin. Drury had to fight to get him a place on a swing among other jostling, fighting kids. As he pushed him back and forth, Agnes stood near and they indulged in a low, bitter quarrel. Money. In twelve hours they had come to rely on the quick sale of the house. Any alternative means of raising money assailed him with terror. He did not want to pursue the matter of the statue. It would activate trouble. Had Michael photographed it before it was stolen? He could ask Aunt Hatta. He was afraid of Tony and Eugene.

Agnes was shrill, but this was a good place to argue. Children's voices absorbed their exchanges, and even Kevin could only hear snatches of them when he came back on the return of the swing. She wanted to go to Peachey right away and talk about legal separation or whatever miserable half-severance the country allowed citizens whose marriages failed. Peachey would be full of I-told-you-so's, although Drury considered that separations of partners of mixed marriages were comparatively rare. The bond created at the outset by the opposition and difficulties heaped upon the unfortunate couples made for stable unions.

Agnes continued to jabber about money as she broke off bits of cheese and handed round apples. They argued as they made their way down to Pearse Station. It was Drury, with his long experience of economizing by reading other people's papers, who first caught sight of the photograph on the front page of an *Evening Herald*. ARMS AND NO ARMS said the caption which matched the main headline ARMS DUMP FOUND IN WEST WICKLOW. He left Agnes in mid-sentence and rushed to buy his own paper. The photograph showed Aunt Hatta's statue looking horribly like a real torso in the company of some grenades and Armalite rifles. The report stated that members of the Special Branch had discovered them in a forestry plantation. The statue was assumed to be stolen property. Had there been a tip-off? Had anyone been arrested? There was no mention. He strode back to Agnes.

"I hope you're satisfied."

She never gave up. That evening she produced another hare-brained scheme. Aunt Hatta still knew nothing about the value of the statue, and Drury had better go along and offer to buy it for a little more than Michael had offered for it all those weeks before. In the end he lost his temper and snarled at her. He'd been angrier many times in the past; now it was depressing to see how her aggressive mood subsided in fear.

He went to see Aunt Hatta next day, to learn from her lips about the statue's recovery and offer his congratulations. At the gateway to Eagle's Nest, Dempsey let him in and his tyres crunched on gravel. Dogs barked. He got a bad fright when he saw Michael's Rolls standing outside the front door beside the hydrangeas. Aunt Hatta leaned one hand on her stick and raised the other in a gesture of farewell as Maire Kenny, looking very grim, started up the engine. Turning at the top of the narrow space originally meant for governess carts was not easy for a woman unfamiliar with the big car she was driving, very angry, and trying to avoid dogs snapping at tyres and a Morris Minor.

When she had gone Aunt Hatta ceased her regal waving and led him into the drawing room, where she poured him the remains of the coffee she had offered her departed guest.

"That woman is a pot of poison."

"Mrs Kenny? What did she want?" He was trembling.

"I suppose you heard the lovely news about my statue? I'm so pleased, even though they didn't catch the beastly people who killed Rascal." She seemed very cheerful. "Do you know that bad-tempered hag came here to say that the statue belongs to her?"

His terrors rebounded. "But it does, doesn't it? As Michael Kenny's widow? I suppose you gave him some sort of written acknowledgement that he had paid for it?"

"That's what she says. She gave me this." He was shown a photocopy of a receipt she had signed. "She wouldn't trust me with the original. I asked her why she was so eager to have the ugly old thing. And she hummed and hawed and said it was Mr Kenny's last wishes, and if necessary she would take me to court about it. And then, do you know, it came out. I don't know if she meant to say it, but she was getting very angry. Do you know what she said?"

"No."

"She said that the statue is extremely valuable. Mr Kenny had apparently already bought Silver Sally, which we gave to the Sherlocks."

"I told you that."

"Yes, well he had in some experts who said it was worth a lot of money. And that's why he very dishonestly bought mine, which is apparently worth just as much."

"You'll have to let her have it."

"That's what she kept saying. She kept shouting that since she had the receipt she could prove it belonged to her."

"It does."

"Oh no, not at all. I certainly shan't let her have it back. I told her that it would not look good to show publicly how her husband tried to rob an old woman. But she didn't seem to worry about her husband's posthumous reputation." Aunt Hatta looked up at the portrait of Uncle Jack. "As the poet says, 'Pious thoughts which visit at new graves will cease to go so duly and so oft.'"

"You'll have to give it back to her." He felt desperate. Litigation and open quarrels would lead to revelations.

"I most certainly will not. I shall give it to the Museum."

"Museum?"

"The one in Kildare Street. She can try and get it back from there. I remember your grandfather giving a number of things to it."

"But it's worth thousands!"

She seemed extraordinarily happy. It was rather more than that—she was radiant. She continued gazing at Uncle Jack's photograph.

"It will be a memorial to him. Isn't it marvellous? It justifies all his work."

"What work?" He had always been under the impression that Uncle Jack was an idle old man who spent his life checking his portfolio of stocks and shares and sailing his yacht.

"His work with Lord Cloncurry's papers."

"What was that?" He accepted more cold bitter coffee.

"All those papers about the Cloncurry shipwreck. Didn't your parents ever talk about it?"

"No."

"They never paid enough attention to what Jack was doing." In fact they had never got on with Uncle Jack, which was why he himself had been obliged to make such efforts with Aunt Hatta in order to charm her. "It happened in 1800 or thereabouts. A ship called the *Princess Caroline* with a cargo full of antiquities belonging to Lord Cloncurry sank in Killiney Bay. You can see the place from here." She pointed to Uncle Jack's shrine in the bay window. "Jack's mother was connected to the Lawless family—that was the Cloncurry name—and at some point our family inherited a portion of the Cloncurry papers. I suppose they should have stayed in that gloomy old house in Kildare that the Cloncurrys lived in, but there you are. They came to us, bundles and bundles of old papers."

"What were they about?"

"Letters mostly, and documents about this shipwreck. Jack got interested in the whole affair. There was the coincidence of having all these papers in his possession and being actually able to see the spot where the ship sank from up here, as well as his hobby of diving. It made sense of the whole thing that he should go out searching for treasure."

Drury went over to the window and looked across at the blue waters of the bay. He did not try to use the brass telescope which was set to Uncle Jack's nearsighted focus, unchanged since his death fifteen years before. On the wall beside it was a yachting cap and a sailorly portrait of the old man in pencil by Sean O'Sullivan. He examined the photographs of yachts and their crews which stood in silver frames on an inlaid Chinese table. Here was Uncle Jack still youthful in his diving suit, holding the helmet like a football. Even the table lamp, an early eighteenth-century K'ang Hsi bottle, with a hole for the electric flex, the elegant curve of the rim hidden by a brown plastic bulb-holder, had a connection with Uncle Jack's interests. The lampshade was one of the family documents that Aunt Hatta had fitted as shades on most of the lights in the house. He began to read it, his head swaying as his eyes followed the circulating copperplate handwriting. It was spaced neatly in some sort of list.

"Item. 1 God Mercury from Herculaneum.

Item. 2 Marble Pillars ibid. Bought of Gallileo Battisti.

Item. 1 bust of Roman nobleman from ye villa of Hadrian . . ."

"What is it?"

"An inventory of all the things that went down in the ship. There was another in Italian; this is only the translation, but it's so much easier to read. It was made before the *Princess Caroline* sailed from Genoa. I thought it would be fun to have it here."

"Is there any mention of the statues?" he added, determined to be brutal. "You know the one you gave the Sherlocks is just as valuable."

"That foul Mrs Kenny said as much during her horrible row."

"You realize you gave away a small fortune to the Sherlocks just for a joke?"

She was unperturbed. "Half a loaf. The main thing is that Jack's efforts are justified at last. After all the disappointment. Everyone was so scornful. We never managed to match up the shabby old bits and pieces with anything on the list. The two marble bodies Jack dredged up could have been Mercury, and there's a mention of Venus and I don't know who else, the whole Olympic pantheon."

"Did you call in any experts to look at them?"

"Oh lots. People from the Museum and the National Gallery. And Mr Grogan who had that bookshop in Nassau Street. None of them were very encouraging. They all thought they must be Roman copies in poor condition or, more likely, eighteenth-century copies, the sort people brought back from the Grand Tour. None of them were sure, of course. They kept saying that it wasn't really their field. But you could tell none of them were keen."

"Didn't they look at this list at all? Was it already made into a lampshade?" "No, that wasn't until I got Switzer's terrible estimates for making new shades. That was years later. But it was so difficult to match up the list to those two torsos. They all had a look at it and they all said it was inconclusive. One or two advised contacting someone in England. But the war was on then, you see. And by the time it was over Jack wasn't interested in Lord Cloncurry's shipwreck any more. He had been put off after all his work and expense and the fact that all he could come up with were these wretched bits of bodies. And also by then, do you see, he had become interested in stone circles and the winter solstice."

High up beside a black mark burnt by a light bulb Drury could read "Item. A nymph and a God. Marble. Found in ye Baths of Titus." "But there's no doubt he managed to locate the shipwreck?"

"Of course not. He studied papers and old Admiralty charts and got what he thought were good bearings on the spot where the ship went down. And he went diving. It was all so much more difficult in those days. Nowadays I've watched young men on television putting on their goggles and an oxygen tank on their shoulders and swimming about without any trouble. Before the war people who wanted to dive had to wear a terrible Martian outfit. You can see Jack wearing the great heavy thing in that picture. He didn't do much of the diving since he was directing operations."

"Who did?"

"Dempsey. He was rather keen. Of course it was long before he went gaga. It made a nice change from driving the car and he liked the little extra that Jack gave him. The expense of everything! All that summer he took out the *Hiawatha* and his crew and went round the bay looking for the right sandbank on which the *Princess Caroline* had sunk."

"Wasn't there any publicity?"

"Jack kept rather quiet about the whole thing. He was a wee bit nervous in case one of the Lawless connections should get to hear about it and make a fuss. A few local people around Dalkey and Bullock harbour did show interest, but not after they saw that the only things that came out of the whole expedition were these hideous bodies. There was an item about them in an evening paper, I forget which, we have it somewhere. Something else was happening on the same day, Hitler invading Poland or something, and no-one took any notice. Jack hoped to get up more things, but the winter storms stopped work that year. The following year nothing was possible because of the war."

"Have you any more documents about the shipwreck?"

"Peachey has them. Letters and things about it. 'My lord, with sorrow I have to inform you . . . the cream of your collection . . . rolling heavy seas . . .' Poor Jack found it fascinating."

"I'm sure he did. I'd like to have a look at them sometime. We should really try and track down more about the origins of your statue."

"The Museum can do that."

"I think you should hold on to it." His voice sounded despairing.

"And have to give it away to Mrs Kenny? I suppose the burglar who stole it really did me a good turn, although of course it doesn't make up for poor Rascal. Won't you stay for luncheon?"

"I've a busy old afternoon ahead of me, thanks all the same." She'd only give him fish fingers.

CHAPTER 11

Although so many things threatened to topple him, he continued to balance on his tightrope. Wherever he went in Killiney or Dublin he looked out for the youth in brown, scanning faces on the train, peering down from buses for his shabby figure, keeping constantly on the alert like a zebra on the Serengeti plain. He dared not open a newspaper. Had Eugene or Tony been arrested, or had they been in voluntary contact with the police so that the statue would be connected with Agnes? Had Aunt Hatta got it back or given it to the Museum? What was Maire Kenny doing?

Agnes moved out with cries of "I can't stand it!" She didn't even ask if she could take the car. Drury suspected a new lover. She went not to Connacht, not to Poona, but to some place in Dublin. She left him a telephone number to contact her when the house was sold since she would have to sign a consent form before the transaction went through. No sale, no money for her, and at the most only a couple of thousand if and when some fool purchased Goleen Park. He couldn't give her any money now. He was virtually penniless. She managed to subsidize herself by selling her cannabis plants, which were nearing harvest. He had read that one plant could yield as much as a hundred pounds in money worth of pot. He doubted if she got a quarter of that, but evidently she received some readies. A bearded man in a closed van called and took them away. The kitchen looked a lot lighter. A landscape gardener once told him that such plants would make ideal ground cover in suburban gardens.

He gave Kevin a pound and promised to take him to the zoo in a week or two. When they had gone the days seemed very long. He filled in some hours by seeking information on the two marble fragments that had survived twenty-three centuries in Greece and Italy, a hundred and fifty years under the cold Irish Sea and forty years of mistreatment by his relatives. Would it be worth going out into Killiney Bay in search of more of Lord Cloncurry's possessions? If they could be located and retrieved in 1939, how much easier, given modern diving methods, would it be to bring them to the surface today? He remembered the wreck of the *John Tayleur*, a clipper that sank off Ireland's Eye about 1854 with the loss of 300 lives, mostly emigrants on their way to Melbourne. During the early 1970s some skin divers had recovered some of her cargo, and a good many items were acquired by the Civic Museum. He went to South William Street and examined the pieces of cheap china, the assorted domestic utensils, and the collection of brass dog collars embossed with stylized greyhounds that were intended to be sold in Australia. How Uncle Jack would have loved to find them, rather than the things he did find. How would all Lord Cloncurry's other antiquities compare? "The cream of your Lordship's collection?"

Had Uncle Jack left any notes or a log about the location of the wreck? It was unlikely there would be more things of the quality of the Praxiteles group at the bottom of the sea. Would pillars from the tomb of Hadrian and unspecified statues of Mercury be worth searching for? He would have to consider the matter when he had capital.

He spent days in the National Library in Kildare Street (a refuge) under the domed ceiling edged with smirking naked cherubs. The obvious source of information was the *Dictionary of National Biography*. It made no mention of the shipwreck, only details of Lord Cloncurry's career. But, in his own *Personal Recollections* he waffled on about his possessions and included a tantalizing note, "The largest and most valuable of the treasures of art were . . . lost by shipwreck in Killiney Bay within two hours' sailing time of Dublin."

He learned that Valentine Lawless, Lord Cloncurry, lived for some time in Rome during the great age of collectors. A contemporary had been Sir William Hamilton, Emma's husband, who had sent back from Naples to England a seven-ton Roman vase which was later bought by the Earl of Warwick. That was now worth half a million. Sir William, too, lost his favourite antiquities in a shipwreck; transport of heavy marble material by sea was evidently a hazardous undertaking.

Several other Anglo-Irish peers collected avidly in Italy, like Lord Charlemont and the Earl of Milltown, who was an ennobled brewer. Lord Cloncurry also had a background in commerce, since his father was a Dublin grocer. Another collector was the eccentric Earl Bishop of Derry, Lord Hervey, a strange gaitered eccentric who died in Rome and was shipped back to England on the man-of-war *Monmouth* wrapped as a piece of antique statuary in deference to the superstitions of the sailors. In his lifetime, in spite of his vast private income, he always ensured that by the end of each month his debts exceeded his assets. Once he was down to his last bottle of Orvieto. At such times his belongings in the form of his newly-purchased antiques were sold off. Was that the way Lord Cloncurry acquired Apollo and Daphne?

Drury read on. What a pleasant time Lord Cloncurry seemed to have had. Rome was going through a harsh economic period, and this affluent Irish milord managed to rent the Palazzo Accarola, situated close to the Quirinal, complete with fountains, gardens and fifteen principal bedrooms, for a derisory ninety-six pounds a year. When he was not playing a round of whist with a cardinal (a favourite pastime) he went in search of the antique. This was not always easy since there were so many foreigners in Rome engaged in a similar pursuit. Antiques were in demand; some were even forgeries. But his successes had included four immense red granite pillars from Hadrian's Villa which he bought and sent over to Ireland where they were set up in the portico of his principal seat, Lyons House. They are still there. He also obtained permission from the Pope himself to excavate the Baths of Titus. Ah! That was what Aunt Hatta's lampshade had mentioned. A nymph and a god. Found by ye Baths of Titus.

He thought of Rome as depicted in the Piranesi prints on the stairs of Eagle's Nest. His Lordship sitting in his rented palazzo by an open window overlooking the terrace and fountains. A powdered footman ushering in the workman who was overseer to the excavations. After siesta, going in his carriage to wherever the Baths of Titus were. Bay horses, smell of old leather and filthy cobbled streets. The foreman, billycock hat in hand, leading Milord to where sweating workmen dug through mounds of rubble to reveal two marble torsos. Had he recognized their worth any more than Uncle Jack did? He had put them on the *Princess Caroline* as part of the consignment from Genoa. "The cream of Your Lordship's Collection."

Research took quite a lot of time, although his interest in the origins of the statues was academic since they were out of his possession. The frustration of not having them was eased by the fact that Michael was no longer here to humiliate and threaten him. But the worries that had replaced Michael's threats still created problems with sleep. He visited a doctor, one patient among scores during a busy morning session, and obtained a prescription for barbiturates after a few weary questions. Why had he postponed it so long? What had he been expecting? A session under blazing spotlights? Hypnosis revealing horrible truths?

Before the house in Goleen Park came up for sale, he spent three days cleaning it. Agnes had taken few things away with her, declaring as she went that possessions were unimportant, at the same time reminding him of his money commitments. He dug out her kitchen utensils, wooden spoons, rolling pins, peppermills, garlic crusher and wooden bowls. There had been a time when she had regarded them as having their own spiritual being and labelled the kitchen drawers "wood beings" and "metal beings". Now that she had deserted the little darlings, he piled them into rubbish sacks, together with old clothes, magazines, broken toys and dried flower arrangements. He kept some of the glass jars full of herbs and beans for display on the dresser. In addition he had to keep most of her hideous posters since they hid wall stains, while the goatskin rugs and numdahs had to be moved around to hide holes and marks in the carpets. Smells lessened or became more pleasing as he sprayed the strongest scented polish he could buy over every hard surface in the house. Every morning he painted out the damp spot over the living room fireplace that was the result of poor structural work by the builder of the house, and twenty-four hours later, with the aid of early autumn drizzle, it would reappear. It brought a little bit of a musty smell with it, which had to be dispelled with a shot of central heating. His tank outside still contained some of the oil that had been a Christmas present from Michael three years ago. The heating had to be turned off well in advance of the arrival of a viewer who would be suspicious of unnecessary warmth for the time of year.

The first set of advertisements displayed the house among Georgian mansions, stud farms and luxury bungalows. On the Saturday it appeared, three couples came to inspect it, two of whom were curious neighbours. During the next ten days no more interest was shown in the property, and he saw himself imprisoned here for the forseeable future. If he could not sell it, perhaps he might make an income from letting it? He made sums on scraps of paper.

The opening of term at Prospect was imminent. Like every English-orientated private school it began the year with the autumn equinox. Three weeks had gone by since Agnes left, six since he had committed murder. Nowadays the telephone hardly rang at all, except on the rare occasions when the estate agent wished to inform him of impending viewers. When he was woken one morning by its persistent bell, his fears took some seconds to infiltrate his pill-induced sleep. Half-past seven in the morning?

"Mr James, Mr James? Is it you, Mr James?"

"Who's that?"

"It's Mr James I'm after."

"What number do you want?"

"Mr James, sir. This is Angela, sir."

"Angela?" For a moment he could only associate the name with hockey-playing schoolgirls. Then he remembered. This was Aunt Hatta's maid.

"Oh, sir, the mistress is took bad. She's sick, sir. Breathing heavy and moaning like."

"Have you called Dr Waters?"

"I have, sir. He's coming over, sir."

"I'll be there as soon as I can."

He did not hurry. As he shaved and dressed he hummed a little tune. She was a grand old lady. The mould that made her was broken. We'd never see her like again. He lingered over his breakfast before he drove up to Eagle's Nest.

An ambulance was parked outside the front door, along with two cars. Two cars? One was Dr Waters's. He had been her family doctor for a long time and was very nearly as old as she was. He still kept up his practice for the benefit of his very oldest patients. On his visits he'd prescribe penicillin, whatever the ailment, since like a number of doctors of his age group who had been dazzled by the wonder drug at its first appearance, he still believed that it would cure everything. Then he would sit beside the bed and chat restfully about old times. When anything serious in the way of an illness threatened he had enough sense to bring in a second opinion. He had done so in this case. The glossy Audi whose window was pasted with little notices showing entwined snakes and permission to park at Trinity College and the Royal Dublin Society indicated confident authority.

Both doctors were in Aunt Hatta's bedroom, together with ambulance men, Angela in distress and Aunt Hatta herself being lowered onto a stretcher. The small white dog, the favourite who slept on her bed, had been removed, and its barks were audible from the basement where it was confined. There had been difficulty in approaching the invalid while it sat on the eiderdown yapping and snapping. This was the first time Drury had been in Aunt Hatta's bedroom since it had been converted from the dining room a decade ago. It contained the usual dusty clutter, supplemented by clusters of photographs in silver frames—there was one of him in short trousers and school cap—a big double bed with plenty of room for Uncle Jack, a Teasmade and the big television resting on an elliptical satinwood side table.

The younger doctor was asking about her medical history. He was only a few years older than Drury, who recognized him from school days and his years at Trinity. Trench. A former player of rugby football who would soon be able to afford his own yacht in Dun Laoghaire harbour. How had he done so well? Probably Daddy's practice. Old Waters was saying she'd been splendidly healthy considering her age, apart from a spot of high blood pressure, "but something's got to give sometime." Drury thought she had probably been miserly about her blood pressure pills. If she had lived in a country that offered comprehensive social medicine, she might have lived for ever.

"This place was far too big for her. But she refused to consider leaving it."

"Easy, lads, easy as you lift her." Although her life was pretty well without stress, she had had a bit of good news lately. Drury had read somewhere that good news could cause as much strain as bad. She was very white as she opened her eyes.

"You'll take care of everything, won't you, James?"

"Yes, of course. Don't you worry about anything. Hurry up and get well." She didn't look well at all. They put her in the black-windowed ambulance which departed with flashing blue lights and noise quite unnecessary in Killiney. Mee-maw, mee-maw! She was taken to her favourite little hospital where Sister Halligan met the ambulance. He followed, stopping on the way to buy flowers. He hung around to be told she was resting, before going back to Goleen Park to collect his things. It took less than a quarter of an hour to collect a few possessions and drive up to Eagle's Nest.

He chose one of the large bedrooms upstairs above the drawing room with a matching bay window overlooking the sea and a similar view of the watery grave of the *Princess Caroline*. He spent the afternoon cleaning, running the old carpet-sweeper over the Axminster, polishing away the dust. He went round the house collecting attractive ornaments and pictures from the other rooms which he brought upstairs and arranged. This would be his headquarters for a time. Someone must stay here to guard against burglars. Poor old Angela was well past it.

Over the next few days he settled down. Angela spoiled him. It had been a long time since she had a man in the house to feed. After his morning had begun with a cup of tea prepared in the Teasmade, he descended to collect a fry from her quivering old hands. She could not make the stairs from basement to ground floor more than once a day, and he disliked eating in the kitchen. They worked out a system that involved trays and one of the spring bells that dated from the past. He helped in his way, sometimes washing up, occasionally pushing her away from the stove while he cooked himself a steak.

He made his bedroom as pleasant as possible, summoning Dempsey to help him move in some choice pieces of furniture from elsewhere, a Carlton House desk, or a wing-backed chair. The little O'Connor moonlight scene and the Breton landscape with children by Walter Osborne looked most attractive arranged beside the gilded Chippendale mirror with birds that he brought up from the drawing room. Although it was too soon for fires, he found the little one-bar that Aunt Hatta had used provided the correct degree of comfort in the evening. The nights were a little chilly, and her electric blanket, a fearsome old gridiron dating back to Uncle Jack's time, pleasantly warmed his bed before he lay down. (He made quite certain to switch it off first.) The

Teasmade was invaluable. His sleeping problems improved immediately, and he could count on seven hours' sleep at night.

Most mornings he toured the house. He noted the drink in the dining room and earmarked a modest whiskey for his evening nip. He opened cabinets, taking out china, gold-rimmed flowered tea services and groups of shepherds, maidens and china animals, all filthy and covered with sticky dust. He decided to clean them all, Red Anchor, Gold Anchor, Derby, Bow. As he was washing a shepherdess in warm water and Fairy Liquid, Mrs Keogh, making her once-weekly gestures of dusting, paused as she took round the carpet sweeper.

"Don't bother about my room, Mrs Keogh. I'll manage."

"I'm not allowed upstairs, sir." He remembered Aunt Hatta hid the tea caddy and other kitchen stores from her. She did not seem to mind the slur. Was it a slur? In the dining room, counting felt-wrapped silver in drawers lined with green baize, he found a number of sets of forks and spoons that appeared to be short. There would be eleven when you would think there should have been twelve. Was silver Mrs Keogh's weakness? Was he wrong in his long-held assumption that Aunt Hatta never went upstairs herself and never missed things that were lost? She may have thought of Mrs Keogh as the culprit. But if so, why had she not dismissed her? Perhaps her role as purveyor of news in the neighbourhood had become essential. Possibly the challenge of the hunt inspired Aunt Hatta with a wish to catch her pilfering. Most likely it was that she did not want to break a long-established habit; Mrs Keogh had been coming here for more than thirty years, dating back to Uncle Jack's time. If she did indeed share Drury's weakness for picking and stealing, they had been of mutual benefit to each other.

The afternoons he spent digging in the garden. It was therapeutic, and such a lot of things waited to be done, the flowerbeds with their perpetual weeding and all those jobs left by the handyman who had last come five years ago. Dempsey appeared to have given up work altogether when Aunt Hatta was taken away, and retired into the gate lodge, emerging once weekly for his pay. Quite often he sneaked up to the kitchen for the odd meal with Angela. When the time came Drury would inquire into his so-called rights to the gate lodge. Meanwhile all his hours were filled up. Every day he visited Aunt Hatta. She hardly talked at all, just a wan smile as he told her news. She lay looking very pale, occasional nurses in white lace-up shoes clumping over to view her, poor soul.

He was short of money. Peachey had contacted him a few days after he moved in, agreeing that it was important to have someone in the house as caretaker. Drury mentioned everyday living expenses, special ones incurred by the problems of living in Eagle's Nest. Very well, if he sent in receipts and monthly returns, Peachey and Keane would honour them. This did not solve immediate problems. Angela had to be paid her salary and Dempsey his, which was ten times as much. Mrs Keogh had to be paid on the nail. He needed funds to feed himself and Angela, not to mention the dogs. Aunt Hatta had no account with local shops, except for her butcher in Dalkey, the last in the world, probably, who delivered meat. He took advantage of this, and for the time being lived on hunks of roast or grilled meat like an Argentine cowhand. It could not last for ever. And when he summoned a television engineer to put a connection in his room so that Aunt Hatta's set could be moved upstairs the swine had demanded (and received) twenty pounds.

He had spent his last monthly cheque from Prospect and could hardly expect another. Perhaps he had been a little precipitate. He never turned up on the first day of term. All his plans about making a dignified or amusing exit were discarded, and he just did not go, but lay in bed luxuriating as the minutes passed and the time for the first assembly of the school year ticked by. Praise my Soul the King of Heaven. Headmaster could not get in touch with him, since he did not know where he was.

Although Agnes did not yet know about his move to Eagle's Nest, she would soon have to be placated. The money situation became more urgent after she demanded a subsidy which he obtained by selling off some of the incomplete sets of silver. The sale of Goleen Park was an ongoing situation. The place could not be entirely abandoned, since thieves and vandals would learn about it. He had to pay regular visits, and once every three or four nights he slept there, roaming round the seedy little rooms turning lights on and off. Then he got what seemed to be a brilliant idea and left one of Aunt Hatta's dogs there for the night to act as watchdog. But it made such a mess and did so much destruction that the experiment had to be curtailed. The chewed-up rugs were replaced with a couple of Oriental carpets from Eagle's Nest which brightened up the house. But still it did not sell. He hated staying in it even for an hour, and on the nights he slept there spectres waited to haunt him, and sleeping problems recurred.

He visited Peachey again in his skimpy office. Deed boxes of distinguished clients lined the walls, painted with their names in white letters, Lord This, Sir That. He noticed a black box marked SKIBBEREEN ONLY and imagined how the documents inside signified Billy Skibbereen's wealth. In contrast the box labelled DRURY contained parchments, wills, conveyances and leases with SURRENDERED written across them that charted generations of failure.

Peachey made out a cheque for expenses to Mrs Good's unprepossessing great-nephew. Drury pocketed it and asked if the office had by any chance an inventory of the contents of Eagle's Nest. It might be useful at this stage. Peachey called in his spinster secretary to bring down the box with the white letters showing Mrs Good's name. He riffled through the parchments and through flimsy pages in a beige folder that contained lists of her securities. No, there seemed to be nothing of the sort here. Had Drury tried her insurance company? No, said Drury, immensely relieved. In fact this was not quite correct. In his tours of Eagle's Nest he had gone through cupboards and desks, found keys and opened drawers. He had come upon what appeared to be the household insurance policy made out decades ago at premiums that were grotesquely out of date. He rang the insurance company which confirmed that the unlisted contents of the house were valued at £5,000, while the turreted bulk of Eagle's Nest itself was insured for £12,000.

Peachey made a note and Drury summoned up courage to ask about his expectations. Agnes had wanted him to do this for years, but how the hell could he? Now however, in the circumstances . . . his aunt not being well . . . he would have to change his lifestyle . . . he had been led to believe . . . he would be grateful for advice. Peachey glared. It would be quite improper to discuss the subject at this time. You must understand that I cannot possibly divulge the contents of the will. Premature. However, you may rest assured that you can look forward to a substantial private income. Far more than most hardworking young men of your age can expect.

Income! Drury almost shrieked. Certainly. Naturally any family property had to be retained in the form of a trust. You must be well aware that your own immediate family never ever considered handling their securities and property in any other way. Of course the disposal of the house and its contents would be subject to the approval of the trustees.

Drury did not deign to ask who they could be. He took the cheque to the bank and cashed it before retiring to Neary's to brood over whiskey. Why a trust? Was it for Kevin's future benefit? Naturally, though he doubted if anyone concerned had Kevin in the forefront of their minds. No, relying on trusts was a matter of habit. His family had formed trusts for generations, originally to guard against the activities of spendthrift sons. They were the devil, and Peachey as trustee had always been the embodiment of caution and disaster. It was he who had advised his grandfather to sell up all those years ago. At other times he had restrained, restricted, sold out shares here, lost securities there, advised the disposal of property everywhere. Dishonest? Unlikely, merely a cautious fool. Michael used to sneer at his activities. If only Michael was alive! He always claimed that he could get hold of good pushy lawyers capable of breaking trusts. Would there be any point in trying to persuade Aunt Hatta at this stage to leave out the trust aspect of her legacy?

"Hello, Jim!" Here was that terrible Maurice from the Museum. "I'm sorry to learn about your aunt's illness."

"How did you hear about it?"

"Oh dear . . . I hope it's not a secret? We were doing a little transaction with her, actually . . ."

"The Greek statue?"

"You know about it? She bequeathed it to the Museum. Most generous of her, I may say."

"She's already left it to you?"

"Her illness has put off the signing of the deed of gift. So I suppose it is a little selfish of us to wish her well in all senses of the word."

"You know the thing's worth a fortune?"

"I wouldn't go so far as to say that. Some of the claims for it may be exaggerated. We are having it examined by various experts since the police have kindly allowed us to take unofficial possession of it."

"What experts?"

"Oh, some of our colleagues from the other side of the water."

"What do they think of it?"

Maurice paused. "One or two are quite enthusiastic . . ." He could never keep his mouth shut.

Drury asked, "What are you going to do with it? Put it on display?"

"Between you and me, Jim, it's all a little awkward. The thinking is that a piece of this quality that has no direct bearing on our culture is rather out of place in an Irish national museum."

"You'll get rid of it then? You'll sell it?"

"Good heavens, we certainly won't sell it. I really can't say. We'll just have to see when the time comes."

Drury snarled, "You'll hum and haw for a couple of years and then you'll hand it over to the Greeks on a long-term loan, most likely on a feeble exchange for something pertinent. Some wretched Celtic artefacts brought to Attica by Phoenicians, something like that."

"I really wouldn't like to comment at this stage."

"Isn't there a dispute over ownership? A little bird told me that Maire Kenny was claiming that Michael had bought it from my aunt."

"I understand she has decided it is not worth her while to take the matter to court. Well, I'd best be hurrying on. Give my regards to Mrs Good when you see her."

Drury ordered another drink. If Aunt Hatta passed away before signing over the statue to the Museum, it would revert to him. Or rather, to the bloody estate. He might manage to do a deal with Maire Kenny involving the other part of the statuary group, since it was so obviously a case of two heads being better than one. Even Peachey in his role of trustee could scarcely object.

He went out to Bray to visit Aunt Hatta who wasn't well enough to be told anything. Old friends had come in to see her bringing pots of cyclamen and azaleas. She lay among flowers as if she was already a corpse. When he drove back to Eagle's Nest, the sight of it gave him some of the thrill of ownership. He would be perfectly happy to potter around here for the rest of his life like Uncle Jack had done. There was really no need to sell the place for millions as a site for multi-storey flats. (Peachey would take some persuading.)

He had to make arrangements in order to keep going. He thought Angela's presence here was *de trop*. He rang up Peachey who thought that his idea of retiring her was quite a good one. Mrs Good was leaving her four hundred pounds in her will. This could be provided for in advance out of the estate.

He took Angela round to the hospital to see Aunt Hatta lying very weak and pale, and the next day brought up the subject over bacon and eggs. "As you saw, the Mistress is awfully sick, and won't be back for a long time." Agnes nodded. "So you can understand it will mean changes." She smiled at him, her favourite, and he smiled back. He explained about the extra expenses that rose from keeping the Mistress in hospital. Reductions would be necessary.

"I'm afraid we'll all have to make sacrifices," he told her.

"I have money saved, sir. Would that help keep the Mistress in hospital?"

He had to explain about her legacy, and how he was trying to help her. She began to cry; tears trickled down the tired old face under the white cap. She had been here for so long, since she had come as a young girl from the heart of the country.

"What part of the country?"

"Roscommon, sir."

"Have you any relatives there still?"

"My sister, sir."

That was lucky. Although she was not all that eager to go to her sister, whom she had not seen since 1956, she agreed when she learned that this would be the best thing for the Mistress. The sister was out of the way in a mountainy place where communication was difficult, and he had to get in touch with a parish priest to let her know when Angela was coming. She was grateful when he drove her down to Sean Heuston Station himself and put her on the train, receiving blessings as he pushed parting gifts into the carriage—clothes out of Aunt Hatta's wardrobe and one of the dogs.

Mrs Keogh departed with less trouble. He dismissed her with a mumble about changes, and kept an eye on her all during her last day on the premises. When he advertised for a replacement, six applicants replied immediately to the notice in the newsagents. He was not satisfied with any of them. He wanted no one from the housing estate opposite Goleen Park, no one of the Brady stamp. Then he had a good idea and rang Mrs Hackett. There was nothing Mrs Hackett liked doing better than offering advice and managing other people's affairs, and she soon sent round a garrulous woman with dental problems who liked to follow him around pointing to her gums. However, she appeared to clean efficiently. He did not know what to do about Dempsey. For the moment he paid him resentfully; at least when Angela left he had cut off a major source of his food supply.

He missed Angela, the way she served his breakfast, the smiles, the gossip and the affection. However, it was time she went. Before she left he was beginning to get enraged by the slowness of her movements as she waddled round the kitchen. She had done one very useful job, and that had been the sacred feeding of the dogs. There were still seven of them around, a horrible nuisance, savage, dirty and noisy. One in particular, since Angela had taken its friend away, now kept up a constant despairing yapping which threatened to destroy his newfound capacity for sleep. Another was Rex, perpetually wagging his tail, hanging out his tongue, leaping on his clothes, reminding him of Michael. When he put an advertisement in the *Times*, "Good home wanted, owner sick," no one replied. He thought of taking them all up to the Dublin Mountains and letting them out on the Feather Bed. But that would be cruel. When he rang a vet—not a local one, but a man with a practice on the north side—and asked him the rate for putting down an unwanted dog, he was horrified to learn that it was seven pounds an animal. He went over to Bray to see Aunt Hatta lying asleep, very weak. When he got back he bundled all the dogs into the Morris. (The cats had to stay, because he could not catch them.) After a nightmare drive into the city he delivered them to the Dogs' Home in Grand Canal Street.

When he got back Peachey rang him up. He was concerned that there was no inventory of the contents of Eagle's Nest. Usually he could be relied upon to be the personification of the law's delays, but now it seemed he had been checking with the insurance company. He was arranging for someone to come out tomorrow to make a list.

"Could you make it next week? After I'm back?"

"Oh, are you going away?"

His eyes scanned the What's On column in the *Times*. (He bought it every day now.) "I'm going down to Wexford for a couple of days for the Festival."

"I may see you there. I'll arrange for next Monday, then."

If the question ever came up, he'd have to say he'd been ill and unable to go. Flu. An unspecified range of symptoms. Meanwhile he had to act quickly. He went to the attic and found a leather suitcase full of tropical clothes preserved in camphor-smelling tissue paper. He brought down suitcase and paper and went round the house from room to room. He chose carefully, china groups from the backs of cabinets, some silver with good hallmarks, two small paintings in the drawing room by Chinnery and various odds and ends. In Aunt Hatta's bedroom he found a little clock on the mantelpiece, its white face set in a frame of blue enamel and silver beading. He blew away dust to examine the filigree arrowheads on the hands pointing to neat black figures and the Cyrillic lettering announcing the maker's name. Although he had decided not to touch anything in here, the temptation was too great.

He would go over to London on the mailboat and come back quickly. Suppose Customs should stop him and search? There was no law against carrying your own personal property from one place to another, although he suspected that the load he intended to take over would invite awkward questions. He was getting used to taking risks. In his own way he was indulging inherited warrior instincts. Risk was the backbone of war, the main ingredient of bravery. When his grandfather threw himself over the top at the Somme and his father trundled around the desert in a tank, they had been taking risks. He managed to put a surprising amount of things in the suitcase. The house looked less cluttered.

Before he left he paid his daily visit to Aunt Hatta. It was teatime, and she was propped up on pillows, eyes glazed and mouth open being spoonfed by a nurse talking baby talk. He went down to Dun Laoghaire. Flying would have been so much easier, but invited more risks at customs. He was dressed carefully in casual sports jacket and clean shirt. (He had taken to using a laundry.) Long hair, beards and anorak invited customs men's attention. He had been to a barber for a haircut.

He boarded around a quarter to nine, shuffling along in the midst of a reassuringly large crowd set on competing for the leatherette seats, the cafeteria chicken and peas, and the pinball machines. He went to the bar and mingled with hitchhiking youths carrying haversacks balanced on ladders and returning countrymen. As he finished his first stout *British Rail 2* began to move. He took a short walk on deck, noting the necking couples, the squalling gulls and the cold wind. He wanted to arrive alert and refreshed in London. But no-one who has travelled on the Irish Mail has ever arrived alert and refreshed.

At Holyhead the passengers shouldered their way on shore as if the ship was on fire. He shoved with them, terrified of dropping his suitcase, but eager to keep in the crowd centre. A couple of customs officers crouched in wait like lions watching migrating antelope. He carried his case safely past them. His relief made him slow, and the berth he intended to take was booked by the time he got to the train, and he was lucky to get a seat in the packed carriages. The snoring man beside him smelt of vomit. An English family returning from a tour of Ireland complained for a hundred miles, and by the time the train reached Chester he had heard about every indigestible meal of their holiday.

Sleep came painfully slowly among the clatter of rails and the ghostly stations full of creeping figures and sodium lights.

He woke in morning light as the train clicked through high walls towards Euston. Giving his reflex glance round for the youth in brown, he stumbled out onto the platform and walked to the central station that rang with dulcet broadcast announcements. He washed and shaved in the WC, emerging more prepared for a strenuous day. A cigarette and breakfast helped. He checked the names of dealers and fine art houses that he had noted down from *Country Life*. He did not wish to sell the things all together. Something here, something there. A little family piece. An oddment I wish to dispose of. My wife's not partial to it.

He took the tube to Piccadilly Circus and went into Swan and Edgar where he obtained a carrier bag by making a small purchase. Then he toured Bond Street and its environs, decanting each object he intended to dispose of into the bag from the suitcase, since he wished to give the impression that he only had one item for sale at each place he went into. It would have been nice to dump the suitcase, but he could not think how to. But he managed pretty well. He found that Aunt Hatta's belongings attracted discreet admiration, and the offers made to him seemed to be for a lot of money. But was three hundred pounds a fair price for the silver teapot with the pineapple on the lid? The Chelsea tureen in the shape of a rabbit: he had always thought it hideous, and had hesitated to bring it over because of its size. Was it naive to accept five hundred for it? In his old life he had handled so little of real worth that now he simply could not tell. He noticed that none of the dealers he approached advised him to consult a nearby auction house. Not that he wanted to. Delays. Addresses had to be exchanged. The Property of a Gentleman. He took two thousand pounds for the Fabergé clock, although he knew it was worth more. These are not easy times for the antique trade.

At the end of the day he had a bundle of English cheques, totalling just under five thousand pounds. He would put most of them in his

Post Office account when he got back. Thank goodness he had never quite closed it at the end of the last bank strike. He could draw out fifty pounds at a time from any Post Office in Ireland. He returned to Dublin the same evening, a journey that was just as rugged as the voyage out. In the morning he disembarked at Dun Laoghaire with his empty suitcase and drove back to Killiney in the Morris, which he had parked near the pier the day before yesterday. (Perhaps he would use the cheque for the clock to get a proper car.) He was glad to get back to Eagle's Nest, although the house was rather chilly since the Aga had gone out. He would get it converted to paraffin. (Perhaps he would risk putting a few cheques in his bank account after all.) The place was a little lonely. He would rather like to have Kevin running round, and a woman. Not Agnes, some lovely quiet girl.

He made some of the fresh coffee he liked to have nowadays and boiled two eggs. When the telephone rang he went upstairs and answered it reluctantly. The house agent had a couple who were interested in a semi-detached house in the Killiney-Ballbrack area. He agreed to show them round Goleen Park the next day. The sale of the house was still a nagging worry.

He went out to Bray to see Aunt Hatta. He drove down the front, past the house where James Joyce's family had quarrelled about Parnell, past the amusement arcades and the boarding houses, Stella Maris, Novarra, Kylemore, Glengarriff. Here was Brenan Terrace where his maternal grandmother used to spend summer holidays during her childhood. Bray had even less to offer in those days. She once told him of the excitement when Lord and Lady Meath came down from their big house on the outskirts of the town to the promenade in a car that carried their bicycles. The noble couple would mount their machines held by chauffeur and footman, and would ride up and down beside the sea smilingly acknowledging the attention of onlookers. Later his great-grandparents decided that Bray was too garish for a member of the clergy to spend his vacation, and they moved down to Greystones for August. Greystones was the place where the elephants went to die.

The hallway of Bettyview was covered with a vivid floral carpet and the walls were hung with maroon flock wallpaper. He smelt disinfectant and urine. He opened the door to Aunt Hatta's room very gently. She was sitting up, her hair in a net, writing a letter. A transistor by her bed was broadcasting Woman's Hour. When she saw him she turned off the soothing voice.

"Hello, James. How nice to see you at last."

"I was here . . . oh . . . three days ago. I had to go to England."

"Why?"

"Why? A job. Possibility of getting a job in a public school."

"Where?"

"Where? Charterhouse. I had an interview."

"Who's been looking after the dogs?"

"Who? Angela. It was only for a couple of nights."

"Poor old Angela's getting rather tottery. I hope she took good care of them?"

"Oh yes."

"You're a good boy, looking after everything for me. I'm longing to see them. Dr Waters thinks I'll be able to go home next week."

"You can't! You can't leave here! You're not well. You need to be taken care of!"

"I want to be taken care of in familiar surroundings."

"Someone would have to nurse you night and day."

"Of course someone would have to nurse me. Matron and Nurse Halligan have been most helpful in getting people. Just as soon as they're able to arrange a day nurse, a night nurse and a relief, I'll be able to come home."

"But the expense!"

"It's quite awful. But not any more than staying here. You'd think after all these years . . . Next year I'm not showing my garden for the benefit of these people." She closed her eyes. "Water!"

He held up a glass and she sipped. He rang the bell beside her bed. "You're still not at all well, Aunt Hatta. You mustn't dream of going home yet."

"Dr Waters thinks it's a good idea."

"He probably wants you out of here so that he can use the bed."

"No he doesn't."

"Suppose you get another attack. They've got all the right things to take care of you here."

She put the writing pad and biro on the sliding bed-tray in front of her. "I don't say I have an awful lot longer. But I'm going back to the comfort of my own home among my own things. Will you ask Angela and Mrs Keogh to prepare a couple of the spare rooms upstairs for the nurses? They'll be sleeping there part of the time. And tell Angela to expect me early next week. You'll be able to return to your own little house."

Nurse Halligan came in full of smiles. "Isn't she a wonderful old lady?" she said, talking as if she wasn't there. Such a miracle, they had been expecting the worst. She'd known recoveries like this before which usually happened with stern-willed old people. Marvellous. No, she wasn't rambling when she talked about going home. Wasn't it far better for her to go back to what she was familiar with? She was still very weak, of course. To be honest, Mr Drury, although she's looking that much better, she hasn't all that much time left in this world. Who's in charge of her case? Dr Waters—hasn't he been her doctor a good while? Oh yes, he believes she'd be more comfortable in her own bed. She should be home early next week, D.V.

When he got back to Eagle's Nest he rang the Dogs' Home. Too late, they'd all snuffed it. He toyed with the idea of looking for seven substitute dogs, ringers of the departed. He could recall Angela from Roscommon with a story that he had given her a holiday and she had not understood. Mrs Keogh had been dismissed for pilfering.

He wandered through rooms which looked so much more elegant now they were less cluttered. They would really be better with even less. Those Chinese vases, for instance, were rather hideous. He did not really like Chinese things. But they had been much too big to carry all the way to London. In the drawing room the items that were left looked really beautiful at last, now you could see them properly on their own. He could always fill up the cabinets again with pieces from upstairs. Would she notice? The absence of the Chinnerys would be hard to explain, although he could say that he had sent them to the National Gallery to be cleaned. Or valued. No, not valued, cleaned. Probably she would be too ill to come into the drawing room at all. Would she want to peep in just to take a look at Uncle Jack's shrine? He hadn't touched anything in the window. He should never have yielded to the temptation of taking the clock from her bedroom. Sadly he went from one big graceful room to the next, standing in front of the high windows bathed in greenish light from the sea. Could he find a substitute for one dog at least, the fluffy white creature she liked to have on her bed?

Later he went to the supermarket, not a local one, but a place quite a distance away, towards Dundrum. A part of it was devoted to selling drink, the display having spread out from the corner where it was once confined with fungoid swiftness. He looked at it for a long time before choosing a half bottle of champagne. In the hardware section he saw some champagne glasses; he had to take six because they came in sets. He put a selection of other items in his basket before making for the checkouts where there were long queues since this was late afternoon at the end of the week. Beside the cashier some long-lasting razor blades were hung on a display stand. He shaved with throwaway razors, but now he bought a packet of three blades.

In the car he wrapped three of the champagne glasses in a couple of polythene supermarket bags and broke them into very small pieces with the handle of his jack. He deposited the fragments in a litter bin. When he returned to Eagle's Nest he went to his bedroom and found the bottle that contained his sleeping pills. Since he had been staying here, he had needed them less, and it was more than half full. He got a laminated table mat from the dining room and a darning needle from the ivory and silk-lined sewing cabinet in the drawing room. He cut each ultramarine-coloured pill in two and scratched out its contents with a needle. What harm would eighteen do to an enfeebled consti-tution? What would the symptoms be? Would she go out like a light or would there be retching and gasping? Was the stuff soluble or would it lie in powder at the bottom of a glass? There were elements of risk. She was in the sole charge of Dr Waters.

Next day he chose to go and see her in the early afternoon, the time when nurses had fed their charges and had retired to feed themselves. Bettyview was informal about visitors, and its door was on the latch so that any stranger could go in without summoning the staff. A com-mando raid. He tiptoed past the wrought iron table in the hall with its display of dried flowers dyed the colour of blood and the two crude pic-tures of children with tears in their eyes. The lounge door was open a crack. In its overheated interior he could see a circle of sleepy old ladies sitting before the big television which happened to be tuned to a sta-tion broadcasting a commentary on a horse race. They did not see him go by. When he opened the door into Aunt Hatta's room she was doz-ing. He shut it quietly behind him, and went over and shook her awake. A little celebration? What a lovely thought! He took out the champagne bottle and two wide brimmed glasses from another super-market bag. The powdery insides of the sleeping pills were in the tube he carried in his top pocket. He emptied them into one glass without being observed. About a teaspoon full. When he opened the half bottle of champagne, he muffled the pop in a towel, as both he and Aunt Hatta giggled and made sh . . . ing noises. Aunt Hatta put her finger to her lips. The champagne poured out bubbling and frothing, and they toasted her recovery and her future. She drank it all, and then lay down again and closed her eyes. He examined her glass, which was quite empty, before he packed it away with his own, together with the bottle and the cork in the supermarket bag. He crept out, closing the door behind him, and hurried past the lounge and out of the front door. Fortune favoured the brave.

He had bought an *Independent* that morning. As the most widely-read newspaper in Ireland, it was a suitable wrapper for the three remaining glasses (the third had been a spare) which he now pounded to powder. He deposited them and the bottle and cork in different litter tins at distances round and about south County Dublin. Then he had to go to Goleen Park and meet the house-hunters sent along by the agents. He tried not to worry. As soon as he got rid of one lot of prob-lems, more surfaced. Would his action bring about the desired effect, peaceful and painless? Would Dr Waters stir himself and call in another opinion? Or perhaps demand an autopsy? Not if the nurses in Bettyview could help it. It was strange—in Michael's case alcohol in the stomach allayed suspicion, while in this case it would do the opposite.

His little Moorish home, distinguishable from others round it by the FOR SALE sign like a becalmed flag, seemed smaller and shabbier than ever. In the hall were two letters he did not open, one bearing a crest featuring legless and armless eagles and addressed in a faded typewriter ribbon that signified a communication from Prospect. The other fat envelope bore Agnes's handwriting. He had always felt miserable in this house. He should really sleep here again this evening to make his presence felt, since it was nearly a week since he had last done so.

The doorbell chimed. The people from the agency were early for their appointment. He delayed for a few moments, running round and rubbing furniture polish on exposed surfaces before opening up. The youth in brown was standing just a little way back from the doorstep. Behind him were two stern-faced men who had stepped from a big dark-coloured official car at which the neighbours were already staring.

Peter Somerville-Large was educated in Dublin, and after leaving Trinity College spent a decade working abroad. His jobs ranged from Lecturer in English at the Royal Military Academy in Kabul, Afghanistan, to gold miner in Kalgoorlie, Australia, and wharfee on the docks of Wellington, New Zealand. He then turned to writing and journalism, and journeys to the Yemen and northern Iran gave him material for his first two books. He has since written four books about his native Ireland, three thrillers, and a ghost story. He lives in County Wicklow with his wife and daughter. A LIVING DOG is his first novel for the Crime Club.